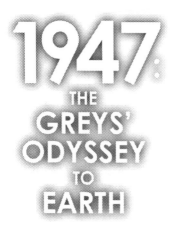

1947: THE GREYS' ODYSSEY TO EARTH

They came to Earth in 1947 and crashed near Roswell, New Mexico. But who were the Greys, and where did they come from? Why did they come? What did they want? What did they think of us?

1947:

THE GREYS' ODYSSEY TO EARTH

Gus V.

ARCHWAY
PUBLISHING

Archway Publishing books may be ordered through booksellers or by contacting:

Archway Publishing
1663 Liberty Drive
Bloomington, IN 47403
www.archwaypublishing.com
1 (888) 242-5904

Artwork by Roberta Lerman, photographs by Lester Overstreet.

ISBN: 978-1-4808-8418-2 (sc)
ISBN: 978-1-4808-8416-8 (hc)
ISBN: 978-1-4808-8417-5 (e)

Library of Congress Control Number: 2019918206

Print information available on the last page.

Archway Publishing rev. date: 11/25/2019

CONTENTS

PREFACE

Since his early childhood, the author has been fascinated by the starry skies above us and the subject of humanity reaching out to those starry skies. For many years, space exploration has been a driver of science education. Ask scientists and engineers, like the author, what motivated them in their careers. In many cases they were inspired by NASA's space program and by the science fiction books, movies, and television shows that fed off of it. Space exploration has also been a driver of technology—satellite communications, weather forecasting, global positioning systems, computers, robotics, digital photography and video, and more.

One big question many of us ask ourselves is, 'Are we alone in the universe? Not likely. There are several billion stars in our galaxy and billions of galaxies in the universe. That should make for perhaps hundreds of planets where life could come together and, after billions of years, evolve toward technological creatures like ourselves. Then the big question becomes when we'll have the technological means to reach out and contact other intelligent beings. Other big questions would be, Are these other beings looking for other intelligent life like ourselves? and, Do they have peaceful intentions?

In this book, *1947: The Greys' Odyssey to Earth*, the author narrates a fictional journey of the Greys from their home planet to their crash near Roswell, New Mexico. The Greys are described as an advanced and peaceful race. Chapter 1 starts in the year 2065 with an interview of three old Greys familiar with their 1940s journey. In chapter 2, the Greys begin their story by telling of an invasion of their home planet of Zeta in 1944 by an aggressive alien species called Reptoids, just as the Greys' spaceship, *Zeta's Hope*, is about to be launched on an expedition to the uninhabited planet of Avalonia with fifty colonists—made up of both Greys and their human-like allies from planet Amigo.

The Greys and their Amigo allies journey across several planets: Avalonia, Terruno, Sapiens, Verde, and Proxima. At these planets they are faced with various issues—the life-threatening wilderness of Avalonia, a repressive dictatorship in Terruno, addiction of a crewmate in Sapiens, and terrorism in Verde. During this time, romance, families, and long-lasting friendships are formed among the members of the crew. They share the pain and misery of bad times and the joy and laughter of good times. Eventually, with the support of the Interplanetary Alliance—made up of planets Sapiens, Verde, and Proxima—they embark on a mission from Proxima to Earth in mid-1947, with the intention of reaching out to humans and establishing formal relations. Unfortunately, things do not go as planned.

Model depicting crash at Roswell UFO Museum (Photo by Lester Overstreet)

Specific inspiration for this book came from the Roswell UFO (Unidentified Flying Object) crash at a ranch near Roswell, New Mexico, in 1947. Following wide media and public interest in this reportedly crashed UFO, the American military reported that it was just a weather balloon. Years later, ufologists began promoting a number of theories about the event, claiming that an extraterrestrial aircraft had crashed. Today, there is an International UFO Museum and Research Center in Roswell, visited by the author and a photographer friend back in 2016. The author's gratitude goes to those who operate and maintain the museum; to ufologists, who study UFO phenomena and seek for the truth; to my sci-fi buddy Rick Targett, for his insight and comments on the original draft of this book; and to the many thousands of aerospace workers who are paving the way for humanity to further explore our galaxy, the Milky Way.

In order of appearance, recurring characters are,

C. A. Wyatt (an earthling interviewing three old Greys in 2065 about their 1940s journey)
Noah Zambuto (Grey Captain of *Zeta's Hope*)
Faith (Grey Communications Officer of *Zeta's Hope*)
Akina (Grey Medical Officer of *Zeta's Hope*)
Romo Agrox (Amigo First Officer of *Zeta's Hope*)
Jang Tauls (Grey Chief Engineer of *Zeta's Hope*)
Ben (Amigo Helmsman of *Zeta's Hope*)
Boudica (Grey Quartermaster of *Zeta's Hope*)
Chaika (an alien friendly to the Greys who traveled to Earth's future)
Nova (Banacan political refugee who serves as nurse of *Zeta's Hope*)
Rick Patel (Sapiens who serves as Interplanetary Alliance Liaison with the Greys and Amigos)
Neo (an identity theft specialist, low-level drug dealer, and wannabe terrorist from planet Verde)

Fictional Map of Cluster of Habitable Planets near Earth

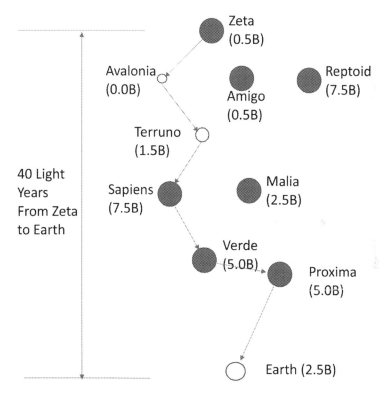

Zeta (0.5B)

Avalonia (0.0B)

Amigo (0.5B)

Reptoid (7.5B)

Terruno (1.5B)

40 Light Years From Zeta to Earth

Sapiens (7.5B)

Malia (2.5B)

Verde (5.0B)

Proxima (5.0B)

Earth (2.5B)

Notes:
1944 Spacefaring Planets shown Solid.
Planet size proportional to development.
Planet population in parenthesis.
Grey's journey from Zeta to Earth shown by arrows.

CHAPTER ONE

INTERVIEW WITH THE GREYS

Ever since the days of my childhood, I've been a stargazer. Early in the evening of my fifth birthday in 2015, Grandpa Gus took me to the front yard of his home and pointed to the heavens. In my hands I held my cherished toy space shuttle. Grandpa said, "Look, C.A.! It's a half moon tonight!"

Then, pointing to the heavens, he said, "There! That's Venus, the brightest body in the night sky other than the moon."

My eyes followed his hand, bewildered by the beauty of the shiny lights in the heavens. "One day during your lifetime," Grandpa went on, "humanity will explore the stars and establish contact with the peoples that live by those shiny points. We'll make friends with them, trade, and go vacationing to their home worlds. And they'll come here to visit us too!"

Full of curiosity to learn more about our future extraterrestrial friends, I asked, "Grandpa, will there be good guys and bad guys among them?"

Grandpa looked at me, reflected for a few seconds, and

replied, "Many will be good, gentle, and kind knights in shining armor. Perhaps a few will be bad knights. And people all over the galaxy may have character defects, such as getting upset if things don't go their way. So most of them will be in various shades of gray!"

By the time of this writing, in the year 2065, fifty years had passed after that talk with Grandpa on my fifth birthday. A year had passed since Earth formally made friends with several extraterrestrial races. A new age of peace, economic prosperity, and enlightenment flourished. Life had gotten better for most, though not all problems were solved; some were still affected by hunger, disease, and poverty. But I had an eerie feeling that this was the calm before a storm. Was there some diabolical threat lurking in those beautiful starry skies above us?

Before getting into our story, let me tell you about myself. I became interested in spaceflight through my grandpa, an engineer who worked for more than thirty years on various aerospace projects before he retired in 2008. I remember gazing at the stars with him when I was a kid. I fondly recall the time he took me on a tour of NASA's Kennedy Space Center Visitor Complex in my native Florida. They featured exhibits and displays of historic spacecraft going back to the seven Mercury astronauts, and a bus tour took us to replicas from the old Apollo firing rooms and launchpads to those of more recent programs.

Grandpa passed on to me old issues of technical magazines, planting in me a seed of interest for the subjects of science and engineering. When I was a preteen, he bought me old classic science fiction novels, from authors such as Jules Verne, H. G. Wells, George Orwell, Isaac Asimov, and Philip K. Dick. And together we saw many *Star Trek* reruns, from the original series to *Enterprise*. Sometimes I would let my imagination go, daydreaming of being a space explorer and traveling on faraway missions through the stars.

My eventual profession was journalism. Science fiction and space technology and exploration were frequent topics of my work. My current project was a book about the 1940s Greys' odyssey from their home world, planet Zeta, to Earth. To further the project, I was interviewing several of them about that journey.

At first, there was speculation that these extraterrestrials wanted to become our friends because they were threatened by an enemy that gave no quarter to other species. One of the friendly alien groups, the Greys, told us an incredible story of their world being invaded by creatures called Reptoids. During initial contact, the Greys traded medical equipment, technology, jewelry, and rare metals with them. The Reptoids had a closed society, and travelers there were not allowed outside their capital, so the Greys knew very little about the Reptoids' culture. But to the Greys' surprise, the Reptoids invaded their home planet of Zeta without any warning.

The Greys' home world fell to this threat in a few days. By order of their leadership, only twenty-five Greys escaped in the nick of time. They left behind kin and other loved ones who were either murdered or enslaved by the invaders. It must have been painful deciding to leave the land of their birth, where they had made lifelong friendships, were married, and settled down in the homes of their dreams. The Greys I was to meet knew this sad story from the beginning. And one of them, Admiral Noah Zambuto, not only was their leader in the journey that brought them to Roswell, but he was also in charge of the technology transfer program to Earth.

On that cool early November evening in 2065, I was to have dinner with the Greys' Admiral Noah; his wife, Faith; and their friend, Dr. Akina, at a restaurant located by the ocean in Cocoa Beach. The sea breeze blended with the sound of a classic mellow rock song by the Red Hot Chili Peppers called "Under the Bridge."

On that beachside resort, we would conduct our interview about their home world and their journey through the galaxy.

These notable Greys were all about 150 years old, comparable to seventy-five-year-old humans. At the time, Noah was nearing his retirement, and I had been fortunate to connect with him through an old college buddy who worked in public relations at NASA. My friend described the Greys' attitude and behavior as reminiscent of the rational Vulcans in *Star Trek*, albeit a bit more lighthearted. I was then fifty-five.

The average Grey was about five and a half feet tall. They were amphibians who gave birth to live young. On land, they didn't have the athletic abilities of humans, but in water they swam skillfully with the aid of their webbed hands and feet. They had a well-developed sonar system, like dolphins, that helped them detect predators or prey. They also had strong empathic abilities; they could sense the emotions of a person or animal. There was an air of seriousness and distinction to their faces, their lizard-like skin slightly wrinkled with the passing of years.

Noah was slim, with long, thin limbs. He had five fingers on each hand and five toes on their feet, with some webbing between the digits. His head was large and hairless, with slightly slanted, almond-shaped black eyes, two tiny nostrils, and a small mouth and ears. Noah looking distinguished in his black suit, and so did the ladies in their purple evening gowns. As I sat for dinner with them, I had a fond memory of when my dearly beloved schizophrenic mother told me she had imaginary friends who looked like Greys.

As our soup-and-salad dinner ended, Noah drank a sip of coffee and took a draw of his cigar as he relaxed for our interview. From my observations, he did not drink any alcohol, which made me feel at ease, for I had had to carry my last drunken interviewee out of a restaurant.

Flirtatiously, Dr. Akina asked me, "Do you have a wife or girlfriend?"

"No," I replied quickly and nervously, afraid of the ramifications of my answer.

"Have you ever considered dating an experienced 150-year-old Grey lady?" Akina asked, with a smile and a flirting wink.

Her friend Faith giggled and added, "And you know what they say: once you go Grey, you will go astray!"

As the ladies laughed heartily, I blushed and thought, *Are they just messing with me?* Then, turning to Noah for rescue, I abruptly began our interview by asking him, "Why do you want me to write your story?"

Faith interrupted. "My husband needs some serious help. He can barely write his own name! He's all math, physics, drawings, nuts, and bolts. But he's good in the sack and a good daddy and provider. And that's why I've kept him!"

Noah smiled and said, "Please forgive my companions! They are both very mischievous! But deep in their hearts, they are good people and loving and caring moms. And that's why I've kept my wife, Faith!"

I chuckled. Then, out of curiosity, I asked, "Is Noah a family name? How did you get it?"

"My maternal grandpa was a captain with the merchant marines. My parents wanted to name me after him, particularly my mom, who read the Holy Scriptures from our world every day. Dad was a real cool guy, and he was thrilled when I first turned out to be a pilot and later an astronaut."

I prompted him to go on. "Tell me about your education and experience before the start of your journey."

"In 1936 I attained an undergraduate degree in mechanical engineering with a minor in computer science, while simultaneously training as a pilot. During my first four years in the space agency, I was an astronaut pilot for our space transportation system, which resembled the US X-33 experimental vehicle. During the four years preceding the launch from our home world in 1944, I was the lead for the test program of the spaceship *Zeta's Hope*, the vehicle I was to command. By the time my first mission was scheduled, I'd finished a graduate degree in engineering management and was happily married to Faith, the ship's communications officer."

"What about the Greys and their home world?"

Noah reflected with nostalgia, answering, "Zeta is the name of our home world. It's a planet about forty light-years from Earth in what you call the Zeta Reticuli star system. That is more than two hundred trillion miles from here! Ancient writings dating back a hundred thousand years tell that our race originated from a group of two dozen space colonists from planet Eden. The Grey colonists accidentally shot through a wormhole and crashed on the other side of it in the deep waters near the shore of a large island on planet Zeta.

"Initially, life was tough. The daily tasks of farming, fishing, hunting, mining, cloth making, and tending a camp of primitive huts was a hard routine. Back then, there was no convenient infrastructure of contemporary living—motor vehicles, roads, bridges, aqueducts, and modern housing with electricity and climate control. We spread over our new unexplored world. Our civilization grew into separate city states and nations. By the early nineteen forties, the nine constitutional republics in our planet agreed to exist under a central government based on the principles of universal rights and shared our knowledge and resources, including our experience of nearly two centuries of space exploration."

Curious about their apparent spiritual nature, I interrupted with a question: "What about the Greys' concepts of religion and justice?"

"We have diverse ideas of religion and justice. But most Greys believe in a loving and caring universal God. And we have a tolerant system of justice, where only those who steal or hurt others are jailed. Habitual sinners are not punished for gambling, for getting intoxicated, or for having consensual sex. It's not our belief that the state is to be the guardian of the morality of any particular group of people. As for God's system of justice, punishment in an eternal hell only comes to those who hurt others and freeloaders that live off the sweat of others. For example, we believe that historical figures on Earth who committed mass genocide—such as Hitler, Stalin, and Mao—together share the worst level of punishment in hell. Small-time thieves receive a much lower level of punishment. Big-time corrupt politicians are somewhere in between."

Still curious about their peaceful nature, I inquired, "Any recent wars in your history?"

Noah's wife Faith took up the answer. "By the early nineteen forties, we had enjoyed four centuries of peace among our nations, with rare disruptions of peace by terrorists and violent criminals. No countries on our world had a standing army, much like countries on Earth such as Costa Rica and Iceland. Through space travel, we had trade and cultural relations with another planet called Amigo. Although our weapons were at a late nineteenth-century human level, we were capable of space travel at about a hundred times the speed of light. This meant we could make the round trip to Neptune and back to Earth, a distance of over five billion miles, in about six minutes! We were close to a century ahead of Earth in computers, communications systems, power generation, and medical technology."

I went on with more questions. "How does your world compare to Earth?"

Noah smiled proudly. "Zeta is about two thirds the size of Earth. Our planet is in the Goldilocks Zone, which is an area of space in which a planet is just the right distance from its home star so that its surface is neither too hot nor too cold for liquid water. The planet's surface is 90 percent covered with water, and its atmosphere is about 80 percent nitrogen and 20 percent oxygen. Most of the landmass consists of island archipelagos, like the Caribbean islands, with most of the population, about half a billion inhabitants, living near the planet's shores, rivers, and lakes.

"It has a magnetosphere like Earth's, which protects our planet from the charged particles of the solar wind and cosmic rays. Otherwise they would strip away the ozone layer shielding us from the ultraviolet radiation of our binary star system in Zeta Reticuli. Our spaceship, *Zeta's Hope*, has a magnetosphere created by our engines to protect against ultraviolet radiation and micrometeorites up to the size of a softball. Our advanced guidance and navigation helped us avoid collisions with larger meteorites."

Curious, I asked, "How did a typical Grey make a living? How about housing?"

"Despite a strong free market and going through industrial, computer, and telecommunications revolutions, much of our people's work is not much different than in developed countries in Earth. Most common jobs were in retail sales and in food preparation and service. And with the average lifespan of Greys going over 150 years, there was growth in the healthcare industry. Environmentally friendly sources of power were available, such as solar, wind, and gasohol for motor vehicles. Though we primarily eat vegetables, we'll also consume small fish, shellfish, snails, worms, and insects as our primitive ancestors did.

"Because most of our population lived in temperate and tropical climates, most houses were structured like large one or two-story igloos, a design that stood strong winds from hurricanes and tornadoes. In cities, apartment buildings and condominiums were common. Construction materials used included steel framing, concrete, wood, stone, and adobe. As on Earth, utilities included water, electrical power, television, and internet."

Then I asked an obvious question: "What about the aerospace industry?"

"In the aerospace industry, the main type of work was for scientists, engineers, and technicians. As a hardware engineer, you could be responsible for designing, building, and testing equipment and mechanisms for spacecraft and supporting ground systems. As a software engineer, you could be responsible for building technology with a wide range of uses, from collecting information to analyzing data, and writing code for control systems and to protect data infrastructure. What impressed me most about my aerospace coworkers was their teamwork and dedication to work and help others in the team to succeed."

I further inquired, "What about recreational activities and other forms of entertainment?"

Enthusiastically, Faith raised one of her webbed hands and answered, "Sports included swimming, surfing, fishing, camping, and sports resembling volleyball and water polo. Families would often gather at home to play indoor games that resembled Monopoly, Parcheesi, cards, backgammon, dominoes, chess, and checkers. We also enjoyed music, theater, singing, and dancing. Each of the nine constitutional republics on the planet had annual festivities similar to arts and craft fairs and Mardi Gras. After Mardi Gras, membership in substance abuse recovery groups drastically increased."

I interrupted with one final hard question: "Tell me about the arrival of the Reptoids to Zeta."

Noah's face saddened for a moment. Taking a long draw on his cigar, he replied, "Near the peak of our civilization by mid-1944, a crew of twenty-five human-like aliens came from a friendly neighboring planet called Amigo to join us on a joint venture to planet Avalonia. They were as intelligent and as advanced as we Greys. The Amigos told us of a catastrophic event in their home world a couple of days before they arrived on our world. They were invaded by an alien race of Reptoids. The aggressors brought with them hundreds of armored vehicles and fighter-bombers. Like the Greys, the Amigos had not fought a war in several centuries, and their weaponry was at a level comparable to ours. In a matter of days, the invading soldiers overran their home worlds like Nazi Germany did the Low Countries in World War 2 and either murdered or enslaved their inhabitants. Our Amigo refugees feared that this army of invaders would embark across the universe to conquer other species and obtain their technologies."

Noah paused briefly, nervously studied his cigar, and continued. "Within two days of the arrival of the Amigos, our orbital long-range sensors showed a large fleet of ships approaching Zeta. Before then an asteroid shower brought infectious agents from space, which might have caused a pandemic if not for our advanced medical technology's ability to contain it. But we had no idea that would follow was the beginning of the end of our civilization as we knew it! This was in mid-1944, when we were to embark on our first long journey to another planet. To those of us who survived and escaped the invasion, it was the beginning of a long and arduous odyssey that would eventually bring us in contact with humans on Earth, and many other intelligent species along the way."

CHAPTER TWO

THE LAST DAY ON PLANET ZETA

Captain Noah told me that zero hour for launch was midnight on that summer evening of 1944 in planet Zeta. The Greys' Space Center doubled as a wildlife reserve. "One of my former drinking buddies took that literally, and even had a bumper sticker on his car that read 'Support the Wildlife, Party Every Day.' What can I say about the poor, confused fellow? He wound up in rehab after a few years of partying."

The flight crew boarded the launch vehicle on schedule. The Greys had outfitted the cargo bay of the launch vehicle to carry up to fifty passengers. Cryogenic propellants would be loaded into the vehicle a few hours before liftoff. The launch vehicle was similar to the X-33 single-stage-to-orbit reusable launch system developed by the United States in the late 1990s. But while the United States' program had failed in 2001 due to failure of its composite fuel tank material during cryogenic fuel testing, the Greys were able to develop light composite materials to reduce vehicle weight and make a more efficient liftoff engine. Now 100 percent of vehicle hardware was reusable, making access to space more cost-efficient. Captain Noah told me,

"Private industry was the engine through which more than ninety percent of the work was done in aerospace and defense projects, and over a thousand private industry contractors supported the design, development, ground processing, and launch of our space vehicle. Space agency managers will tell you that people are the most important asset of any organization, and I felt that I was in good company. There I was, an inexperienced young adult given the kind of responsibility typical of someone more senior. I was grateful to be in the company of such dedicated and experienced teammates as I navigated the learning curve that would ultimately lead to this launch.

"After all, you have to remember that new space programs are just concepts in the minds of an engineering team, who then visualize it for others through diagrams, conceptual drawings and write-ups of operational concepts, and top-level requirements documents, project plans, block diagrams, and interface control documents. Planning includes preparation of budgets, schedules, and contract statements. From this baseline flows more detailed documentation, such as cable-interconnect diagrams, schematics, fabrication and installation drawings, testing and operating procedures, software coding and documentation, user guides, safety and reliability analyses, problem reports, contracts to industry, change requests, and more. After all this is developed, the result is the hardware and software products that we see come together for the ground processing and launch of a new space vehicle.

"The launch vehicle took the crew to a space station orbiting planet Zeta. The space station was a Greys' version of the International Space Station from Earth's early twenty-first century, the big difference being a large dock for the spaceship Zeta's Hope. From the space station, the crew would board the spaceship docked to the station. The spaceship resembled a WW2 submarine in shape and living space limitations. The crew included the twenty-five humanoid astronauts from nearby Amigo, which had been taken over by the Reptoids. Flying at a hundred times the speed of light, in about three weeks *Zeta's Hope* would carry the crew of colonists to the orbit of Avalonia, a habitable planet that they would explore and where they would establish a small colony."

Before Noah went on with his story, he paused to report with enthusiasm that since his preteen days he had loved science fiction books and television shows. He dreamed about being part of his planet's quest for the stars after he grew up, and he also felt that a lot of his crewmates shared that vision. When he was hired in the Greys' space agency, old-timers instilled in him values that influenced him for the rest of his life. They were committed to the design and development of equipment that was cost-efficient, safe, and reliable. They valued diversity in their engineering teams, both in the makeup of a team and in the opinions of its members. They valued excellence and ingenuity in their technical work. And their value system encompassed a high work ethic that included unquestionable honesty, open-mindedness, nonjudgmental trust among teammates, and a strong dedication to the task at hand. "If you ask me, our agency might have hired those guys out of some idealistic sci-fi TV series! And their core values were as essential to the agency's success as technology, public support, and funding."

Back to the launch. The countdown sequence went flawlessly from a well shielded control room that was not connected to the internet to reduce security concerns. The flight crew felt confident and lighthearted at that time.

Captain Noah turned to Romo, his first officer, and mentioned an old aerospace fact: "Is not it wonderful to know that we are sitting on top of a rocket built by the lowest bidder?"

Romo chuckled at Noah's remark.

During the T-minus-nine minutes hold prior to the start of the countdown, the weather officer reported, "Long-range orbital sensors show what appears to be a number of large objects approaching our planet. Each object seems to be about the size of a city block. This could be some sort of large meteorite shower. At present speed, these objects are estimated to arrive here within thirty minutes."

The launch director then said, "Let's proceed with the liftoff as scheduled and pass a warning to civil defense to alert all our fellow Greys to go to ground shelters provided with deflector shields."

Thus, most of the folks in cities headed for the designated emergency ground shelters in schools, hospitals, sports complexes, and churches. Most people in remote areas far from the shelters chose to remain home, perhaps trusting a basement, if available. It was chaotic, as the citizenry hurried to get to the designated shelters, taking their loved ones and carrying some of their possessions. Not all of them made it to the shelters. *"May God shelter them from any harm!* was our collective thought."

The launch went well. In the wee of the morning hours, while the ground launch team was loading propellants, a crowd of spectators was gathering on viewing sites six or seven miles from the launch pad. As the sun rose above the horizon, the roar of rocket engines caused a flock of nearby birds to take flight. It was a successful launch on a beautiful morning with clear skies.

About two minutes after the liftoff, the Amigo crew members identified the imagery of the suspected meteorites as a fleet of spaceships from the aggressive alien race known as Reptoids. The same race had invaded the Greys' allies in planet Amigo. Maybe they also intended to conquer Zeta!

Very little was known of them. The Greys' Amigo allies

described the creatures as fairly tall, about seven feet in height. They had unblinking lidless eyes and a scaly skin that changed in color like a chameleon. They were intelligent but had an aggressive demeanor.

Shortly after their appearance, the Reptoids discharged about twenty nuclear electromagnetic pulse (EMP) weapons scattered above the surface of Zeta at an altitude of 250 miles. America conducted similar high-altitude nuclear tests in 1962, known as Starfish Prime. The magnetic fields caused by these explosions resulted in disruptions of electrical power, communications systems, and transport without damaging building infrastructures or hurting people.

As the result of these high-altitude nuclear blasts, the Greys' home world sank into a massive blackout. Electrical surges caused fires and incapacitated traffic control and emergency dispatch systems. Police and firefighters were unable to respond to emergencies and were limited in their efforts, as most of their vehicles had been impaired by the EMP attack. A vast humanitarian effort followed the attack, but it was not enough to keep nearly two hundred million inhabitants from death by the starvation, exposure, or lack of medicine that followed. Overnight, Zeta receded into a Dark Age.

But the worst was yet to come. The initial landing parties of the Reptoids, totaling one hundred thousand soldiers, arrived in the largest nine inhabited islands in planet Zeta. Within seven days their spaceships were able to bring an additional million Reptoid soldiers, with air, naval, and armor assets superior to the antiquated weaponry of the Greys. Not having had a war in centuries and have no standing army or artillery (except in museums), many disabled command and control centers, and strict gun control laws, most Greys were slaughtered with little resistance. The few that had guns, mostly police officers, valiantly fought the advance of an enemy, well-equipped with armor, heavy artillery, and airborne bombers.

The attackers overwhelmed the inhabitants of Zeta. Within two weeks the Greys were overrun. Over 75 percent of them were mercilessly slaughtered, as the emotionless Reptoids thought them an unworthy, weak species and believed that letting many survive would present a threat of rebellion. Numerous families escaped into the jungles, swamps, and mountainous areas, where they planned to survive by hunting, fishing, and fruit gathering.

Sensing their demise, Zeta's President Datcher called on the Greys' spaceship: "Captain Zambuto, I order you to escape our home world's orbit, head to planet Avalonia, and save your crew, who may become the only survivors of our species."

With a sad face, Noah heard in silence and understood the order too well. After a few moments of reflection, he replied, "Yes, Madame President. I understand your decision. I'll embark on our mission to Avalonia and start a colony as planned. Our top priority will be our survival, whether on Avalonia or any other planet in the Milky Way. May God look after any surviving Greys in our home world of Zeta. May God bless you all! Zambuto out."

From now on, our story focuses on that spaceship that escaped, commanded by Captain Noah Zambuto. A crew of fifty (twenty-five Greys, and twenty-five humanoids from planet Amigo), escaped in his prototype spaceship capable of traveling at one hundred times the speed of light, a speed that the enemy spaceships were decades away from attaining. Captain Noah's ship, *Zeta's Hope*, had advanced propulsion, structural deflector shields, computers, communications equipment, and remote sensor technologies. Among the escapees were prominent scientists and designers and about an equal number of skilled technicians. A linguistic expert was also brought along. They also took with them enough food and fuel to last a year and four food replicators capable of turning any organic material into consumable soups and juices.

Before the fall of their planet to the Reptoids, the Greys destroyed all drawings and specifications of their prototype spaceship, thus blocking this advanced space flight technology from their conquerors. Many had retreated, with whatever weapons they had, to their capital, Zeta City, for a last stand. Roads in and out of the city were barricaded with vehicles, where citizens fought with antiquated guns. They had also rigged some old artillery, obtained from museums, which could be used fairly effectively as either anti-air or anti-armor weapons at short range. The fighting was furious, and they were inflicting many casualties on the invaders. The Greys were holding them off.

From a viewing window on their spaceship, the crew and passengers took a last glimpse of their planet. They saw what appeared to be a sudden, gigantic explosion that engulfed their capital, Zeta City, where the last pocket of Grey resistance was fighting.

Communications Officer Faith asked, "What's going on? That looked like a large explosion!"

First Officer Romo replied, "Our sensors detect a high level of radiation coming from Zeta City. —Oh my God! The invaders exploded a nuclear device to destroy our last pocket of resistance."

Romo paused momentarily, and said, "The Reptoids wanted to cut their casualties and used an atomic bomb."

Faith had patched into a traffic intersection security camera about three miles outside Zeta City, a city of about a hundred thousand inhabitants. She was recording data from the camera and replayed the video. The initial image showed the skyline of Zeta City, with perhaps half the buildings showing some damage from the Reptoids' previous aerial bombing and artillery shelling. A couple of enemy tanks were in place, apparently guarding the road where the camera was at. Suddenly a bright flash filled the whole video screen, shortly followed by the sound of an explosion. As a mushroom cloud was forming, they could hear the rumbling roar of the ground shaking.

Sorrow engulfed the hearts of all the crew members. They had left behind kin and other loved ones that had now been murdered by the invaders. The Greys and Amigos huddled together, praying and embracing each other, with tears in their eyes. They all kept nostalgically looking out the spaceships' windows, sensing in some way that this was the last time in their lives that they would see the Greys' home world.

It must have been a tough decision to leave the land of their birth, where they had made lifelong friendships, gotten married, settled down in the homes of their dreams, and decided to raise families. But they were ordered to escape and survive, by whatever means, somewhere in the galaxy.

Faith turned to her husband. "Noah, will we ever come back to Zeta?"

He replied, "I don't know, dear. This race of Reptoids has powerful weapons, from bomber planes and armored vehicles to nuclear devices. We've been ordered to escape, do the best to stay away from them, and survive."

Noah knew that President Datcher rationalized that if they could not fight the enemy, they could outrun them! For the next few years they were to become a band of space gypsies. Their interstellar journey would begin at their first stop on planet Avalonia and would eventually take them to Earth.

CHAPTER THREE

DEATH OF CAPTAIN NOAH'S PARENTS

After witnessing from orbit the invasion of his home world, planet Zeta, on a summer day of 1944, the Greys' Captain Noah Zambuto retired to his quarters. He'd been ordered to continue on his exploration and colonization mission to planet Avalonia. After all, his vessel was not a warship, and it had no weaponry.

In the Captain's cabin, Noah checked on his electronic mail via desktop. He found one from his nineteen-year-old brother, Ozzie, who still lived with their parents and worked as a technician at the Greys' launch center. On an email sent a few minutes earlier, Ozzie updated him on the events of the last day:

> Dear Brother:
>
> May God bless and protect you and the members of your crew in these moments of great peril caused by the invaders. Hope that the launch of our space vehicle, *Zeta's Hope*, went well and that you are on your way to settling in on that new

planet of Avalonia. The hope of our people rests with you guys!

After the launch, we were directed to underground shelters to survive what we thought was a meteor shower but turned out to be an invading armada of Reptoids!

Shortly after their appearance, the Reptoids exploded about twenty nuclear electromagnetic pulse (EMP) weapons orbiting above the surface of Zeta at an altitude of two hundred and fifty miles. The resulting magnetic fields caused unimaginable disruption of electrical power, communications systems, and transport without damaging building infrastructures or hurting people.

Our home world sank into a massive blackout! Some electrical surges caused fires and incapacitated traffic control and emergency dispatch systems. Police and firefighting workers were unable to fully respond to resulting emergencies and were limited in their efforts because many of their vehicles had been impaired by the EMP attack.

Overnight, Zeta receded into a Dark Age! Fortunately, most of the equipment at the launch center was protected against that initial energy spike caused by the EMP attack without suffering any damage. The same applied to some important government facilities and a few private citizens.

In the space center, our last order was to destroy drawings and specifications of your prototype spaceship, thus denying our attacker this advanced space technology. As the sun fell in the early evening, management allowed nonessential personnel to go home, so I walked to my building's protected indoor parking and rode my motorcycle to our parents' home ten miles away. Before departing I called them, but their phones were apparently disabled by the attack. On the way there, traffic was light, and a police officer was directing traffic at a moderately busy intersection where the signal was out.

Further down, I spotted a column of smoke from the direction of our parents' home. Rain started to drizzle, accompanied by intermittent lightning strikes. My concern for our parents' well-being increased as I saw a few burnt vehicles on the road, as if they had been hit by explosives.

I rode my bike, regarding little but the road ahead of me as the sun slowly set, painting the horizon with mixed shades of yellow, orange, and purple. On the side of the road, I could see the green foliage of a subtropical forest of tall oaks and pine trees surrounded by palmettos, cabbage palms, pepperbushes, and wildflowers. Nature seemed indifferent with its innate magnificent beauty as creatures fought for dominance in its realm. By the time I neared our parents' home, a full moon was glowing in the early evening.

A large object making a steady thudding sound as it moved swiftly through the bushes bordering our parents' home came to my attention. I stopped my bike and took shelter in a shallow ditch that contained about an inch of water.

What I saw next was the scary sight of a noisy armored vehicle under the moonlight and the strobe light effect of intermittent lightning. My heart was thumping like a drum. Alongside the vehicle were four Reptoid soldiers, cautiously moving about.

Suddenly, the vehicle partially sank into the septic tank and drain field of our parent's home. Then the Reptoids came under small arms fire from the neighbor's house across the street, a bullet hitting one of the enemies, who fell to the ground. Two of the other soldiers returned fire and the third one aimed his large directed-energy rifle on the neighbor's home, setting it on fire. As the neighbor, his wife, and two preteen children came out, hands up, escaping the flames, the Reptoids shot them dead!

The horror that I had just witnessed momentarily paralyzed me! But then I wondered about our parents' well-being. I crawled out of the ditch and moved through the bushes in the direction of the backyard of their home, speculating that was my best course to go unnoticed by the soldiers as they moved away across the street. By then, the armored vehicle unstuck itself from the septic tank and drain field and moved out into the street. Under the light of the full moon, I was able to reach our parents' back porch and froze with fear as I discovered that the back glass sliding door had been broken thru.

Regaining my composure, I moved into the house through the broken glass. My worst fears became reality as I found the bodies of both our parents in the dining room. I knelt first next to Mom and moved on to Dad, hoping that they might still be alive, but to no avail. I stayed on my knees for a few minutes, tears in my eyes, praying for their souls.

All of a sudden, I heard the sound of feet crushing the broken glass on the floor. I turned around with my pocketknife, thinking that I was been surprised by one of the Reptoids.

But after a quick look, I recognized the sixty-five-year-old retired widower police officer who lived alone in a house about half a mile away. He was standing by the back-sliding door in hunter's camouflage apparel, packing a side-arm. He was one of those survivalist preppers who was ready for any catastrophic event. As he lit a cigarette, he said, "Calm down, Ozzie. It's your neighbor, Abdul!"

Taking a drag of his cigarette, Abdul handed me his spare gun and said, "This revolver may come in handier than that pocketknife you've got!"

"Thank God it's you, Abdul! My parents are dead! So is the family across the street! What a terrible day this has turned out to be. An army of alien soldiers is wiping out our civilization! This must be some sort of Armageddon for our home world!"

I then told him, "I hope you have lots of am-munition back in your house, because I would like to kill as many of these Reptoids as I can!"

Abdul put a hand on my shoulder and replied, "Sorry about your parents. They were among the nicest people I ever met."

With a sigh, he continued, "I saw you pass by my house on your way to your parents'. I believe that we are the only ones left alive in this rural neighborhood. I suggest we stay the night in here, as the Reptoids already checked out this end of the neighborhood. But the most important thing we can do tonight is to survive, not kill any Reptoids without some good reason other than revenge! This is a battle for survival!"

I resigned myself to accept the reality of the day's events. Looking back at our parents' dead bodies, I said to Abdul, "Help me move their bodies upstairs. They deserve to rest in their beds."

He replied, "Let's do that tomorrow. We may then bury them. I fear that in an hour or two the Reptoids will do a sweep of the neighborhood before they leave. They'll know we are here if we move the bodies now. May God bless their souls!"

Then he asked, "Son, are you hungry? I've got a chunk of cheese and some dry beef sticks with me."

"Sure, Abdul. I've not had anything to eat since noon! We can chase your food with a couple wine bottles in the kitchen. There may be some milk, hard-boiled eggs, bread, butter, cereal, and other ready-to-eat food for tomorrow."

So, we sat down and ate and drank ourselves silly to bury our sorrows and any feelings of despair. After we finished our improvised dinner of cheese and dry beef sticks, we went upstairs to finish the wine and settle down for the evening.

As we looked out the second-story window, in the distance we could see fires that

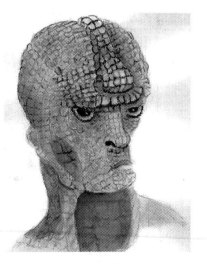

**Depiction of Reptoid
(by Roberta Lerman)**

were dwindling as an effect of the mild rain. Under the moonlight, we could see the ruins of gutted homes and blackened trees on the road downhill. There was a truck driven by one of the Reptoids collecting dead Grey bodies. What were they going to do with them? Incinerate them? Eat them? Save their organs and other body parts? But eventually we were overcome by fatigue and fell asleep.

Ozzie ended his email by promising to update Noah in about twenty-four hours. Noah replied to the email, updating Ozzie on the status of the flight mission to planet Avalonia and letting him know that he looked forward to Ozzie's next electronic mail tomorrow. After logging out of his computer, Noah silently mourned the death of his parents with slow-moving tears dripping from his eyes.

CHAPTER FOUR

CAPTAIN NOAH'S REMEMBRANCE OF HIS PARENTS

Captain Noah was overwhelmed by the violent death of his parents as a result of the Reptoid invasion in 1944, when more than 80 percent of the Greys perished. Many in his crew were undergoing the same grieving process for the death of their loved ones. Noah's initial reaction was to return to planet Zeta and fight. But he was bound by duty and understood the decision of President Datcher to send off his spaceship. After all, their vessel was just a fast space transport. It wasn't a warship, and it had no weaponry. The President's order ensured the survival of the crew and prevented their Reptoid enemy from getting hold of their advanced space flight technology.

After he'd brooded for about an hour, his wife, Faith, the ship's communications officer, walked into their cabin and sat down next to him on the bed. She massaged his tense shoulders in hopes of comforting him.

"Thanks, Faith! I guess I needed some support in this moment of distress."

"No need to mention it, my love. I know how close you were to your parents. I was fortunate that mine lived in a remote area of Zeta and escaped the initial Reptoid onslaught. I hope and pray for all the survivors of this genocide."

Noah said, "At this point in time, hoping and praying is all we can do, dear. The fact that Ozzie and Abdul have survived gives me hope that many of those living in remote areas will survive. It seems that the Reptoids focused their attacks on urban centers and strategic targets like the space center."

He started to share with Faith his memories of his parents. About his mother, Captain Noah had mixed memories of good times and painful moments. His mother was a loving, caring, and light-hearted individual. And they had a good time enjoying anything from board games and playing mini-golf to sharing a dinner or simply watching a good movie. On the other hand, since childhood he'd had difficulty dealing with his mom's mental health. Noah shared with Faith how in 1935 he had taken his fifty-year-old mom to a psychiatrist, who diagnosed her with schizoaffective disorder. This condition caused loss of contact with reality and mood swings between normal and manic. Some of her symptoms were problems concentrating; incoherent, disorganized speech; occasional agitation, trouble sleeping; and occasional hallucinations.

(Noah later told me that the couple of times that his dad and the family institutionalized his mom were painful for everyone. In his younger drinking days, he felt some shame that his mother had twice "graduated" from mental institutions! These were times that required love, patience, and tolerance. But despite minor difficulties, it seemed that Noah and his parents took good care of each other.)

Not giving his mom the joy of having a grandchild before she died was one of Noah's greatest regrets. A few days before her

death, his mom told him that she wished he had married and
formed a family with a high school sweetheart who committed
suicide in 1936. Instead, he moved on, got a few years of recovery
under his belt, and married his college sweetheart, Faith. But his
mom seemed still obsessed with memories of "what if" with his
old girlfriend.

Just a few days before the launch, while he and his mom
were watching television, with mom, she turned to him during a
commercial break and said, "Son, I think of Mary on occasion.
Did you love her?"

"Yes, Mom, I loved her."

"Did you ever tell her? You could have married her, made
some grandbabies for me, and lived happily ever after!"

Noah's gaze moved from the TV to her, as he reflected on
what she said. His failure to sire grandchildren seemed to have
come up every few months during the last year. Giving her grandbabies was not the kind of thing one added to the grocery list! It
had been eight years since Mary passed away!

"No, I don't recall telling her that I loved her," he finally
replied. "By the time I realized I loved her, I was several months
clean. But Mary was still going out and drinking herself silly until
closing time at the clubs. Then I would get a phone call to come
and get her at the bar and drive her home. I tried to get her help
and took her to a couple of recovery meetings back in August of
'thirty-five, but she was not willing to live a recovery program, and
she left me for a drinking buddy of hers. Had she stayed with me
and put together as little as ninety days clean, I would have asked
her to marry me."

"Son, you should have married her and given me grandchildren! Your brother is too young, and it may be a few years before
he settles down. It's your duty as the eldest brother to get going
and give me grandkids soon while I'm still here!"

Noah kept quiet and turned back to the TV. Mom could not
understand that it wasn't advisable for an addict in recovery to

maintain a relationship with an old drunk girlfriend who was not willing to get clean. Accepting that fact was not Mom's forte. But he understood her desire to have grandchildren and feared that he would regret her passing away without grandchildren.

After some reflection, he said, "Too late now, Mom. A friend told me that Mary committed suicide eight years ago, back in 1936, about nine months after she left me. I wish I could change the past, but I can't. Now I'm now married to Faith, a good woman that I love and consider my best friend. We'll eventually make you some grandbabies!"

With that said, their attention turned back to the television program. That would turn out to be the last time he saw her.

On the other hand, Noah's dad was his life's hero, idol, and role model, the wise anchor that held the family together. He was born in 1878, at a time when the Greys' home world of Zeta had enjoyed over three centuries of peace and prosperity.

His pop was an easygoing fellow with an engaging personality and a quick wit, who retired from his small-town law practice after a span of over four decades. Who knows, perhaps he could have been a stand-up comedian instead of a lawyer! He loved games that resembled softball and dominoes on Earth. Those who knew Noah's dad in his younger days described him as a handsome ladies' man. His good looks were enhanced by his preference for dressing elegantly. And Dad was also a functional drinker of alcohol, mentoring Noah on the art of drinking in his younger days.

His dad had a great understanding of history, literature, and geography, and Noah had access to a large home library on those subjects during his growing years. By the time he graduated high school, Noah had also read many classical works—including a number of science fiction books. But his dad's greatest legacy was his love for democratic institutions, political liberties, the free enterprise system, and a strong work ethic. Though not religious, his pop had traditional ethical values from which Noah learned—whether this was achieved through playing sports and board games or just discussing literature and politics.

Noah's dad had great love for his family—and there was a strong loving and caring bond between them. If Noah had a child and had half the love for him or her that his dad had for him, he would be the second-best dad in the world! But all good things come to an end. His dad's health kept deteriorating due to his diabetes, which caused him to quit working in 1943 at the age of sixty-five. During the last two years of his life, his pop seemed to age twenty years, and this physical deterioration seemed to slow him down, and it affected his once alert and savvy state of mind.

Many years into the future, about three decades after dad's death, Noah too would develop diabetes—a metabolic disease in which a person has high blood sugar, either because the pancreas does not produce enough insulin or because the body's cells do not respond to the insulin that is produced. With diabetes, the excess glucose is stored as fat in the body. Long-term complications include cardiovascular disease, chronic renal failure, retinal damage that can lead to blindness, erectile dysfunction, and gangrene, which can lead to amputation of the toes or feet. These complications are less common among people who exercise, eat moderately, and control their blood sugar levels with medication.

Noah's father accepted the fact that he had little time to live. Maybe his utter honesty was his way of facing the imminence of death. What little time Pop had he spent mostly with Mom. He would also help himself to an occasional drink—beer, wine, and sometimes a beverage with a bit more alcohol. Pop continued to crack jokes until a few days before his death—perhaps that was his own way of dealing with the painful advent of the grim reaper. Unfortunately, his murder and mom's by the invading Reptoid armada in the summer of 1944 cut short their lives by a few years. May God bless their souls!

CHAPTER FIVE

STAYING ALIVE

Two days after the invasion of their home world in the summer of 1944, the Greys' Captain Noah retired to his quarters. He slept better the second night, despite learning of the death of his parents. But the knowledge that his brother, Ozzie, had survived the initial onslaught of the Reptoids had brought him some comfort. Noah went to check on his electronic mail and was glad to find a second one from his brother. Ozzie updated him on the events of the last day as follows:

> Dear Brother:
>
> God bless and protect you and the members of your crew in these moments of great peril. Hope that the mission to planet Avalonia by your space vehicle is going well and that you are on your way to settling that new world.
>
> Depressed by the drama and chaos, including the death of our parents, my neighbor Abdul

and I shared a bottle of wine after dinner, which promptly put us to sleep. I did not sleep well, having nightmares about the invaders and the death of our parents at their hands.

We were awakened early the next morning by the noise of the Reptoids coming into the first floor of the house. We were in fear of being found out. But the Reptoids did not check upstairs, where we spent the night. From the second floor of our parents' home, we peeked out one of the windows. A slight drizzle was coming down, accompanied by intermittent lightning strikes. This time around, we did not see any armored vehicles, but the soldiers outnumbered us two to one. And one of them seemed to be in constant communications on his radio with neighboring units.

Abdul and I saw a pickup truck where the Reptoid soldiers were loading the dead bodies of our parents and those of four neighbors from across the street whom they had killed the previous day. The inside of my young and passionate nineteen-year-old heart raged with anger!

Amid feelings for revenge, I felt like going downstairs to confront them and whispered to Abdul, "We should go down and shoot them!"

But the older and more level-headed Abdul put his left hand on my right shoulder. As my head turned around, his right index finger was over his mouth, signaling me to remain quiet. I opted to wisely comply with Abdul's silent request. He whispered to me, "Listen, Ozzie. Even if we kill the four soldiers outside, more will come if they don't hear from them. Be quiet; your parents would have wanted you to stay alive!"

Abdul was right. It was too risky for us to take on those Reptoid soldiers. It seemed that our best course was to remain quiet until they left. On the previous evening, Abdul wanted to go back to his house and pick up more food, a rifle he left there, and some ammunition. Then he wanted to call his forty-year-old daughter and her family; he had contacted them yesterday on his cell phone. He also wanted to check on his girlfriend, Chloe. Heck, I had neither close kin left alive that I knew of nor a girlfriend in our home world. I figured I might as well tag on to Abdul!

Before they left, the Reptoids buried their only casualty from the fighting the previous day right in the front yard of our parents' home, putting a wooden stake as a grave marker on it, after a one-minute burial ceremony honoring their fallen companion.

It bothered me that we could not properly bury our parents. What were they going to do with their bodies? Incinerate them? Eat them? Save their organs and other parts? I bit my lips and stayed put, as the older and wiser Abdul had directed me. At sixty-five, he was a retired Special Weapons and Tactics law enforcement officer, and I figured that he knew what was best for our survival.

We waited for about ten minutes after they left and started digging up the body of the dead Reptoid to learn more about our enemy. By then the rain had stopped. Although the ground was a bit wet, the disturbed dirt was soft and easy to remove. The dead Reptoid had a headset, a bionic right eye, and a bionic arm, which we removed for storage in our attic and further analysis later. Then we covered the grave again, leaving the wooden stake in the same position, and headed to Abdul's home. We avoided the open road, walking under the cover of the trees and brush.

Once we arrived at Abdul's home, he told me that the Reptoids had apparently been there, for he noticed that a couple of fresh fish were missing from the refrigerator, which now lacked power. Also missing was a box of ammunition that he'd left on the kitchen table. But they did not take the rifle and additional hundreds of rounds of ammunition that he had in the attic, which they did not search. They had also left untouched most other food. This included some cheese, butter, cooking oil, eggs, cereal, bread, crackers, nuts, vitamins, a dozen bottles of water, and some cans of salmon, spam, tuna, soup, and vegetables. He also had several candles, a supply of wooden matches, dry firewood, and a couple of lighters and flashlights. Abdul even had a hand water pump in his backyard!

I said to Abdul, "It seems that you were prepared for a catastrophic situation."

He looked at me, smiled, and replied, "Yes. I was. But I would have preferred a tropical storm to an alien invasion!"

He then led me to a small ten-by-ten-foot room that he had protected against electromagnetic interference (EMI), where equipment was protected from the electromagnetic pulse (EMP) preceding the alien invasion. There, he not only had his personal computer hooked to the internet, not currently operating because of the EMP explosions, but also had his amateur radio system. By then, it was nearly noon, and we could hear gunfire and explosions in the distance, apparently coming from the space center.

Abdul picked up his smartphone and called his fifty-five-year-old girlfriend working security there, "Chloe! This is Abdul calling from home. How are you guys holding out at the space center?"

"Abdul! I'm glad to hear your voice! Hundreds of these Reptoid soldiers are pouring into the space center, with support from helicopters and armored vehicles. Two other security guards and I are holding out in the Launch Equipment Test Facility, where we test swing arms and umbilicals. I believe it may only be minutes before we are overrun. The main attack is on the north side, where they have taken over most of the industrial area and the launch pads. I have lost communication with all other security personnel in the space center."

"Listen. You guys each get a bottle of water, break into the candy machine for snacks, and retreat into the woods on the south edge of the facility. Stay out of sight in the brush, away from any buildings the Reptoids may be checking out. You guys may have to spend the night in the bushes, but with some caution you can get to my house on foot by tomorrow. I'll leave the sliding door in the back unlocked. Love you, sweetheart! Abdul out."

Surprised at the sudden end of the conversation, I gave Abdul a puzzled look. He said, "The call had to be quick. I didn't want the Reptoids to have time to trace the call here. But just in case, we'll grab some water and food and head back to your parents' home a mile down the road."

Before we left, Abdul called his daughter, told her to hold out in the basement of her home, and said he would call again the next day to check on her.

With that said, we picked up some water and food and headed back to my more remotely located parents' home. We went upstairs and did some reading under the afternoon sunrays coming through a window. We had tuna sandwiches for dinner and listened to some music on a battery powered CD player that Abdul had brought from his EMI sheltered office. Overcome by fatigue, we started to fall asleep.

Ozzie ended his email telling Captain Noah that he would update him in about twenty-four hours. Noah replied, updating Ozzie on the status of the mission to planet Avalonia and saying he looked forward to Ozzie's next message the following day. He was relieved that Ozzie and Abdul had done well so far, surviving the initial attack by the Reptoids.

CHAPTER SIX

A GORY STORY

Captain Noah was depressed after watching events from his spaceship as the Reptoids conquered his home world within a matter of days. He retired to his quarters and checked on his electronic mail. He had a message from Chloe, who was Deputy Chief of Security at the Greys' Launch Center. She updated him about the events on Zeta:

> Dear Captain:
>
> May God bless and protect you and your crewmates in these moments of peril caused by the invaders. Glad to see that the launch of our space vehicle went well and that you are on your way to that new world of planet Avalonia!
>
> After the successful launch, management allowed nonessential personnel to go home. They would be driving at the tail end of a crowd of 100,000 visitors who had come to view the launch!

We had no idea of the Reptoids landing around us about twenty minutes after the launch. Your brother Ozzie was lucky to make it out in time!

From the security control room, we saw that first wave of armored gunship helicopters that the invaders sent, spraying machine gun fire all over. Then ground support planes started dropping napalm and mustard gas. It was a horrendous sight! Those not burned by the napalm died of exposure to the mustard gas, which affected their skin and lungs. There were burned-out vehicles and dead bodies strewn throughout several miles of roads! It was estimated that two thirds of the visitors who witnessed the launch perished!

The Reptoids landed many craft with about a thousand of their soldiers south of the space center. They had many armored vehicles and advanced on us. In terror, we watched as they shot unarmed tourists leaving after the launch, many of them women and children. We were first attacked by a contingent numbering about 300 in the mostly deserted industrial area where I was. But the bulk of them, perhaps another 700, proceeded north to engage our security forces in the launch complex, where my boss, the Chief of Security, was with most of our hundred security guards.

There were no more than twenty security guards in the industrial area, where I was. We fought valiantly but had a losing battle, as we were outgunned and outnumbered. I retreated with two other officers into the Launch Equipment Test Facility. The last command I heard from the Chief of Security was "Everybody is to abandon your posts! Retreat into the woods!" It was then that I had a phone call from my boyfriend, Abdul, retired former leader of the SWAT team. He was alive and safe in his remotely located rural home. Abdul suggested that we abandon our positions and retreat into the woods south of the center and head for shelter to his home about fifteen miles away.

We retreated into the woods. After two hours, we arrived at a house isolated in the middle of the woods owned by my companion Rib's parents; he was one of the two guards who escaped the onslaught with me. His mom, a sweet woman aged in her late sixties, received us. After urgently bandaging a skin wound on Rib's arm, she turned to us and said, "What a terrible day! No electricity or water! But thank God, we have supplies for a few days and a hand water pump in our backyard! My husband walked over a mile up toward the highway, hiding in the bushes as he saw two enemy helicopters heading toward the space center. From his hideout, he spotted an invading column of armor and alien-looking mobile infantry heading toward the space center."

After catching her breath, she asked, "Are these the nasty folks who invaded our friends on planet Amigo?"

I replied, "Yes. The Reptoids also overran us at the space center within about an hour. From early reports, we estimate that they have killed several thousand of our fellow Greys, including many tourist families who were viewing the launch."

After a pause to digest the shocking news, Rib's mom added with a sad tone, "Dear God! I hope and pray that our neighbors who went to view the launch survived. I also have been trying to hear news in our battery-operated radio all day, but all I hear is static. We had the radio stored in a metallic file cabinet, and my husband told me that it was protected from any electromagnetic interference. I was hoping to hear our president to give a speech about a day of infamy as President Frankie did when the militaristic Sakitas attacked us by surprise four centuries ago! Thank God we all became friends after they adopted a constitutional monarchy to govern themselves!" She then went into a kind of trance and slowly repeated: "But all I heard was static!"

After some reflection, she said, "But what a terrible host I am! May I serve you any drinks or snacks? And please feel free to crash here!" After some small chitchat, we accepted her invitation to spend the night.

The next morning. Stout, the other guard, and I continued our journey to Adbul's house about eight miles away, which would take us nearly a full day.

After the destruction of the launch complex, Stout and I were saddened by the fact that we did not know if any of our loved ones had survived the Reptoid onslaught. We worked our way through the thick brush to avoid contact with our enemies. During our journey, we heard distant gunfire and explosions, but we stuck to our plan about going to Abdul's. After all, he was the only close friend we both had who had survived the attack.

Stout and I kept to the brush as we approached Abdul's house. As the sun was setting, we spotted a convenience store that was about two miles from his home. Thirsty and hungry, we broke into the store through the back door, out of view of about forty Reptoid soldiers and an armored vehicle that guarded a highway overpass fifty yards from the storefront. We cautiously entered the store and found nobody inside. After looking around for a few seconds, I told him, "Somebody has already plundered the store for supplies! Perhaps it was the Reptoids by the highway overpass."

Stout added, "Chloe, it seems that they took all the beer, wine, and canned beans. But they left plenty of other goodies for us!"

We grabbed milk, fruit juices, bread, and a few snacks and stuffed them into our backpacks. It was dusk. We figured that our adversaries had poor visibility into the store. We crept toward the front of the store to see what they were up to.

By the highway underpass a small gathering of enemy soldiers appeared to be cooking. They had a red flag with a white circle in the middle containing the black silhouette of a Reptoid with a spear and a shield.

With my binoculars, I observed a nightmarish vision. They brought in the dead body of a Grey, who was wearing the garb of a clergyman. They disrobed, skinned, and dismembered his body. I watched in horror as they roasted the trunk of the corpse on a rotisserie rod over a firepit, the same way we would a pig! One of them seemed to be pouring white wine over the body. Another Reptoid soldier was cutting chunks of meat and serving them around on paper plates. He was wearing a collar made from severed fingers of his Grey victims!

My companion Stout exclaimed, "Those sons of guns are feeding on our people—and wearing body parts as war trophies!"

The Reptoids were laughing, apparently trading jokes and boozing it up with the beer and wine they'd seized from the convenience store.

We were disgusted at this gory sight of a fellow Grey being cooked! Stout said out loud, "Oh, my God! I wonder if the poor Grey being roasted was a loved one! We should take on these guys, but they outnumber us twenty to one, and they've got a tank!" As he finished talking, I vomited over my clothes. I went to the bathroom to clean up.

When I came back to the front of the store, two of the Reptoids, apparently their leaders, got on top of a pickup truck with a loudspeaker and started to address the others. I did not have any idea of who these two guys were. But they must have been important, as two others with video cameras positioned themselves in the crowd. I decided to turn on the recorder in my cell phone and record their speech, which we translated a few hours later at Abdul's.

The first Reptoid addressed the crowd, "Companions. It is a great honor for this humble lieutenant to introduce one of the leaders of the Nationalist Socialist Union, our vice-president and army commander—Heinrik Beriangly."

The small group of soldiers applauded and shouted, "Heinrik! Heinrik!"

Then the leader moved forward and began speaking, "Companions. It's such a delight to see you today as we vanquish our enemies!"

He paused and pointed to the sun, as it was about to set on the horizon. "Our triumphant troops shine like the sun on their rolling march to victory! A few days ago, victory in Amigo! Today, victory in Zeta! And in a few days, victory in Avalonia!"

The soldiers cheered, saying, "Viva Heinrik! Beloved commander, command us!"

Heinrik crossed his arms and smiled, as he gazed through the crowd. He went on, "My dear companions. We've been together in this struggle for a long time. At the end of the Great Reptoid War on our home world fifteen years ago, we were sold out by democratically elected corrupt politicians who agreed to pay an enormous war debt to fund the industrial military complex, the main beneficiaries of the war!"

Many in the crowd yelled, "Down with the capitalists! Power to the people!"

Heinrik's expression changed to one of disdain. Then he continued, "Out of control government spending, subsidies to preferred industries, reckless printing of worthless money, easy credit, and trade wars among the states in our home world resulted in high inflation and unemployment. And those self-centered imperialist capitalists only watched for their own interest at the expense of the little guys! Lawlessness and violence prevailed, including rape of our women. Democracy as we know it consists solely of elections rigged by the rich and professional politicians. It's not the voters who count. What's most important for the capitalists is the people who count the votes. And democracy, as we know, consists solely of elections rigged by the rich and professional politicians!"

Heinrik paused as the crowd applauded, then went on. "Guns for what? Our communist ideas are mightier than guns! Why should we let potential enemies of the people have guns? And who needs a biased media, multiparty elections, property, religion, and gun rights? With these tools, democracy and capitalism failed! But the people prevailed during our glorious revolution ten years ago when our Reptoid Nationalist Socialist Union came to power! The party took over the corrupt independent media, the puppet labor and student unions, who catered to special interests. We seized all businesses and land holdings, including church properties. Who needs religion anyhow? After all, religion is the opiate of the masses! And don't worry about the devil! I've been told that he's a good communist!"

Loud laughter came from the crowd. Heinrik stopped talking for a brief moment. He resumed: "Together, we developed industries and technology better than our enemies', from tanks and aircraft to long-range missiles and nuclear weapons! We jailed and castrated all violent criminals! But read my lips, we will not fail you! We'll put the people first, and we'll all share the spoils of our victorious revolution!"

The crowd broke into cheers, and they started chanting, "Heinrik, hit the capitalists hard! Heinrik, hit the capitalists hard!"

He paused, smiled, and went on. "This war with the Greys and Amigos began when diplomacy failed. Our enemies were charging us exorbitant prices for food and energy resources that our motherland needed. And they would not share their high technology either! These capitalists were leading us on the road to bankruptcy and turning us into their slaves. Unfair trade was their means of conquest! To get what we need to survive, war was our only option! But what do we need in our hearts in order to survive?"

While the guys with the video cameras scanned the crowd, many in the gathering yelled, "Reptoids, yes! Greys, no! Reptoids, yes! Greys, no!"

I wonder what would happen to anybody who did not cheer with enthusiasm in front of the cameras!

Heinrik momentarily stopped, his eyes scanning his audience, and then closed his bombastic speech. "We need hatred! Hatred is an element of the struggle; a relentless hatred of the adversary, transforming us into a cold and effective killing machine. Our soldiers must be thus, for a people without hatred cannot vanquish a brutal enemy. To choose one's victims, to prepare one's plan in detail, to implement our vengeance, and then to go to bed and sleep like babies—there is nothing sweeter in the world! Keep marching on the road to total victory! Fatherland or death; we shall overcome!" The crowd again broke into cheers. Heinrik climbed down from the pickup truck and then shook hands with a few soldiers and posed for a few photos.

From my empath abilities, typical of Greys, I sensed that Heinrik was a person of intelligence. I also sensed he had great pride and personal ambition, coupled with an evil self-will, which meant he'd stop at nothing to get his way. If I hadn't known about the atrocities committed in his name, I might have followed such a persuasive and charismatic leader. But a wise teacher once told me to follow leaders who live by virtuous principles and to beware of those with flamboyant and charismatic personalities!

No longer having to remain hidden in the convenience store, we loaded our supplies and decided to leave for Abdul's place before it got too dark.

We left through the back door and took a path across the brush that led us near the dead-end road where Abdul's home is located. On our way there, we saw houses and cars burned down, plus many dead Greys. The bodies of the dead were surrounded by scavenging animals, mostly vultures or rodents. The destruction caused by the Reptoids was a sad and terrible sight! *Did their arrival signal the end of our civilization?*

We made it to Abdul's house at nightfall and found him and Ozzie waiting. We traded our stories of survival and made short-term plans that included another visit to the convenience store the next day for more goods and a fishing trip to a nearby river. Despite the traumatic events of the last couple of days, we are determined to survive!

Chloe ended her email telling Captain Noah that she would update him on how they were doing within a few days. Noah replied by updating her on the status of the mission to planet Avalonia and said he looked forward to her next electronic mail. As a matter of fact, Chloe and her friends did well for the better part of the next few days. Perhaps there was hope for them to survive their ordeal!

CHAPTER SEVEN

TRIP TO PLANET AVALONIA

The evening after Zeta fell to the invasion of the Reptoids, the crew of *Zeta's Hope* could hardly sleep with the traumatic memories of the conquest of their home world. As directed by their now presumed dead President Datcher, the Greys and their Amigo allies were now en route to establish a small colony on an unexplored planet called Avalonia.

The Greys had decided to take this space journey after nearly four centuries of peace, when their society first engaged in space exploration. They had developed advanced technologies in healthcare, computers, communications, power generation, and space travel that were nearly two centuries ahead of Earth. By the late 1930s, space probes had surveyed a planet in a neighboring star system that had an atmosphere rich in oxygen and nitrogen and had a flora and fauna similar to Zeta. The Greys named this planet Avalonia.

The people on Zeta were enthusiastic about this discovery and embarked on a mission to explore and colonize this planet. By that time, a Grey called Jang Tauls had developed a space vehicle propulsion system capable of traveling at a hundred times the speed of light. He was the Grey's modern rocketry father, the equivalent of Robert Goddard and Werner von Braun in America—or Konstantin Tsiolkovsky and Sergei Korolev in Russia.

Going to planet Avalonia was a topic dominant in Grey social media for several years before they launched the mission there. A similar period in Earth's history was when President Kennedy committed to go to the moon back in the 1960s and when President Harkness did the same for a manned mission to Mars in the late 2020s.

For the day after the launch, Captain Noah had scheduled a staff meeting. The nine bridge officers were present: four males, four females, and an android. Other than Noah, they were Mr. Romo (an Amigo science officer who doubled as First Officer), Chief Engineer Jang, Doctor Akina, Quartermaster Boudica, Ben at helm (an Amigo), Navigator Nax (an Amigo), Faith (Noah's wife, the communications officer), and Security Chief Amie. There were three non-Grey bridge officers—human-like Amigos, experienced in space travel, who had escaped days before the Reptoids' invasion of their home world.

Though some of these officers' regular stations were not on the bridge, the chief engineer, the doctor, and the quartermaster were considered bridge officers. It was a diverse group in race, sex, education, and experience. But this diversity helped provide different perspectives, together with willingness to work together, that were a key to their success and survival as a team.

Mr. Romo Agrox was second in command. He was a baby-faced male in his mid-twenties, who had the looks of a young college student. He thought highly of the more experienced crew members and years later told Captain Noah, "Those old-timers instilled in me values that influenced me for the rest of my life. They were committed to the safe and reliable design, development, and operation of the spaceship. They valued diversity in their engineering teams, whether in the makeup of a team or the opinions of its members. They valued excellence and ingenuity in their technical work. And their value system encompassed a high work ethic that included unquestionable honesty, open-mindedness, nonjudgmental trust among teammates, and a strong dedication to the task at hand. They were serious about their work, but they also had the lightheartedness required to stay sane in a high-stress environment. If you ask me, the space agency might have hired those guys out of some idealistic sci-fi TV series! But their core values were as important to the space agency's success as technology, public support, and funding."

Something humorous happened when Romo first came to the initial staff meeting back on planet Zeta. Chief Engineer Jang, not knowing that Romo outranked him, thought that Romo was a young aide and asked him to procure a cup of coffee for him. And Romo actually went off and did so! Jang was a bit embarrassed when told that he had ordered a higher-ranking officer to get him a cup of coffee.

But despite his youthful looks, Romo was responsible for the overall systems design, development, and integration of the Greys' space vehicle. Nobody knew the spaceship's systems better than he did. And he had some basic project management skills required for leading design, development, test, and space operations teams—skills like planning and execution of user technical requirements, budgets, and schedules; communications skills to create a project vision; and organizing and motivating others. He also had an uncanny ability to identify safety, reliability, and quality issues. He could write good contracts, specifications, procedures, and technical reports. Despite being naïve about the ways of life and lacking in the art of politics, when it came to technical and aerospace business skills, Noah considered Romo his right hand and the most valuable member of his crew.

Captain Noah started the meeting by welcoming all of *Zeta's Hope's* bridge officers. Communications Officer Faith, who doubled as the ship's chaplain, offered the following prayer: "God, thank you for another day alive, free, and of good health and spirits. Bless those less fortunate who have died or been hurt or are suffering under slavery in our home world. Give us good health and good spirits for another day."

Noah then yielded to Navigator Nax for a progress report on the mission to planet Avalonia. She was a female humanoid aged thirty-five, the oldest member of the crew. The Amigo humanoids were close in appearance to humans in Earth, except that their stomachs were off centered to the right about an inch. (You might ask your friends for a tummy check to see if you have a human from Amigo among you!)

Nax gave her mission progress report. "Launch went well with no damage. Current velocity is about one hundred times light speed. Fuel consumption is at the specified nominal rate. Arrival at planet Avalonia is estimated at twenty days from now."

The Greys' attitude was welcoming, accepting, and supportive toward the humanoids. They were glad that they were peaceful people like themselves and not ruthless aggressors like the Reptoids that had conquered both their home planets.

Noah nodded. "Thanks for your report, Nax. Now Quartermaster Boudica"—a Grey female— "will proceed with her report."

"We have ample food supplies and fuel for six months. After our twenty-day trip to planet Avalonia, we were originally scheduled to go back to Zeta, but that will not be possible after the Reptoids' takeover. I propose that after we survey Avalonia for a week, we then reconvene to draw up a new plan for utilization of resources. I volunteer to lead that effort."

Noah thanked Boudica and moved on to introduce First Officer Romo for a report on forming a colony after the landing at planet Avalonia. Like the other bridge officers, he had a minimum of three years' experience in the aerospace industry. Like him, most of the crew was made up of recent college grads and technicians who averaged about twenty-five years of age, with no more than three to four years of aerospace experience.

Romo, who was in charge of setting up the initial camp, gave his report: "The day before arriving on planet Avalonia with our landing module, we'll have selected a preliminary base camp where I'll lead a crew of four for our first ten days there. The four-person team for our landing party includes Doctor Akina, Chief of Security Amie, and Quartermaster Boudica, who'll serve as an additional armed member of security. At the moment we are not aware of any large land predators on the island where we plan to land, but I recommend that we act with some caution anyhow."

Romo stopped for a drink of water and went on. "Despite the fact that probes previously sent to Avalonia showed that the air, soil, and water are similar to our home worlds, we'll err on the side of caution on our initial landing. During the first two hours, our android Chief of Security Amie will sample air, soil, and water for any unknown microorganisms that may endanger the crew. Once we determine we have a safe environment, the rest of us will disembark. We'll then establish a fishing base camp and explore about a mile and a half perimeter on foot. From the base camp, we'll explore our surroundings and assess the area for hunting, fishing, fruit gathering, farming, and fuel resources. When we're all back at the landing module, we'll go through the decontamination showers and breathe disinfectant vapor to minimize any danger from microorganisms. We'll also have medical examinations by Doctor Akina. We want all members of the landing party to stay healthy and free from any harmful microbial life."

Romo stopped and asked, "Any questions so far?"

After a few seconds, he resumed. "In the meanwhile, *Zeta's Hope* will survey the planet from orbit and suggest any alternative sites for a permanent settlement, where we can set up a few tents for the colonists who will follow. After a couple of days, we'll reconvene in the ship and replan as required. When anyone is exploring the surroundings of our base camp on foot, either

Security Officer Amie or another member of security—Boudica—is required to go with them. That is all!"

Noah thanked Romo for his report and asked, "Any problems or any other items that the group wants to discuss before we adjourn?" After a pause, he declared the meeting adjourned.

Security Chief Amie was a fifteen-year-old model of an android who had stirred a widespread interest in robotics. Although she was an artificially intelligent robot who looked human, like any member of security, she was required to carry a gun. Her level of sophistication was a notch lower than that of the robot in the 1960s American TV series *Lost in Space*. In simple words, she was an analytical computer with flexible rubber skin, arms, legs, sensors, and a feminine voice. She had no subjective judgment and no feelings of any kind, such as love, joy, envy, pity, sadness, anger, pride, mockery, shame, or fear. She had no desire to control or manipulate others; conquer, kill, or rob anyone; get high; or have sex.

Amie resembled the designer's college-age daughter and combined the physical abilities of a martial arts master with the stamina of a long-distance runner. In addition, she had the extra feature of a stainless-steel exoskeleton that protected her from dangers like projectiles and sharp objects. The exoskeleton was covered with a skinlike material that resembled a human's skin but possessed a few minute sensors for air sampling and gauging pressure and temperature, and these fed into Amie's "brain." Most of these sensors were located on the middle and lower part of her torso, since she had no digestive system. Instead, she had batteries and a large data acquisition and control system, which made her ideal to explore new worlds on foot. For simplicity's sake, she had no sex organs.

Prior to the takeover by the Reptoids, Amie's designer had

destroyed her design documentation; thus, the android aboard *Zeta's Hope* was the only one of her kind. Everybody thought that detailed schematics and hardware assembly drawings for creating duplicates had been destroyed. But Captain Noah and First Officer Romo had discovered a memory ship in Amie's head that contained all this information. They each made a copy of this memory chip and kept it in their personal safes in their quarters, telling no one else of their find.

When Amie arrived at Zeta with the Amigo humanoids, her arrival caused some controversy. Religious people and nature lovers alike raised objections to the idea of a physically superior artificial life. Some speculated that this android would be duplicated and commit acts of violence against the people. President Datcher ended such concerns when she directed that Amie be placed under the command of Captain Noah and First Officer Romo. They supervised her reprogramming, which directed her to protect the life and welfare of any Grey and humanoid life forms over her own.

After a twenty-day trip, *Zeta's Hope* finally arrived at planet Avalonia and began orbiting around it. Remote sensors had confirmed that the planet had an atmosphere similar to Zeta and Amigo, about 80 percent nitrogen and 20 percent oxygen. There was also a hilly area where sensors had shown an abundant source of fuel resources. Mr. Romo had recruited four members of the crew for the landing module, which included Doctor Akina, Chief of Security Amie, and Quartermaster Boudica, who would serve as an additional armed member for security purposes. After a few days, Romo intended to bring down additional crew members after establishing a fishing base camp and the initial exploration on foot.

They landed on a deserted beach on the north side of a large island about the size of Cuba. There were trees that resembled cabbage palms and pine trees; the underbrush was sparse enough to allow people to walk about without the help of a machete to clear the way.

An hour before sundown, Mr. Romo reported back: "Captain, from the beach, we can observe life on the ocean, from sharks and dolphinlike creatures to schools of small fish. The flora consists of a few cactuses to orchids and an abundance of bromeliads. This includes some edible types, like pineapple plants, which may also provide textile fiber. Some trees resemble citrus, mangoes, papayas, avocadoes, guavas, and coconuts. We have seen some birds, deerlike creatures, rodents, iguanas, frogs, lizards, honeybees, and many other harmless animals."

As he finishes his last sentence, Romo felt an itch on his forearm, swatted a small bug, and added, "I would like to add mosquitoes to my report. I'll ask Doctor Akina to provide a daily physical exam and a blood test for each of us before we rest every evening for our first few days here."

Noah chuckled and replied, "Well done! When you all get back to the landing module, go use the decontamination showers and breathe the disinfectant vapor. You all go and have your medical examination by Doctor Akina. We want you all to stay healthy and free from any harmful microbial life. After that, you guys settle for the night and get back to us tomorrow morning."

Within ninety days, a road was cleared, and a crew set out for a hilly site inland, where they began mining fuel ore for *Zeta's Hope*'s engines. Another crew was left at the initial site to hunt deer and obtain fresh marine life provisions, which included snapper, lobster, crabs, sardines, and shrimplike crustaceans.

In general, it seemed that the Greys and their friends from planet Amigo had reached a planet that could be the closest thing to paradise!

CHAPTER EIGHT

A TASTE OF PARADISE?

A few days after first Officer Romo went down to planet Avalonia's surface with a small landing team of Grey space colonists, remote sensors had shown that there were no dangerous land predators to be concerned about on the large island where they had landed. After a brief ceremony, they named the island New Zeta. Additional crew members were brought down to establish a fishing base camp, and begin initial exploration on foot.

Romo's team landed on a beach in a narrow peninsula on the northern side of New Zeta. The planet's flora resembled a subtropical forest that offered dazzling sights of pine trees, palmettos, oaks, and cabbage palms. The underbrush was sparse enough to allow people to walk about without the use of a machete. Deer and hogs had cleared paths through the brush. Squirrels and lizards fed on plants resembling pepperbushes with their plentiful berries. The visitors also saw birds, frogs, and other small creatures.

"From the beach," Captain Noah later told me, "our landing team observed life roaming on the undulating waves of the boundless ocean surface, most of the time small groups of highly sociable dolphinlike creatures, the acrobatic pranksters of the seas. In the distance, barrier coral reefs protecting the coastline were visible, their rich ecosystem hosting a large variety of marine life. Further out, the blue sky and water merged into a perfect horizon line. A nearby inlet led into a canal, with thick mangroves adorning its shores. There our landing team spotted a large shark, apparently a female about to give birth."

The crews at the base camp worked like busy bees. After four weeks, they had cleared, with axes and machetes, about ten acres for the cultivation of crops like corn, potatoes, beans, and some citrus. They also gathered wild fruits that resembled avocado, guava, and papaya. Pineapple-like fruits were collected and their fiber used to make textiles. There were even plants like coffee and tobacco, which caused great joy to Captain Noah and a few other smokers and coffee drinkers.

They hunted deer and hogs on land, and fished in the ocean. Within ninety days, a road was cleared, and a crew of six headed to a hilly site, nine miles inland, where they began mining for metals and fuel resources.

With plentiful provisions of fresh food and beautiful subtropical weather to enjoy, they organized weekly picnics. They served venison burgers, barbecue pork, and fish along with fruit and vegetables. They cleared an area near their camp and played group games similar to volleyball and stickball.

The joint Grey-Amigo Space Agency (GASA) had a policy of not allowing alcohol in their spaceships. It had been more than three months since their departure from Zeta. But none of the few drinkers in the crew had experience making alcohol. That was fine with Captain Noah and a few other fellow recovering alcoholics in the group. Although nobody was getting drunk, attendance at the recovery meetings remained steady, as a significant part of their recovery program was spiritual. And the Greys and Amigos were by nature a very spiritual people.

Romo wrote in his memoirs about taking a walk on the beach with his wife Luciet. Young and naïve, in their mid-twenties, they resembled the Gidget and Moondoggie characters from Earth's late 'fifties surf culture. They began dating in their last year of high school, stayed together through college, and then worked together in aerospace. They were best friends and lovers and greatly enjoyed each other's company. Like Noah and others in the crew, they were depressed for months because of their loved ones lost to the Reptoid invasion of their home worlds. They had not had been intimate for the last three months. Had the time at last arrived for a little loving?

As they walked on the beach, they tenderly held hands like high school sweethearts. The cool sea breeze caressed them with the gentle touch of a lover's kiss. The soft sound of waves lapping the sandy shores lent a soothing ambiance. They walked into a Florida snow grass flower bed so thick that it was impossible not to step on them. Thanks to a music recorder from one of the Greys nearby, they could hear a romantic tune that sounded like the theme from the 1959 movie *A Summer Place.*

Luciet said to Romo, "Do you think we should be settling down in this planet? It seems as though we have found paradise!"

"Yes. It has a great climate and many wonderful sights." Romo took a deep breath, looked at Luciet playfully, kissed her hand, and added, "We must be in paradise, and you are my Eve."

Luciet smiled. "Maybe we should plan on building ourselves a little house. Perhaps a small two-bedroom chalet on top of a hill with a view of the beach."

"Yes! And we may need extra room for little ones," he added mischievously.

Luciet looked at him, a bit surprised at her husband's parental yearning. Her mind wandered for a few seconds, and then she asked, "Will you love me years from now, when I'm old, fat, and ugly?"

"Honey, I'll get old, fat, and ugly with you!" he replied. "And I'll love you forever."

Luciet giggled. She brought her face closer to his and said, "What are we waiting for? Let's get started on the baby-making!"

Romo grinned. "Someone told me that God created sex to give us a taste of paradise! And this aviator is ready for some heavy bombardment!"

The beautiful, soft light of the sun low on the horizon set the scene for a long-awaited kiss. First there was that deep, penetrating look into each other's eyes, which acted as magnets in alignment. Their eyelashes slowly fluttered, as if mimicking the motion of butterflies. Their breathing and pulse quickened as their anticipation grew. Luciet smiled, licked her lips, tilted her head a bit to the side, and raised one hand to gently run it over Romo's hair. Overcome with desire, they extended their arms to encircle each other's torsos, feeling the shared warmth of their bodies.

They again gazed tenderly into each other's eyes. Then their soft, wet lips met and each slowly explored the other's mouth. Over the next few moments, they seemed to melt in each other's arms. It was a long, lingering, entrancing kiss, the kind that makes you dizzy, as though you are floating in the clouds, and leaves you yearning for more. They continued kissing for what seemed like hours, the intensity never lessening, as they were overcome by the passion of the moment. At the end of their lovemaking session, their faces glowed with radiant happiness.

Not far from Romo and Luciet, with fishing equipment in hand, the Grey couple of Jang and Akina set off on a rubber raft. Jang

Tauls had graduate degrees in both physics and computer engineering, and he was an authority in thermodynamics. He had designed and developed *Zeta's Hope*'s propulsion system, which was capable of traveling at a hundred times the speed of light. As the Greys' father of modern rocketry, he had volunteered to be the chief engineer on *Zeta's Hope*. His wife Akina was the ship's Medical Officer. She was a skilled surgeon and an authority in microorganisms.

They rowed in their raft away from shore with no idea what they would run into, as they were unfamiliar with the planet's sea life. They passed by and waved hello to Luciet, who was splashing around in the water. Romo had dozed off while sunbathing.

After Akina and Jang sat in the raft for a while, she raised a question. "Honey, how do you like the idea of having a child?"

Jang smiled, his eyes wide. He took Akina's hand, kissed it, and asked, "Are we having a child—my queen, eternal companion, and future fellow parent of our children? Having a child with you will be a great privilege! Are we pregnant, dear?"

"Yes, about seven weeks along now," she said, as her eyes shining at the prospect of motherhood. Then she sighed and added, "I feel I could bear you a hundred kids!"

Suddenly an image came to Jang's mind of him doing push-ups on top of Akina, shouting out loud, "Ninety-eight, ninety-nine, and one hundred!? He then imagined collapsing on top of her as he called the last number.

"What's on your mind?" Akina inquired, bringing him down from the clouds.

He reflected for a few seconds, smiled, and exclaimed, "I think we are going to need a few dozen tents for the children and a warehouse for the diapers!"

They laughed together and then shared a tender kiss. As they sat back to continue their fishing expedition, Jang noticed the large dorsal fin of a shark in the ocean. For millennia, man and Grey had reigned supreme over land, thanks to their wits. But for millions of years, sharks were kings of the seas, thanks to their jaws and their tenacity in the hunt for prey.

The beast swam a few feet from their raft as it passed by. It was five yards in length, its stocky shape resembling that of an oversized bull shark. From the raft, Akina and Jang could see its large saw-toothed jaws and cold round eyes. This was a dangerous eating machine that resulted from millions of years of evolution.

Suddenly panicking, Jang turned his head to Luciet about twenty yards away and screamed, "Shark! Shark!"

By the time Luciet turned around, the shark was upon her, and she could not get away. The shark first bumped into the petrified Luciet, as if checking her out. Then it swam away a few feet. Then it came in for the kill! In horror, Akina and Jang watched the shark attack, the nearby water turning red with the victim's blood. The shark had bit Luciet in her torso, which caused fatal internal injuries and intense bleeding. During that time, Akina threw a shark repellent grenade in the water, but it was too late for poor Luciet. The shark eventually got spooked by the chemicals in the repellent grenade and went away. What a terrible way to die!

Romo, who had fallen asleep, was awakened by the shouting around him and courageously plunged into the water in a futile attempt to rescue his wife. He recovered Luciet's body within a minute, but she was dead from blood loss and internal wounds. Everybody was horrified at the violent death of their crewmate.

A million thoughts ran through Romo's mind. He was shocked and dumbfounded by the tragedy of his wife's death. He grew detached from his surroundings. He went into a deep depression and was barely able to put two sentences together. The terrible memory of her violent death persisted and would torture him for years. Their dreams of a house with white picket fences and a happy family were shattered.

Her tree pod burial was late morning the next day. The grave site was in a clearing thirty yards inland. Crew members excavated a resting place for Luciet and placed in it a biodegradable capsule enclosing her body. The biodegradable pod would serve as a seed and grow into a tree. This method returned the body to the earth in an environmentally friendly way.

Her sobbing husband Romo threw a wreath of wild flowers on her lifeless corpse, saying his farewell. 'I'll meet you in the afterlife, my dear wife.'

Then all approached the grave and sank on bended knee.

Noah said a final prayer as follows, "Oh God, whose love and compassion are infinite, accept our prayers on behalf of thy humble servant Luciet and grant her entrance into the land of enlightenment and happiness." Then the funeral party rose and went back to the base camp to share some food and memories of the deceased until the late evening.

Life was tough on planet Avalonia. The daily tasks of farming, fishing, hunting, mining, cloth making, and tending a camp of primitive tents was a hard routine. There was no convenient infrastructure of contemporary living—no asphalt roads, bridges, aqueducts, or robust modern housing with electricity and climate control. And losing a crewmember to a sea predator was depressing to all. Things were not easy in paradise for these space pioneers!

CHAPTER NINE

CHAIKA WHO?

Two days after mourning the passing of his wife Luciet in September 1944 on planet Avalonia, First Officer Romo felt it was time to continue his usual routine. After his eight-hour shift, he challenged Noah to a game of chess after dinner at the captain's tent. It was a long game, and Noah was ahead by a pawn near the game's end.

Noah smiled, drew on his cigar, and jokingly said, "I have to admit I'm cheating. The cigar telepathically tells me the best move."

Romo chuckled at Noah's silly claim. But just then came a ghostly-looking apparition.

A three-foot-tall Greylike creature materialized in the form of a hologram alongside them. With a voice of a five-year-old girl, the alien being cheerfully announced, "Interesting game! I'll play the winner! If you win, I'll give you an electronic copy of the earthling book *World's Championship Matches, 1921 and 1927.* It has some of the best games played by earthling world champions

Lasker, Capablanca, and Alekhine. And if I win, I get to eat the loser. Just kidding!"

With a startled look, Noah and Romo gazed at the alien. Romo finally broke the silence. "Look, Noah! A mini-Grey!"

The creature reacted, "What's the matter with you guys? You act as if you're seeing a ghost! Do I look spooky? Don't laugh, Noah. I could be a distant relative of yours!"

Not certain whether to laugh, Noah maintained his composure. He laid his cigar on an ashtray and said, "Welcome! I'm Captain Noah Zambuto. And you?"

The alien replied, "Call me Chaika. I come from a peaceful civilization more than a thousand light-years away that engages in space exploration and trade. I'm soon to return to my home planet from exploring and mapping your part of the galaxy. I'm also a time traveler and an interstellar music, film, and literature distributor. May I interest you in any of my modestly priced art merchandise?"

Noah and Romo chuckle upon hearing this. Chaika reacts with a loud voice, "Hey, I have a mortgage to pay off and three kids to put through college! And that deadbeat husband of mine ripped me off and left me penniless when he ran off with a young stripper! Anyhow, I'll be out of your communications range within thirty minutes. So, I have no time for bull, and we have to be expedient in our business."

Noah interrupted, "Well. You must be an intelligent being with peaceful intentions. But you startled us with your sudden surprise appearance out of thin air!"

Romo added, "And your technology is better than ours! You got through our sensors and shields. You must have advanced technologies for projecting image and voice communications over large distances! But what business are we talking about?"

Chaika smiled, but within seconds she showed an expression of concern, as she continued, "I come to warn you that by this time tomorrow a large armada of Reptoids will land here to finish the genocide they left incomplete on planet Zeta because of your escape. And they want your spaceflight technology! They know you came to planet Avalonia. It was all over your press and social media prior to their invasion!"

After a pause, the alien continued, "Though their weaponry and numbers are superior to yours, their ships are relatively slow. It took them about three months to catch up! Your sensors will detect them at sunup. You guys had better finish your game soon and call it an early evening. You will be busy tomorrow packing up and leaving this wonderful planet!"

Noah said, "Kind of you to warn us of the Reptoids! If you dislike them and possess technology more advanced than ours, why don't you take them on?"

Chaika flashed a smile. "I command an exploration vessel from a star system in a part of the Milky Way remote from here. We carry no weapons. But our ship is faster, and our communications systems, deflector shields and remote sensor systems are superior to both yours and our adversaries. However, I've been instructed by my superior officer to provide you with any kind of data or intelligence that ensures your survival. But information on our home world and our advanced technology is classified."

She paused briefly, as if reflecting on what to say next. She continued, with some passion in her voice, "It's not in our interest to have this aggressive Reptoid army taking over this portion of the galaxy! They are led by a charming, witty, manipulating, and charismatic leader called Heinrik. But don't let his attractive external mannerisms fool you. He's a cruel fellow who is leading his people on a path of bloody conquest!"

Chaika stopped talking, took a deep breath, and resumed. "We know that your contingency plan calls for you to get out of here in case they show up."

She then pointed to a holographic chart showing this sector of the Milky Way. She continued, "Here is a recommended route of travel. You'll receive a transmission with this data in electronic form after I leave. The first civilization that you'll encounter early in your journey is not as advanced as yours. But keep those aggressive but primitive Terrunos at arm's length! Trust the Sapiens, Verdes, and Proximans. They'll become your friends. But beware of those warlike humans in Earth! Still, about a century from now, they'll form an alliance with their neighboring planets that will stop the mighty Reptoids. That's my dollar's worth of advice! I'll check on you guys in a few months!"

Chaika waved goodbye. Then her image vanished.

Noah and Romo continued the chess game for a few minutes. As he made a move, Romo quipped, "That's a cute petite Grey lady. Perhaps she'll ask you to go to her kindergarten prom with her! I promise I won't tell your wife!"

"You and your silly sense of humor," said Noah, glancing at his watch. "We have a busy day tomorrow. Time to go to bed. Captain's orders!"

Early the next morning, the Grey sensor array detected ten Reptoid spaceships twelve hours away from planet Avalonia. By midafternoon, the Greys were packed up and, to throw off their enemies, flew forty-five degrees away from their true heading. The next day they corrected course and headed toward a planet named Terruno, about twenty days away, rich in water, food, and fuel resources.

Thirty minutes after the launch from planet Avalonia, Noah scheduled a staff meeting. All nine bridge officers were present: four males, four females, and the artificially intelligent android.

Noah welcomed all of *Zeta's Hope* bridge officers and quickly moved to the subject at hand, "You all read the report of the encounter with Chaika. She appeared to Romo and me as a holographic image. She seemed an intelligent being with peaceful intentions, possessing advanced technology, advising us on a route to other planets, and identifying obstacles on our way to meet friendly species, which she called the Sapiens, Verdes, and Proximans. The question is: Who is Chaika, and should we trust her advice?"

Chief Engineer Jang answered with his own questions. "We never met this Chaika before. Can we trust her? What if she's guiding us toward a trap, so that she can seize our fast starship and avail herself of our space technology? We could be walking into a trap!"

Doctor Akina interrupted, "Nonsense! She warned us of the approaching enemy ships. And like Moses, she's guiding us on our odyssey to a safe haven."

Navigator Nax added, "Remote sensors confirm the existence of that first planet on her list, Terruno, about twenty days away. It has breathable air and is rich in food, water, and fuel resources. Let's check it out, instead of traveling blindly in unexplored areas where we risk running out of fuel. We estimate that the Milky Way is about a hundred thousand light-years across, but habitable planets may be scattered through it at great distances!"

Helmsman Ben then provided his rationale for trusting Chaika. "The early warning about the Reptoids moving in on us at planet Avalonia is proof that Chaika is out to help us. And why should we blindly navigate around when we can use her charts? Using them will save us years in travel time and prevent us from running out of air, water, food, and fuel. In addition to that, she gave us an electronic database with a lot of information about all the species we'll meet—anything from politics, religion, science, and the arts to the development of philosophy and healthcare!"

Romo interrupted. "I agree with Ben. The valuable data provided by Chaika includes the climatic, political, religious, economic, and military information on the nearby planets we may be visiting. She has given us with a kind of world atlas on this part of the galaxy. She's provided us with maps of this part of the Milky

Way, where we can use the beacons from pulsars as navigation markers, the same way sailors used lighthouses centuries ago."

Captain Noah then reentered the discussion. "Chaika said that it's not in the interest of her people for the aggressive Reptoid army to take over this portion of the galaxy. But if she can travel through time, why have not they gone into the past and wiped out the Reptoids?" He reflected for a moment. "I was wondering if her society has a policy of avoiding direct conflict but finds it permissible to influence others who may help them stop the Reptoid threat. Any other comments?"

Quartermaster Boudica threw in her nickel's worth, "I agree with Doctor Akina, Nax, and First Officer Romo. Obviously, Chaika is as fearful of that murderous Reptoid bunch as we are. They are our common enemy. And I believe in that old proverb telling us that the enemy of my enemy is my friend!"

Boudica paused for a few seconds and then erupted in anger, "Those bastard Reptoids! While grieving, we have kept an utter silence for weeks about the slaughter going on in our home worlds. They have killed many of our loved ones! The blood of millions of our fellow Greys is on their hands. For God's sake, they are cooking us and having us for dinner! Our common bond is our pain and suffering. We should do anything in our power to make allies of our new friends, so that we can fight the Reptoids together and avenge the genocide of our loved ones!"

About a minute of silence followed. Boudica's angry words reflected the feelings of all present. Captain Noah then proposed, "Let's have a vote! Those recommending that we use Chaika's charts to navigate to a safe haven?" Seven hands went up. "Any abstentions?"

The hands of the two remaining officers, Jang and Amie, went up. Jang abstained because he had reservations about Chaika. Amie abstained because she was an android that only voted yea or nay in matters of science, safety, and regulations; she had no subjective judgment on any other subjects and no feelings of any kind.

"So, it's decided," Noah concluded. "We'll use Chaika's charts. Navigator and helmsman, let's move forward on our journey to planet Terruno!"

Chief Engineer Jang, who doubled as Disc Jockey through the ship's public address system, searched for some earthling music in the data base provided by Chaika, who claimed traveling to the future. After a minute, he starting playing a tune titled "Roam" by an earthling new wave band that went by the name of The B-52s.

Fictional Map of Cluster of Habitable Planets near Earth

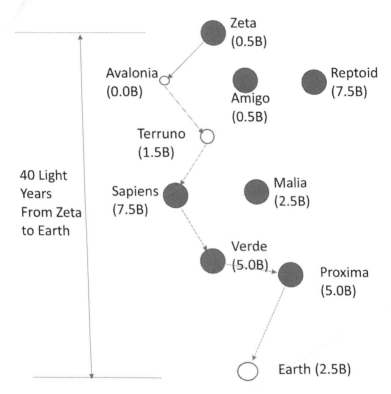

Notes:
1944 Spacefaring Planets shown Solid.
Planet size proportional to development.
Planet population in parenthesis.
Grey's journey from Zeta to Earth shown by arrows.

CHAPTER TEN

EMAILS FROM ABDUL

Because of the appearance of a large armada of the aggressive Reptoids, the Greys left planet Avalonia. *Zeta's Hope* performed well on its way to planet Terruno during the summer of 1944. But on the negative side, Captain Noah's worst fears about his brother Ozzie materialized nearly three months after the invasion of his home world. After liftoff, Noah retired to his quarters and checked on his emails. He found one from Ozzie's neighbor Abdul:

> Dear Captain:
>
> How are you doing? May God bless and protect you and the members of your crew in these moments of peril caused by the Reptoids. It's been a few days since our last contact. From our last communication, you are all doing well and on your way to settling in that new world of Avalonia! I know that your brother Ozzie and my girlfriend Chloe filled you in on all the horrific details about

71

the beginning of the Reptoid invasion. Thus, I'll spare you my version of those events.

However, I regret to inform you that your last living close relative in our home world, your brother Ozzie, died during our attempt to forage for dry goods from the convenience store near our homes. We thought it was abandoned as we approached it from a path in the woods on the backside of the store. Ozzie was point man when several Reptoid soldiers, lurking in the wilderness, opened fire and killed him instantly. I was barely able to escape by firing back and by throwing a Molotov cocktail that set ablaze one of our attackers, and deterred the rest of them from following me for a minute, precious time that I used to escape.

Throughout the years I grew attached to Ozzie and thought of him as a kid brother. He lived the nineteen years of his life with his parents, and they were all loving people and took good care of each other. I saw Ozzie grow from a playful toddler to a responsible young man. On occasion I played softball or cards with him and other neighbors, all of whom regrettably died during the initial days of the Reptoid invasion. I wish I had died instead of him, such a young and promising man!

I also have bad news about our friend Stout. Yesterday, we returned from a fishing trip to his home and found his three-year-old daughter alive, hiding under a pile of clothes in the Groves' apartment where he and his wife lived, several miles north of us. We did not find Stout's wife but found a pool of blood in the living room, which led us to assume that she was killed and her body taken away by the Reptoids. It will take some time for Stout and his daughter to recover from this tragic loss! They live with me now.

Halfway back from Stout's home to my place, we befriended a young family of four, with two small children, living at a remotely located house. The parents were software programmers who had the day off during the first day of the invasion, stayed home, and survived in their isolated location. They had some firearms, a couple of goats, a chicken coop, and plenty of fruit trees within a mile of their home. We intend to keep in touch with them and help each other in any way we can.

Our prayers are with you in this sad time of sorrow for Ozzie's loss.

Sincerely yours,
Abdul Zoudeq
Retired SWAT team Captain,
Grey–Amigo Space Agency

Captain Noah was overwhelmed by the news of his brother's violent death. It was barely three months ago that his parents were killed by the Reptoids! As of now he had no close living kin back in his home world of Zeta. Many in his crew were undergoing the same grieving process for the death of loved ones. Some estimated that the Reptoid invasion resulted in the death of about 90 percent of the Grey population.

Noah's initial impulse was to return to planet Zeta and fight. But he was bound by a sense of duty and understood the decision of the now defunct Grey leadership to send off his spaceship—ensuring the survival of the race and preventing the Reptoids from getting their advanced space flight technology. After all, the Greys' spaceship was five times faster than the Reptoids!

Depressed from the news of his brother's death, Noah prayed for a few minutes. His wife Faith, the ship's communications officer, walked into their room and sat on the bed next to him, massaging his shoulders to comfort him.

"What would I do without you, Faith? I need your support in this moment of sorrow. Thanks for being here for it."

"No need to mention it, my darling. I know how close you were to your brother. I hope and pray for all the remaining survivors of this genocide by the Reptoids. My parents and Quartermaster Boudica's younger brother and his family are the only survivors that we know of in remote areas of our home world."

He added, "For now, hoping and praying is all that we can do!"

Then Noah shared with Faith some good memories of his brother Ozzie. "When Ozzie was a toddler learning to walk and talk, I got carried away in teaching him bad words. He was a few months past two years old, while I was twelve. He repeated every foul word that I taught him. None of those words were decent enough to appear in a dictionary! Though young Ozzie was ignorant of their meaning, he would show his charming smile, chuckle, and with great joy jump around his little playpen, clearly enjoying all this attention from his older sibling. A few times later, Dad caught me in my mischievous education of young Ozzie. I would take off, running out of the house, while Dad coyly faked chasing me for a while, calling out, 'You shameless kid! You little bandit!' I could swear that Dad chuckled, perhaps enjoying the thrill of the playful chase!

"But young Ozzie grew up to be a clean-cut and compassionate person. He showed this trait first when he was three years old, hanging out with Mom and me by the door of our house. Ozzie saw a little three-year-old neighbor girl running out of her house in her birthday suit, being chased by her mom, who quickly caught up with her and took her back into the house. With tears in his eyes, little Ozzie turned to Mom and in a sad voice said, 'Look, Mommy! Poor little girl! She has no pee-pee!'"

Faith giggled.

Noah smiled at her and went on. "My brother grew up to be an easygoing kid with an engaging personality and quick wit, much like Pop. Who knows, perhaps he could have been a great stand-up comedian instead of an aerospace technician! But he was a nuts-and-bolts hands-on type and also loved outdoor games. I remembered many times teaching and playing stickball with him.

"Eventually Ozzie grew into handsomeness in his late teens and became popular with the ladies as a result of his guitar playing and good looks. And his good looks were enhanced by his preference for dressing sharply. He looked like one of those guys modeling in fashion magazines!"

Noah paused and wiped a tear from his eye. "May God bless his soul"!

As the days passed, the Captain kept up a daily exchange of emails with Abdul. Noah told of the Reptoids showing up at planet Avalonia, which caused their quick departure for a new destination, whose coordinates Noah did not identify for fear of the message being intercepted by the Reptoids. The messages were short daily reports on how each party was doing, and Noah was just happy that Abdul, his girlfriend Chloe, Stout, his young daughter, and a few others were able to subsist by collecting fruit and fishing in a nearby river.

Two days after the Greys left planet Avalonia for planet Terruno, Noah got an interesting email in which Abdul and his friends mentioned that they were starting to decode some of the invaders' messages from information encoded electronically in the headset of the deceased Reptoids soldier who was buried in

Abdul's neighborhood. Key to the decoding was the use of the salute "Hail Heinrik" and the posted date and time.

Shortly after that, Noah stopped hearing from Abdul and never did again. Did he perish at the hands of the Reptoids? But after some thought, he speculated that their spaceship had traveled away from their home world 25 trillion miles, a distance that may have been too far for the Grey communications relay satellites to transmit any further messages. Noah hoped and prayed for those left behind in his home world of Zeta.

CHAPTER ELEVEN

MORE ABOUT ZETA'S HOPE AND ITS CAPTAIN

One early October evening of the year 2065, a soft ocean breeze caressed my face as I walked toward the entrance of a restaurant in Cocoa Beach. In the early 1960s the place was a bar frequented by rock legend Jim Morrison, who'd gone to high school in nearby Melbourne. As I crossed the threshold, I could hear Morrison's "Hello, I Love You" playing through the restaurant's stereo system.

I was to meet Grey Admiral Noah, his wife Faith, and their friend Akina for dinner and discussion of the Greys' journey to Earth in the 1940s. At that time, Noah Zambuto was captain of the spaceship *Zeta's Hope*, years before he was promoted to admiral. By now, I had written the first ten manuscript chapters of my book about the 1940s Greys' odyssey to Earth.

A waiter led me to the table where I would spend a couple of hours dining and chatting with original members of Captain Noah's 1940s crew. His wife, Faith, was a retired communications officer, and Akina had been the mission's medical officer. My Grey companions had arrived earlier, and they were engaged in sharing lively stories from working together over the last 120 years. They were drinking coffee, and Noah had already lit a cigar. His sense of humor and mannerisms reminded me of the twentieth-century comedian George Burns, of whom Noah jokingly claimed to be his Grey reincarnation!

During dinner, we continued our interview about the Greys' home world, with emphasis on the design and production of their spaceship *Zeta's Hope*. I took my seat and asked Noah the first question of the interview: "Admiral, what motivated you to work in the space program?"

With a nostalgic look, he pondered for a moment. He then replied, "My arrival to the Grey–Amigo Space Agency was the culmination of a childhood dream that I nurtured up through my college days, when I idolized explorers—from Grey historical figures that on Earth would be the equivalent of Marco Polo or Christopher Columbus to fictional ones like Flash Gordon, Mr. Spock, and Captain Kirk."

"That's nice to hear! I'd love to know something about your education and experience prior to leaving your home world."

Noah answered, "I trained as a pilot during my college days, graduating in 1937 with a degree in mechanical engineering from Zeta Technological Institute. During my first four years in the agency I was selected as a pilot for our space transportation system, which resembled the US Space X-33 single-stage-to-orbit reusable launch system developed by the United States in the late 1990s, but that program was scrapped in 2001 due to failure of its composite fuel tank material during cryogenic fuel testing. But the Greys were able to develop light composite materials to reduce vehicle weight, plus more efficient engines. During the four years before the maiden flight of *Zeta's Hope* in 1944, I was involved in the vehicle test program, for which I became the overall lead after my predecessor retired. By the time the mission to planet Avalonia was scheduled, I had completed an advanced degree in engineering management from Zeta Technological Institute, married Faith, and been selected as the ship's captain. That was just over 120 years ago. I'm an admiral now."

Curious about the specifics of Noah's academic studies, I asked, "What course gave you the most trouble?"

After some thought, he replied, "My computer programming skills were no better than your average engineer. Perhaps the course that gave me the most trouble was Machine and Assembly Language Programming. I remember once getting a terrible headache after writing about a hundred and fifty lines of code in an assigned homework!"

Noah paused for a moment, took a draw from his cigar, and went on. "You know what? One of my classmates told me once that that course separated the men from the boys! Do you know what I told that cocky son of a gun?"

With a puzzled face, I remained silent for a few seconds. Noah then added, mimicking a little boy's voice, "Yes, Daddy-O!"

The ladies giggled at this. I regained my composure. "You were involved in the design and production of the Greys' spaceship *Zeta's Hope*. Tell me about how this revolutionary wonder of space technology came about."

Noah smiled and asked his wife Faith, "Honey, would you like to lead off?"

Faith smiled, threw a kiss to her husband, and led off by saying, "Let me share some general information about how the Greys came to develop the spaceship *Zeta's Hope*. After several centuries of peace, our society decided to engage in space exploration and colonization. Concurrently, we developed new technologies in healthcare, computers, communications, and power generation that were one to two centuries ahead of Earth. Our culture also emphasized music, theater, dancing, and sports. The nine countries on our planet would have annual festivities similar to arts and crafts fairs and Mardi Gras."

I interrupted by asking, "What specifically motivated you to build a space ship such as *Zeta's Hope?*"

Faith smiled, took a sip of coffee, and continued, "Our un-manned space probes had discovered and surveyed a planet in a neighboring star system that had water, a magnetosphere, an atmosphere rich in oxygen and nitrogen, and flora and fauna similar to our home world. We were enthusiastic about these findings and named this planet Avalonia. Our planet's people and democratically elected political leadership were enthusiastic about these findings and decided to embark on a mission to explore and colonize this planet. Going to Avalonia was a topic dominant in our media for a few years before we launched the mission there. A period similar in your history may have been when humans committed to go to the moon back in the 1960s by a young President—Akina, do you remember his name?"

Doctor Akina, 150 years young, answered, "Jack Kennedy. He was a handsome man with a reputation as a womanizer. Too bad he did not meet any Grey ladies. And they say that once you go Grey, you go astray!"

The ladies laughed in unison after Akina's off-the-cuff comment.

I smiled and took a short draw off my cigar, blew it out, and turned to Admiral Noah. "What were important design features of *Zeta's Hope?*"

He smiled, reflected for a few seconds, and after drawing on his cigar, he said, "Important requirements for a spaceship were accommodations for its crew of fifty and its cargo—a communi-cations relay satellite and a landing module. Salient features were its long-range sensors, deflector shields, and a propulsion system capable of traveling at one hundred times the speed of light. This revolutionary propulsion system was designed and developed by our chief engineer, Jang Tauls."

The admiral paused as his wife squeezed the hand of Akina, Jang's widow. Noah then went on. "At that speed, no crew hiber-nation was required for trips between star systems. Also, the crew wore skintight gray uniforms and magnetic boots to walk on the iron alloy floors of the spaceship."

"Noah, tell me about the overall vehicle test program for which you were the lead."

"In the Grey-Amigo Space Agency, we were not able to benefit from the economics of mass production that are common for automobiles or electrical and electronic widgets. For hardware acceptance, a well-documented functional test, with perhaps some shake and bake tests for flight hardware and launch accessories, were considered sufficient. The use of either military grade or commercial off-the-shelf components, when possible, was also common."

Noah momentarily reflected about what he was going to say next.

"For that test team, I recruited several of the engineers and scientists that would be going in the mission to planet Avalonia with me. Their fields of knowledge varied—physical sciences, structural and materials science, chemistry, propellants, electrical power, communication systems, electronic controls and instrumentation, and computer engineering and programming. We also needed a number of hands-on technicians in these fields. For the actual flight mission, I recruited many of these experts and added a couple of members of the design team—First Officer Romo and Chief Engineer Jang. In the latter case, we had to get a waiver from the agency's administrator to hire him. You see, during his first year in college, Jang got intoxicated, went streaking nude across the campus, and got himself arrested. But it helped that he had been sober for seven years by the time of the launch. And eventually we needed a good doctor." Noah smiled and looked toward Doctor Akina.

I went on with the next question. "Would you give me the operational flight sequence from the time of launch to the on-orbit station around your home world?"

Taking a sip of coffee, Noah went on. "We used a vertically launched orbiter vehicle that resembled a large version of the US X-33 experimental vehicle of the late twentieth century. The crew came onboard, and the fuel tank was filled with cryogenic propellants. Additional checks continued until the engines were ready for ignition and launch. Usually, after the orbiter vehicle reached the on-orbit station, to either carry its passengers or deploy its payload, it would return, land, and be processed for reuse."

I popped the next question: "How about the operational sequence from the time you left the on-orbit station to landing on planet Avalonia?"

Taking a short puff from his cigar, Noah answered, "Prior to launch from the on-orbit station, a crew of fifty came onboard *Zeta's Hope*. Living space was about ten thousand square feet. Our fuel was loaded prior to launch. Additional checks were made until the low power thruster engines were ignited for departure. Afterward, at a safe distance from the on-orbit station, full power was applied to the main engines. About twenty days later, upon arrival in orbit around Avalonia, a landing module with a crew of four was deployed."

The house band began playing Bob Marley's song "One Love," with its sensuous slow beat. Faith bounced up from her chair and grabbed Admiral Noah's hand, saying, "Come on honey. Let's dance!"

He turned to me and said, "That is all for today Mr. Wyatt."

I glanced around the room for a few seconds and my eyes ran into Doctor Akina's, who smiled and blew me a kiss. I thought to myself, *Is she just messing with me?*

Her mannerisms faintly reminded me of the 1960s eccentric comedian Phyllis Diller, with her wild wig and colorful clothes. All of a sudden, I mentally pictured me making out with a romance-seeking 150-year-old wrinkled Grey female! Disturbed by this picture, I quickly got up, courteously bowed in Akina's direction, excused myself, and left in a hurry! I planned to call Admiral Noah the next day and schedule a follow-up interview!

Zeta's Hope Layout (by Gus V.)

CHAPTER TWELVE

THE HOLIDAYS BEFORE THE BANACAN REVOLUTION

The Greys' Admiral Noah told me, author C. A. Wyatt, about a political refugee who joined his crew in August 1944 upon the Greys' short stay on planet Terruno. It was inhabited by a humanoid race, called the Bronze because of their skin color. They averaged about five and a half feet tall and had human-like features.

The name of the refugee was Nova. She passed away decades before my interview with Noah in 2065. She had given an electronic copy of memoirs of her home world, specifically about her native country of Banacan. Noah sent me an email containing her memoirs. Nova wrote,

> By the time the Greys arrived, the technology and social development of the Bronze race on planet Terruno resembled that of Earth in the 1890s. My world was going through a phase that resembled Earth's Cold War, a state of political and military tension after a Napoleonic type war against the

old colonial monarchies in the continent of Ropa about ninety years before the Greys' arrival. Two forms of government prevailed after the overthrow of the monarchies. There were the constitutional republics, where the people elected their representatives, who governed according to constitutional law that limited government powers over a citizen's political and property rights. The other type was a statist form of government, where one political party had total control over a citizen's political and property rights. Unfortunately, my native country of Banacan had joined the statist bloc by the time the Greys arrived in August 1944.

As the days of my life pass by, I nostalgically look back to those days of my childhood. The last time all members of our family and extended family got together was on the holidays late in 1937. Holiday dinner gatherings were particularly special, as members of the family from grandparents to grandchildren were all present. Food, drink, music, and noisy kids playing games were the norm for those occasions. The main course featured a pig that had been roasted a whole day by our beer-in-hand fathers. Side dishes consisted of beans and rice, and another vegetable on the side—such as fried plantains or yuca. A salad of lettuce, tomato, avocado, cucumbers, carrots, and radish was common in the old days. And for the grand finale, some sweet dessert would be served, such as flan or guava halves with cream cheese. Despite the atheist dictatorial regime's disdain for religion, many Banacan families kept religious holiday celebrations going, although everything was discreetly kept indoors.

The hosts of our holiday dinner were my maternal grandparents.

Mama was the endearing nickname that my loving and caring mother and her three siblings gave to my maternal grandmother. Two centuries ago, our ancestors settled as farmers in the outskirts of my hometown. These original settlers must have had a very loving nature and prolific reproduction rates, as several hundred in our town shared our last name.

Papa was the endearing nickname that we gave our maternal grandfather. He was a quiet man of gentle manners, who enjoyed his espresso coffee and every now and then a cigar. He was well liked throughout the town, often seen hanging out with his old buddies in one of the fine kiosks and cafes.

At that 1937 holiday dinner, we all gathered around the dining table. Grandma started a prayer: "Lord, we thank you for the food before us. Bring us good health and spiritual joy."

I recall my mother starting a conversation after we'd begun eating. "Where is my brother, Tony?"

My Aunt Karen, Tony's wife, replied, "Fighting with the guerrillas against Fulgen's soldiers at a neighboring town. The rebels now control lots of territory in the central and eastern part of the island. Their victory is imminent within a week or two."

Mama interrupted to say, "Every day I pray for the good health of my son, Tony. May God watch over him!"

After a few seconds of silence, my dad said, "I have a nephew who also joined the guerrillas fighting Fulgen's dictatorship. I also hope and pray that this bloody revolution is not in vain. But I don't trust the leader of the revolution, that egocentric Ledif. A younger college buddy told me that several years ago he shot and wounded a political rival who was running for leader of the student federation, a position that Ledif also aspired to. His millionaire daddy's money bought the silence of the victim's family."

With an expression of horror on her face, my mom said, "There are too many guns in this country! The government must do something about it! Only cops and soldiers should have them!"

With passion in his voice, Grandpa replied, "You want only cops and soldiers of the dictator to have guns? How the heck are we going to fight the dictatorship? With sticks and stones?"

After a few seconds of silence for tempers to simmer down, Grandpa added, "I even have concerns for family members and friends in the event of a triumph by the revolutionaries. Our oldest daughter's husband is an in-law with Fulgen's mayor in this city. Should Fulgen fall, I fear for their welfare. In the confusion that will probably reign in the first few days of a victorious revolution, their house may get ransacked and they may get hurt by overzealous revolutionaries."

My mom retorted, "Nonsense! Let's hope that will not happen. Most people in this town know that she's the sister of a revolutionary. They will not ransack her home!"

Then Grandma then changed the subject back to Uncle Tony. "My son Tony is an underground operative with the Revolutionary Directorate trying to overthrow Fulgen, a corrupt dictator who overthrew the Constitutional Republic in a coup d'état a few years ago. Before Tony directly got involved in the fighting, his primary revolutionary functions were to provide the guerrillas with logistical support with food, medicine, money, and a few small firearms. Other clandestine tasks included public information, recruitment, and raising funds. His struggle against Fulgen's dictatorship consists mainly of clandestine underground operations. But now he has joined the rebels in battle to capture an army barracks at a neighboring town. May God watch over him in these times of danger."

Mama's house was my home away from home. I visited there four or five times a week. It was in the middle of a block of row houses, not far from the center of town. The whole house was probably about thirty feet wide by about a hundred feet deep. It had a large patio in the back with some bushes, a pig, half a dozen chickens, a dog, and a parakeet. It was an interesting inner-city biological niche. The lizards would eat small bugs, the chickens would eat lizards and cockroaches, and the top human predator would eat the chickens. The pig, spiced with garlic, beer, and other condiments, was usually the guest of honor at the holiday dinner table.

A sad childhood memory was when Mama contracted breast cancer. The disease was not detected until it was too late. It spread to her left arm, which swelled to great proportion. Mama seemed content to sit on the rocking chair in her living room, watching her grandchildren play and occasionally chatting with her offspring and in-laws.

The day of Mama's passing in 1940 is my saddest childhood memory. I remember her doctor telling us, "She's in bad shape and may pass away soon. You all should go to her bedside for the last moments of her life!"

My older kin walked into Mama's room and I followed but was blocked by Papa. I said to him, "I'm a mature young lady! I'm fourteen years old and the eldest of the cousins present in the house. I insist on joining the adults by Mama's bedside. I promise that I will not cry!"

Startled by my words, Papa let me through.

Mama's family stood by her bedside in a state of sorrow for what seemed like hours. All of a sudden, she gasped for one last breath and then let go of it. Everybody had tears in their eyes as they silently mourned her passing. This sweet, joyful mother of four and grandmother to many more would be greatly missed by all! I had never seen anybody die in my young life, particularly somebody so close to me. I could not keep my promise not to cry, broke into tears, and wept like a baby! Mama's house would never be the same again without her!

CHAPTER THIRTEEN

UNCLE TONY'S ARREST

In August 1944, Nova, a political refugee from the country of Banacan, joined the Greys' crew during their visit to planet Terruno on their long odyssey to Earth. At that time, the planet had developed technologically to a late 1890s level on Earth. Politically, Terruno was at a stage similar to the Cold War on Earth about the year 1960—a bloc of nations with constitutional republics and a bloc of nations with statist governments.

When I interviewed the 150-year-old Noah in 2065 about their journey, Nova had passed away. But she had given Captain Noah a memory stick with her story about her native country of Banacan on planet Terruno. In one passage of Nova's memoirs, she wrote of the early years after the triumph of the Banacan Revolution when she was aged eleven as follows:

> On that first day of 1938, you could hear cheers, fireworks, and the honking of horns by a crowd welcoming a column of triumphant rebels. Some

threw confetti on the raggedly dressed column. Cars with loudspeakers and people shouted cheers of "Long live the Revolution!" and "Down with Fulgen's rule!" Little did the people know that this was the faint beginning of a propaganda bombardment of military parades, books, films, songs, slogans, and posters never seen before in our country!

The freedom fighters marched in a loose formation from the eastern side of town through Banacan's long central highway. The mostly young soldiers formed a double file of smiling faces in a broken-step march. They all wore olive green army clothing, most had untrimmed black curly beards, and nearly all wore crucifixes and rosaries around their necks to show religious devotion.

At the time of the fall of Fulgen's seven-year reign in January 1938, the overwhelming majority of Banacans celebrated the fall of the dictatorship. They were full of hopes and dreams for a return to the political freedoms of the old constitutional republic. Unfortunately, the temptations of power and prestige paved the way for Ledif's betrayal of the Revolution he led.

Ledif clearly revealed his totalitarian intentions after solidly entrenching himself in power by establishing within eighteen months what he called the "dictatorship of the proletariat." Before the end of January 1938, he took gun rights away from private citizens. Later that year, he ordered "nationalization" of student organizations, labor unions and private businesses—starting with large land holdings. What an odd thing to see—the so-called dictatorship of the proletariat oppressing the proletariat! And the takeover of private enterprises, to be led by political cronies instead of entrepreneurs, had negative long-term effects because of mismanagement and corruption.

Eventually, by mid-1939, he cancelled elections, dismantled a free press, outlawed freedom of expression, and "reformed" the judicial system by making judges out of political cronies. During the same time frame, Ledif stirred up revolts in several neighboring countries—acts that led to sour international relations. Because Ledif centralized the nation's economy under the government and repressed political rights, Banacans were forced to live within a failed political-economic system, constantly preoccupied with obtaining consumer goods, such as food, clothing, and medicine. And those who rebelled were exiled, jailed, or put to death, depending on the gravity of their crimes against the totalitarian state.

Banacan Dictator Ledif
(Artwork by Roberta Lerman)

In late 1939 my uncle Tony, my mother's younger brother, was being held prisoner at the town's nearby police station for passing out flyers critical of Ledif's government. The police station where he was being held was located about fifty yards southeast of my house.

Tony's ten-year-old son Riessi, two years my junior, showed up at the front steps of my house in the middle of the day and said, "Nova, let's rescue my daddy from jail!"

Flattered by Reissi's trust in me, I looked over at the police station and commented, "There must be over a hundred soldiers around your dad, all equipped with rifles."

I knew off the bat that it would be futile for us two kids to attempt rescuing Uncle Tony. But I immediately thought of wild schemes to keep my grieving little cousin too busy to attempt anything foolish.

I said, "We can dig an underground tunnel. But that would take a few days."

I paused for a minute or two and added, "Or we may be able to steal an armored vehicle and break in to rescue Uncle Tony!"

It seemed as if hours passed as we sat on the small wall that bordered the narrow green garden area around my house, facing the police station, staking out the place, keeping count of the soldiers and their weaponry, and dreaming up new rescue schemes.

At nightfall, the phone at my home rang. My mother came out and called, "Reissi! Your mom wants you to come home for dinner!"

Accepting that he was powerless over the situation, Reissi started walking west toward his house. With his head down, he slowly dragged his feet on the ground as if not wanting to increase the distance between him and his incarcerated father. Occasionally he stopped to look back, perhaps hoping to catch a glimpse of his dad, probably wondering if he would ever see him again. Nobody knew what Ledif's kangaroo courts had in store for him—a lifelong prison term? Would my uncle receive the death penalty? I had tears in my eyes as Reissi's small figure disappeared in the distance, heading back to his home, as the sun sank to the horizon. It could have been my dad! It could have been anybody's dad! Fortunately, Uncle Tony was sentenced to only three years of jail for his acts of political dissent.

A few months later, we were allowed by the government to visit my imprisoned uncle Tony. I rode about forty miles in a cab with his wife, Karen, and her children, ten-year-old Reissi and two-year-old Fleebee, to visit Uncle Tony at an old prison in a neighboring town. Other family members pitched in to rent the cab and to contribute some food from their limited rations. This cab was an eight-seat steam-powered vehicle that resembled a French L'Obeissante wagon of the late 1800s on Earth.

Aunt Karen and her two kids sat in the second row of seats with a bag of food for Uncle Tony. Prison rations were meager and often contained bugs and worms. I sat in the front next to the driver, with Reissi behind me. The other four seats in the back were taken up by a family who knew my aunt, consisting of a twenty-five-year-old lady and her three kids. They were going to visit her husband, who also was a political prisoner.

After settling down on her seat, my aunt asked the cabbie, an old family friend, "How fast does this vehicle go? Is this machine safe?"

"It goes twenty miles per hour! It's very safe!" answered the cabbie.

At first, the atmosphere in the car was rather grim and solemn, perhaps because of the trip's painful purpose of going to see a loved one in prison. Suddenly the loving and cheerful mother-and-child interaction between Aunt Karen and her two-year-old toddler broke the silence, as young Fleebee showed off his growing vocabulary to his mom.

My cousin Reissi leaned forward and whispered in my ear, "Shoot! My little brother may start spitting out all those dirty words we taught him while we babysat him!"

Any minute, I expected young Fleebee to spit out a stream of four-letter words. What would Aunt Karen do to us then? Would she punish us by kicking us out of the car and making us walk many miles back to our hometown? Would we be excommunicated by the Church and go to hell? Would we have to go to the mountains and form our own guerrilla group? Would there be posters of cousin Reissi and me in post offices throughout the country, labeling us the Cursing Bandits? Oh well! Those are the typical worries of misbehaving preteens!

During all this time, the cab's radio was playing music. Then the music was interrupted by a commercial break. All of a sudden, our ears were bombarded by the sound of martial songs and government slogans, such as "Down with capitalist imperialism and their lackey worms!"

In a spontaneous manner, young Fleebee started repeating these slogans, unaware of their meaning, much as a pet parrot would. All of us were shocked at the toddler's flawless recitation of the slogans composed by the repressive government who had put his dad in jail!

The cab driver, a man about forty years old, said, "Sorry. I'll switch radio stations!"

But the same songs and slogans were playing on the other station he tuned into. The average Banacan citizen was constantly bombarded with government propaganda through radio, newspapers, street posters, and public loudspeakers.

In a state of frustration, the cabbie loudly exclaimed, "Sorry! It's the same everywhere! All media is owned and controlled by the state! Everywhere you go, you constantly hear a deluge of propaganda! And in school, the kids are subjected to a heavy bombardment of indoctrination!"

Aunt Karen regained her composure and in a loving mother's tone told Fleebee, "No. Don't repeat those bad words!"

The toddler stopped reciting government slogans, perhaps a bit puzzled at the shocking effect they seemed to have on the rest of us.

The cabbie then said, "Karen, while you're visiting your husband, I'll be visiting my older brother, Bernie Sanderon."

Karen asked, "How is he doing?"

"Bernie's doing so-so. His blood pressure is running high. He's no spring chicken anymore!

He's sixty now. I'm taking him blood pressure medicine and a pound of peanuts to snack on."

Karen then asked, "Didn't good old Bernie get arrested a year ago for writing a news article critical of Ledif's taking over the student and labor unions?"

The cabbie replies, "Yes. The commie judges sentenced him to three years in prison. It could have been worse. Commander Huber got twenty years for criticizing Ledif's shift from liberal views to the Fascist Communist bloc. I call them that way because they are both forms of totalitarian dictatorships—regardless of simple, silly labels like left wing or right wing. Their common enemy are free constitutional governments that grant their citizens basic rights—such as free expression, the right to vote, and due process. If government is not transparent and accountable to its citizens, the people are screwed!"

Karen reflected for a few seconds and then said, "Good point. They also sentenced a nephew of my brother-in-law to twenty years for conspiracy against the Rob-Illusion! For a charge like that they might have killed someone else. But he fought on the side of the Revolution to restore the constitutional republic, as did my husband. They are both now in jail."

The cabbie paused, thought for a moment, and then said, "It's such a pity that the government took our gun rights. Now we can't express dissenting opinions, and they can put us in jail for any darned thing, as we have no due process through Ledif's kangaroo courts."

My aunt Karen sighed and said, "The dictatorship sentences people like Bernie, my husband,

and my brother-in-law's nephew as examples for the rest of us. Now we live in fear of been put in jail for any small criticism of the regime. We have become a nation of 'Yessir' people!"

As she finished her last sentence, we arrived at the prison.

It looked like a big, sturdy, rustic building made out of cement, block, and iron bars. Everywhere we looked, there were guards with rifles or sidearms. I don't remember much of our wait there. My father Nino had carefully instructed me not to trust anybody or say anything that might compromise our visit there and to assume that everybody was a potential government informant. It seemed that Pop must have talked to everybody else visiting there, for they all seemed to have the same attitude we had of staying isolated in our own little groups!

Finally, the moment came when my uncle's name was called out by a government official. At a checkpoint, prison personnel lightly frisked us for a few seconds, trying to feel with their hands over our clothes for any extraneous objects that we could smuggle in to the prisoners.

We were led through a spooky-looking enclosed dark and narrow corridor. A chill went through my spine, when ...

"Boo!" my cousin Reissi behind me yelled in my ear.

"Son of a gun! You scared the crap out of me!" I said. I felt like kicking his butt but restrained myself.

We arrived at a well-lit thirty-by-thirty-foot chamber, with walls of mixed cement and stone.

We stood at a lower level, waiting for the guards to bring in Uncle Tony at a level a few feet above us, behind a four-foot-high stone and cement wall and a net we could see through. The whole place gave me the chills. Although divided from Uncle Tony by physical barriers, we could see his expression of great joy when he saw us. During his time in prison, he just lived for those few cherished minutes that he could spend with the family. The short fifteen minutes that we were there visiting him were monopolized by young Fleebee's vocabulary antics.

Fortunately, Uncle Tony got out of prison in good health and spirits, and he and his family were allowed to leave Banacan a few years later for the country of Yuma, where they could enjoy the freedom to say anything they wanted about politicians.

CHAPTER FOURTEEN

THE PASSING OF NOVA'S DAD

Nova continued telling us of her native country of Banacan in planet Terruno:

> By early May 1944 inefficient centralized government production and distribution of consumer goods caused shortages of various food items such as fruit, vegetables, meat, milk, and eggs. This was due to political cronies having replaced the businessmen and farmers who had run our prosperous economy. Shortages gave rise to a black market in goods and services, although some believe that Ledif's regime intentionally kept the rations scarce, as impoverished people spending their days trying to make ends meet don't have time to rebel.
>
> One day, Dad got back home with two steaks he obtained in trade for a banned book critical

of the totalitarian dictatorship. Mom skillfully divided the two steaks equally among the three of us. As Mom fixed dinner, Pop and I went to a neighbor's house to trade two pieces of cake of ours for some extra cooking oil we needed.

As we went past the local central park, Pop pointed to a food store about half a block ahead of us. He said to me, "Nova, do not set foot in that store. The government forbids our entry to that store. In that place, only foreigners and communist party members are allowed to buy unlimited amounts of every product they want. The rest of us go to the regular stores to buy our monthly rations of items such as milk, eggs, rice, and beans, for which we stand in line for many hours under the hot tropical sun. And the same thing happens with hospitals. Only foreigners and communists go to the well-maintained hospitals, get treated by the best doctors, and receive it all free of charge. Meanwhile, the rest of us go to the not-so-good hospitals, have to bring our own bedding and bug spray, and have to pay for any medicines we are prescribed."

As I heard these words about the falseness of Fascist Communism, all that I saw was a new medieval monarchy, where the new nobility was determined by how high you were in the communist party!

As we were within a block of the neighbor we traded with, the president of the block Committee for the Defense of the Revolution came to my father, accompanied by two tall uniformed policemen. They were eyeballing the bag with the black-market dessert Mother made.

Daddy froze. He had been a participant on the food black market for years, so far without any trouble. But he seemed to sense that this time was different. And his face had an expression of worry.

The president of the block committee was upset and voiced his anger at my father. "Companion, your home was the only one in the neighborhood that did not have 100 percent participation in revolutionary activities. Your family's reluctance in joining us is upsetting my record. And if I don't make revolutionaries out of every one of my neighbors, my superiors will think of me as a weak leader! How long do you think I can cover for you?"

After a brief pause, the president of the block committee continued, "We know that you helped that dissident worm Bill, now behind bars, in distributing antirevolutionary flyers! Sorry, comrade. We'll have to take you with us!"

With that said, the policemen grabbed my dad and took him away.

Pop offered no resistance. He turned to me and said, "Don't worry. I'll be out in a day or two. Go home and tell Mom not to worry!"

I went home and told Mother about Father's arrest.

She wept silently for a while and then said, "Nova, I can't help but worry and cry! There is no judicial process in Banacan that protects the accused. When you get arrested, it's not a matter of whenever you are guilty or not. You are presumed guilty when you get arrested in this country. It's a matter of whether you are put to death or else how much time you spend in jail."

After Mom said that, I shed a few tears too. A minute later we started praying together for Dad's welfare.

Nearly a week had passed since my father Nino's arrest. To make matters worse, my mother Caridad had a miscarriage soon thereafter. After a few days of mourning and some sick leave, Mom returned to work at the neighborhood's grocery store, which had been taken over from the original owners by the government the previous year. But things did not get any better the last couple of days, as she helped herself to a bottle of hard liquor that she seemed determined to finish on that sunny mid-May afternoon in 1944.

In the midst of Mom's drinking binge, there was a knock on the door. My half-drunk mother got up from her chair and stumbled a few steps on her way to open the door. I followed a few paces behind to assist her if necessary. As she opened the door, we saw we were been visited by the president of the block Committee for the Defense of the Revolution, the one who had my father arrested for antirevolutionary activities. With him were two uniformed police officers wearing sidearms.

I had a bad feeling about our visitors. Those who worked for Ledif's dictatorial regime were not exactly the type out to lend a helping hand to families of political dissidents, particularly if they were intoxicated. Mother motioned to me to sit down as she prepared to speak to our visitors.

With a serious face, Ernesto, the leader of the block Committee for the Defense of the Revolution, extended a formal greeting. "Good morning Caridad. How are you doing?"

"We are doing fine, Ernesto. How are you doing yourself?" replied Mother as she eyeballed the two rather straight-faced officers, perhaps wondering what the heck they were up to.

"Caridad, we have bad news for you," continued Ernesto. "Your husband Nino passed away from a heart attack after several days in our custody."

A few seconds of complete silence followed, as Mother and I tried to take in the bad news. As tears flowed down my grieving mother's face, she began screaming, "Murderers! You killed him! My dear Nino was diabetic. And being without insulin in jail, he suffered a heart attack! You did not allow visits or calls! Way to kill him, you murdering thugs!" As she finished her last sentence, she puked on Ernesto's fancy dress shirt.

For a few seconds, Ernesto silently stood there in disgust. As his face turned to an expression of anger, he ordered the police officers, "Arrest this woman. Intoxicated in public and disturbing the peace!"

At that moment, they took my mother away.

As I stood there in a state of shock, Ernesto turned to me. "Don't worry about your mom! We'll take her to a psychiatric hospital for treatment in a nearby city. We'll let you in to see her after a few months. In the meanwhile, you can communicate with her through postal mail."

With that said, they left with my mother. I was left alone in my house with no parents, a few months short of turning eighteen.

I was not allowed to see my mother but told I could exchange postal mail with her. Of course, in Banacan all mail was subject to be opened by the government, so you had to be careful with your words. Telephone calls to detainees were not allowed. And humanitarian organizations weren't allowed to visit them either.

A few days later, the viewing of my deceased father Nino took place on a Sunday morning in late May 1944. The dimly lit chapel had a nice aromatic fragrance from the flowers that had been sent by grieving relatives, friends, and neighbors, most of whom were present.

Absent from the funeral was Mom, who'd been traumatized by both her recent miscarriage and the news of Dad's death while in custody in one of Ledif's prison.

In those early days of the Revolution, conditions in Banacan mental institutions were really bad. Many psychiatrists and nurses left the country. They were replaced by unqualified government cronies, who stole the food and clothing from the patients, many of whom died for lack of food and good medical care.

Also absent from the funeral were a couple of my dad's brothers who had already emigrated to Yuma, Ledif's nemesis of freedom to the north. They were not allowed to come. Perhaps the regime feared that my father's funeral would turn into some sort of antigovernment demonstration if they showed up.

Dad's older sisters Maria and Clotilde got up to view his body one last time. They slowly moved forward, their short steps echoing through the small chapel, as they approached the altar where the casket rested. They knelt for one last, grief-filled prayer. For a couple of minutes, they prayed, rosaries in hand, and shed a few last tears. Chins down, they slowly headed back to their seats, as though reluctant to increase the distance between them and my deceased father.

A minute later, a fellow parishioner rose from one of the chapel's benches and quietly approached the microphone that stood a few feet away from my dad's coffin. She stood in silence for a few seconds, her sad eyes gazing into the crowd. Then she broke the silence, singing a funeral song with an angelic voice. With the added beauty of the flowers and the crowd of loving kin and friends, I could not think of a better way to send my father back to our creator.

Her singing was a tough act to follow.

But a smiling priest, who had known my dad for many years, addressed the crowd with a few kind words about him. "Today we gather to bid a last goodbye to Nino before we lay him to rest. He was a good husband and father. Nino was born a few years after the birth of our country and was well versed in our history. He was an easygoing fellow with an engaging personality and a quick wit. Softball and dominoes were his favorite pastimes. Being a small-town lawyer did not pay as well as it would in our nation's capital, but with his income his family managed to live comfortably in their small home."

The priest took a sip of water and went on. "Nino had a great understanding of history, literature, and geography, and his home was full of books on those subjects. His daughter read many of these books, such as the translated works of various famous foreign authors and a couple of science fiction writers. But other than love for family, his greatest legacy was his love for free institutions and political liberties. Though not religious, he had strong ethical values. His daughter tells me that their many shared activities created a close, caring bond between them—whether playing sports or, board games or just enjoying a family get-together. Go in peace, Nino, and may your soul eternally rest in your new home in the heavens!"

After the burial, I was invited for an evening dinner to the home of my uncle Tony and his wife, Karen. Tony was Mom's youngest brother and had just served a few years in prison for possession and distribution of antirevolutionary propaganda.

After finishing our modest rice and beans meal, Uncle Tony says, "Nova, we just received from the government our permission to leave Banacan. They'll come and take possession of our house tomorrow and take us to the airport to board an airplane for Yuma. Here is twenty dollars to help you out for a few days. Please check with your dad's older sisters Maria and Clotilde. They can help you out some. They are currently receiving money and medicine from a couple of your uncles in Yuma. We hate to leave you alone, dear! May God bestow his blessings on you!"

With that said, we bid our last farewells to each other, and I went home alone. Once there, I opened that day's mail. There, I found out that I had just been volunteered to work in some remote farm cooperative for the summer and was asked to report for that duty in a couple of days! There was some alcohol left in the bottle Mom left unfinished. Within an hour, I drank it all and passed out.

CHAPTER FIFTEEN

GOING TO THE FARM COLLECTIVE

As Nova's memoirs continue, they relate how, after her graduation from high school, she was "volunteered'" by the totalitarian Ledif regime to work for the summer at a farm:

> Late in May 1944, all the graduating seniors from my high school were "volunteered" by the dictatorship to work at a vegetable farm in the Cambray Mountains, about fifty miles west of my home town. During our pretrip briefing we were told that the area was infested with antigovernment guerrillas or *banditos*, as the Ledif regime preferred to call them. Government officials assured us that we would be protected by a platoon of soldiers assigned to guard the two-hundred-acre vegetable farm where we would work. In addition to our farming duties, we were told that we would also care for several hundred egg-laying chickens.

Thus, we graduating seniors embarked on a journey to our summer labor camp. We were loaded on a train to the city of Holy Spirit, about twenty miles away from the farm. At Holy Spirit, we were dropped by the train station, where we were asked to drink some water, eat some stale peanuts, and relieve ourselves. We were told that we had to wait for about an hour for several motor vehicles that would take us to the farm collective.

As usual in our beloved country of Banacan, the water from the fountain was very warm, and there was no toilet paper in the bathroom. The government blamed this and nearly every other problem in the land on the economic embargo from our Yuman neighbors, who, despite having been ripped off during the Rob-illusion, were our country's main suppliers of food and medicine through cash payments.

Through a loudspeaker in the train station, we heard some nice music. Some of my schoolmates started moving to its rhythm. About twenty yards away from us on a street corner, two young streetwalkers were also moving to the beat of the music. Within a minute a horse carriage, with a fat fellow of about sixty—perhaps an affluent tourist or government official—stopped and picked up one of the hookers for a few minutes of female company. After the Rob-Illusion, in Banacan this was the highest paid profession a woman could aspire to, paying as high as thirty dollars for an evening, much higher than the average monthly pay of twenty to twenty-five dollars a month or even that of a doctor at sixty-five dollars a month!

I sat on a wooden bench and started to day-dream about my dear mother, her silent, loving smile and magnificent hair. She was sent to a government psychiatric hospital after causing a commotion after being traumatized by both her recent miscarriage and the news of Dad's suspicious death in one of Ledif's prisons. I reflected on the reality of my condition: the daughter of political dissidents who were systematically purged by the dictatorship. But I remained optimistic about my mother's situation and hoped and prayed that she might be released and that I might see her soon.

On a side wall of the train station there was a large five-by-five-foot poster of Chip Guerra, a goon of the dictatorship who had allegedly died fighting to expand our miserable Rob-Illusion to neighboring countries. Members of the regime treated him as some sort of saint of terrorism. And the dictatorship profited from the sales to naïve foreigners of T-shirts with his image and books about him. But political dissidents had named this sadistic murderer "The Butcher of La Cabana Prison." One of over a hundred of his forgotten victims was a kid in his early teens called Ariel; Chip shot him for getting in the way of soldiers during his father's arrest.

That poster was filled with the enigmatic, calm, glowering face of Chip, wearing a beret, black-haired with a well-trimmed mustache and beard. Some of the girls in my class thought he was a handsome man!

My good friend Maria approached me and asked, "Would they have made a poster of Chip if he was an ugly guy?"

I giggled and replied, "I doubt it!"

In the poster he seemed to be in a pensive mood. Maria asked, "Wonder what he was thinking about when they took this picture?"

I turned to her with a smile. "I bet that he was thinking 'Gee, I just took a dump in the middle of the night, and I'm out of toilet paper! I would wipe my butt with my underpants, but it's my last pair! And the government just turned off my water and electricity! How can their spies peeking through the window see anything with no lights? And our darned dictator is on my butt about leaving the country and violently exporting this miserable way of life to our neighbors? Should I take a raft and leave for Yuma and ask for political asylum?'"

Maria laughed heartedly. I was still in deep in reflection about what Chip Guerra must be thinking when our rides arrived. We were loaded into four steam-powered vehicles that resembled a French L'Obeissante wagon of the late 1800s on Earth.

Maria and I sat in the back row of the last vehicle. We'd been good friends since elementary school and were going to room together at the farm. By our first year in high school, her family was hosting get-togethers for her friends. There was plenty of food, drink, and music—some of which had been declared an illegal imperialist influence by the Ledif regime. In the early days of the Revolution, long hair and Yuman music were frowned upon. But her dad was a high-ranking government official, so the regime's guardians did not bother us.

As we started our trip, I broke the silence and said to Maria, "For a few years, there was a shortage of farm laborers after Ledif collectivized the farm system. Those who resisted either landed in jail or died in the hills fighting a large, well-equipped army. Even temporary farm workers from neighboring islands stopped coming to Banacan after Ledif collectivized the farms and expected laborers to work for meager wages!"

I paused. "Maria, do you recall how old we were when we started working on farms during our summer vacations?"

After some thought, Maria replied, "We've been working four to six weeks of our summer vacations on the farm collectives since we were eleven years old, laboring up to eight hours per day. That was about seven years ago! We picked fruits and vegetables back then. But this summer I got myself a cushy job as secretary in the captain's office."

I said, "In the original Revolution in the Old World, the land was initially redistributed to small farmers. But when Papa Joe took over the Fascist Communist Union, he collectivized all farms and killed millions of farmers who rebelled. The same thing is happening now in Banacan, but on a lesser scale because we are a small country."

Maria replied, "At least they don't send us to labor camps for political dissidents, priests, gays, long-haired guys, and musicians who play Yuman music! They really get the shaft!"

About halfway to our destination, we went through a checkpoint where soldiers inspected our vehicles. Maria was the only one carrying a large bag of food, with some canned meat, extra rations of rice and beans, and some cookies. The soldiers asked for her identification, talked to the driver for a few seconds, and let us through.

After about a minute, I turned to Maria and lightly observed, "The soldiers did not mess with you! They normally confiscate bags of food with the excuse that they could wind up in the hands of guerrillas. But they checked your name and talked to the driver and found out your dad is a high-ranking government official."

Maria smiled back at me. "Well, I guess some people are more equal than others in our social-ist paradise! Idealistically I'm a socialist, though I like the idea of allowing small businesses and farms. But as time passes by, any government bu-reaucracy—whether socialist, capitalist, or some-where in between—will become corrupt because of government officials' desires for power, prop-erty, and prestige. And those desires seem to go unchecked in an authoritarian government that is not transparent or accountable to the people. It's not like we are a socialist democracy!"

Maria paused and added, "But don't worry, my friend, I'll share my goodies with you!"

We giggled for a few seconds. Then my eyes opened wide. I asked, "Did you get your record player and your vinyl records sent ahead to the farm?"

"Yes, Nova. I called the farm yesterday, and they assured me that my record player and vinyl records are waiting for us, including your favorite songs by Pablo Anka!"

I smiled. Then I reflected for a few seconds, my eyes nostalgically looking into the distance. A tear came to my eye as I said: "Yes. My boyfriend and I loved a couple of his songs—'Diana' and 'Put Your Head on My Shoulder.' We used to dance to those songs. Too bad my boyfriend got drafted."

I paused to wipe my eyes and added: "He was sent to fight and die for the glory of our leader Ledif in some faraway country a year ago. He was under the command of General Ochoa, who fell out of favor with the regime and was executed. Darn Ledif! It's always a bloody revolution, one after another, in some other faraway country. In a way, all this fighting abroad distracts from the economic misery and political repression here!"

With a loving and caring attitude of a good friend, Maria hugged me, holding me in her arms, as I shed a few more tears. She knew I had been traumatized by the recent deaths of my dad and my boyfriend. In Maria's arms, I wept in silence for nearly the hour it took to get to the farm.

As our vehicle passed through the entrance gate to the farm, we saw a few soldiers posing for a picture. I guessed it was for *Rebel Youth* or some other government newspaper. Heck, all newspapers and radio stations were owned by the regime!

Four of the soldiers were carrying a pole from which hung a small dead young man, tied up the way hunters carry a dead deer. His clothing was covered with dried blood, probably from the gunshots that killed him.

With a sad tone of voice, I said, "Poor guy! Was he a peasant who rebelled after his farm was taken over by the government? Or was he just a dissident that came from a city to join the rebels?"

Then I noticed that one of the men in uniform was Ernesto, the government official who arrested both my parents! He was a captain, perhaps the highest ranking official at the farm. The prospect of spending my summer under the command of Ernesto terrified me!

As I sat petrified in shock, my friend Maria said, "Oh shoot! There's Ernesto! About the last man you would want to see here!"

I froze in my seat as our vehicle slowed to a full stop in front of a two-story house. That was the residence of the captain, his summer secretary Maria, and a roommate of her choice (yours truly).

Maria grabbed me and led me to our room upstairs. It was late afternoon. We had arrived just in time for our evening's meal.

During dinner, Maria made some small talk with Captain Ernesto. I remained silent.

The only conversation that I recollect from that meal is Maria asking Ernesto, "Captain, who was the dead young man that we saw when we came into the camp? Would not it have been better to apprehend him and let the judicial process take place?"

Ernesto's eyes opened wide as he replied with a diabolical smile, "I admire our martyred Commander Chip Guerra! He once said, 'To send men to the firing squad, judicial proof is unnecessary. These procedures are an archaic bourgeois detail. This is a revolution!'"

He paused as if momentarily undergoing some sort of euphoric mystic transcendence when thinking of his unholy and sadistic role model!

He continued after catching his breath, "I love Chip! I shall get one of his books and a T-shirt with his famous picture."

As Ernesto said this, my face turned to an expression of disgust. What can you tell this sadistic goon who rejoiced at the death of those with whom he disagreed? In the reign of terror of a dictatorship, silence and conformity were your best protection to save the life and/or freedom of yourself and your loved ones. After some chitchat, we girls went to sleep. Tomorrow was a workday!

CHAPTER SIXTEEN

THE VOLUNTARY ABDUCTION

Nova's account continues:

Every morning, Captain Ernesto insured that we were awakened about six with a loud yell: "Get up! Let's dedicate a workday to Ledif's glorious Revolution!"

His wake-up call reminded me how years ago my family was always awakened at sunup by a neighbor's rooster crowing. The animal would crow all day to warn off other males. Before coming to the farm, I had not heard the rooster crow for some time. His wake-up call had been replaced by the neighborhood's watch committee record playing through a loudspeaker some martial sounding hymn of the dictatorship, perhaps trying to inspire listeners to work and fight hard for the state. Had the rooster been slaughtered by his hungry owner? Or did he escape to Yuma, the land of opportunity, where he would live as a free rooster? Golly, I missed him dearly!

Back at the farm, we wore thick cotton shirts, work pants, straw hats, and boots. Most students resided at the military-type barracks, which was short of paint and had a palm-leafed roof. When it was not raining, the windows remained open to allow a breeze in. A single light bulb hung over the beds where more than thirty girls slept, with just enough light to see our way around at night. If the light bulb burned out, we had a candle as backup. We washed our faces and clothes in rustic cement sinks. There were two showers and a pit latrine—a row of cubicles with holes in the floor— where we relieved ourselves. A lot of the young high school boys grew moustaches and beards because of a shortage of razor blades. There was never enough food! It was usually of poor quality and often contained a few worms which some joked enhanced its protein value.

By midsummer we were used to our daily routine of harsh farm work and crappy food. The time came for my friend Maria to go to college on August 12 for her first year of premed, a few days before the rest of us girls went home. She had good grades, and her parents were members in good standing of the communist party. But I was glad for her. She was good people and a close friend since elementary school.

Her parents came to pick her up. After her dad went to talk in private to Captain Ernesto, Maria, her mother, and I remained chatting at the front porch of the officer's quarters. While Maria and I sat on a bench, her mother, Tanya, sat on a rocking chair.

After she comfortably settled down on her chair, Tanya gave me a large box and said, "Nova, you've grown fast from a little girl to a future nursing assistant! Here is a cake I made for your eighteenth birthday tomorrow! We'll not be here, as we are leaving within the hour to take Maria to her college, but we'll be with you in spirit."

Tanya paused, smiled, and added, "Is not it nice to have your eighteenth birthday on the same day as our maximum leader Ledif, the thirteenth of August?"

After another pause, she continued, "My husband asked his brother, Captain Ernesto, to give you the day off because of your birthday!"

I just smiled and thought to myself, *What a bummer it is to have a birthday on the same day as your local strongman. But in Banacan, it's pointless to openly whine about anything. It could be interpreted as a criticism of the Rob-Illusion!*

So, I just took the box and said, "Thanks, Tanya! You're so kind! I'll enjoy this birthday!"

I went inside to put the cake in the icebox. Then I returned to the front porch.

By then, Tanya's face turned serious as she told me, "I have bad news."

I had not heard from my mother in weeks. I had a bad premonition.

"Nova, I talked on the phone to the doctor in charge of the hospital where your mother was being treated for alcoholism."

Then Tanya reached in her purse. "Here is a letter that went to your house, and I took the liberty of reading it before I brought it to you. Your mother died from cirrhosis of the liver. They attempted a liver transplant, but she died on the operating table. It's a very complex procedure, and about half the patients die during surgery. Her ashes will be sent to you."

I froze in place on the bench, next to Maria. With the caring attitude of a good friend, Maria held me in her arms as I shed some tears. She knew that I was traumatized by the recent deaths of my father, my boyfriend, and now my mother. I must be the unluckiest eighteen-year-old in the country! In Maria's arms, I wept in silence until I ran out of tears. Mom was cremated too. Typical procedure to hide evidence of physical abuse of dissidents!

About then, Maria's dad came out from his meeting with Ernesto. Maria and her parents left. I went to bed early. But I cried all night and did not fall asleep until just before sunrise.

A knock on the door woke me up about noon on my birthday. It was Captain Ernesto and one of his bodyguards. They brought me the cake and a bottle of champagne. They sat on Maria's empty bed and lit the candles on the cake. I blew them out and sat back on my bed.

Ernesto and his friend then cut three small pieces of the cake and gave me one. As I took my first bite, they passed me a glass of champagne.

Ernesto then said, "Have a drink, Nova! You just turned eighteen! Happy birthday!"

I told them, "What the heck! This may relieve the emotional pain from my mother's death!"

As soon as I took that first glass, I was overcome by the compulsion to have one more, eventually drinking most of the contents of the bottle. After some small talk with my two guests, I felt a little tipsy and went to lie on my bed, closing my eyes. I heard the bodyguard excuse himself and leave.

I felt apprehensive about being alone with Captain Ernesto. My friend Maria and I thought he was a bit creepy. He's just divorced his wife, whom he'd physically abused. And for months he'd given many high school girls in my hometown the elevator look as they passed by him and often made catcalls to them.

But I was drunk and dozed off. Within a minute, I sensed somebody on top of me. It was Ernesto! I tried pushing him off. But I was too dizzy and weak. I was helpless, as he took advantage of my state of intoxication. Eventually, I passed out.

At sunup, I woke up with a hangover. Ernesto, asleep, was sprawled next to me in his birthday suit. I was resentful. The thought of killing him with a knife crossed my mind. But that was the kind of thing my dear mother would not approve of, despite his raping me. I felt dirty and took a shower.

I reflected for about a minute. A life of continuous daily sexual abuse at the hands of the cruel and powerful army officer from my hometown, who had arrested my parents, was a disgusting option. As for taking a raft north to Yuma, we were on the south side of the island. I decided that my best course was to escape and look for guerillas to join in the nearby hills.

I got dressed, took my purse, a knife, and a fishing pole, and went downstairs to the refrigerator. I put some fruit and a couple of hard-boiled eggs in my purse.

As I walked out the door, I told the guard on duty, "I'm going fishing. Captain Ernesto does not want to be awakened for a couple of hours."

Security was light for students working at the farm. And the guard figured that I was the captain's new mistress. So, I was easily allowed to leave the farm alone for the nearest stream. I figured that I had a two-hour head start in my escape before Ernesto woke.

Wading through the shallow edge of the stream by the farm, I headed up the mountains. A couple of miles upstream, I saw soldiers in an observation balloon exchanging fire with somebody on the ground, perhaps guerrillas. The balloon was hit. It slowly lost gas and started going back to its base near the farm. I thought to myself, *Good! There must be guerrillas nearby!*

As the balloon passed me overhead, I saw one of the soldiers in it pointing to me while looking back, perhaps at the rapist captain and his goons on my tracks. I thought *Oh, shoot! The captain and his soldiers may not be far behind!*

I went uphill for a while but ran out of luck. Captain Ernesto, two of his goons, and a tracking dog caught up to me. They knocked me down! And then they threw me on the ground.

As Ernesto got on top of me, he told the others, "Men, you'll have your chance after me! And we might as well kill her after we're done. Apparently, she was going to join the guerrillas!"

But my fortune changed in that instant. Suddenly, a firefight erupted. Ernesto's men and tracking dog were hit and fell to the ground.

When Ernesto reached for his gun, this Grey creature appeared and smashed him in the face with a rifle butt. Seconds later the captain was dead, thanks to a bayonet. For a few seconds, I sat on the ground, confused and amazed, wondering what was going on.

At that moment, a handsome man, one of the Grey's Amigo allies (who I later learned was first officer Romo), stood over me and, using his universal translator, said, "We have to leave this planet! A platoon of soldiers is coming this way! Do you want to come with us?"

I was confused and traumatized by the recent deaths of my father, my boyfriend, and my mother. And only the night before, I'd been raped by a high-ranking army officer. I told my handsome rescuer, "Take me out of this hell! I'll go anywhere with you!"

With that said, my blue prince picked me up and took me inside a landing craft camouflaged about fifty yards away. It was my first time flying!

CHAPTER SEVENTEEN

REACHING SAFE HAVEN

In this chapter, Captain Noah relates how the Greys, with their Amigo allies, reached a safe haven after losing their home worlds and planet Avalonia to hostile invaders.

Their spaceship, *Zeta's Hope*, which was about two hundred feet in length and had a diameter of thirty-three feet. This exploration vessel resembled a WWII submarine more than anything else, except that it could travel at a hundred times the speed of light. After leaving planet Avalonia, they stopped on planet Terruno, where they resupplied their ship with food and fuel. Before they left Terruno, they picked up a stranded political refugee called Nova, who was a nurse in training. The current chapter is an account by then Captain Noah (now an admiral) of their trip from Terruno to planet Sapiens:

> The day after the Greys left planet Terruno on August 14, 1944, I scheduled a staff meeting after dinner. The nine bridge officers were present, four

males, four females, and an android in charge of security. Besides myself, they were Mr. Romo (a humanoid from planet Amigo), Chief Engineer Jang, Doctor Akina, Quartermaster Boudica, Ben at the helm (another Amigo), Navigator Nax (also an Amigo), Faith at communications, and Security Chief Amie. Three of the bridge officers were humans from Amigo, experienced in space travel, who'd escaped from the invasion of their planet. The chief engineer, the doctor, and the quartermaster were considered bridge officers, though their regular stations were not on the bridge. Mr. Romo was second in command. The bridge officers accounted for about a fifth of the spaceship's crew of fifty.

I started the staff meeting by welcoming all the bridge officers.

Communications officer Faith, who doubled as the ship's chaplain, started with a prayer: "God, thank you for another day alive, free, and in good health. Bless those less fortunate who have died or been hurt or are suffering under slavery in our home worlds. We ask that you give us good health and good spirits for another day."

I then yielded to first officer Romo for a progress report on the mission just completed to planet Terruno. Romo said, "During the three days that we were in an abandoned mine at the Cambray Mountains in planet Terruno, we met our targets for mining fuel minerals. We also added three hundred pounds of fish, fruits, and vegetables to our food reserves."

Cheers came from around the table. I smiled and added, "Your shipmates are grateful for your thoughtful collection of fresh food. Many of us were becoming tired of our regular rations and the lack of taste and diversity from the milk, fruit juices, soups, fake meat, and tuberous edible roots we get from our rather primitive food replicators."

Romo smiled and resumed. "About a half hour before we were scheduled to leave an old abandoned mine at the country of Banacan in planet Terruno, we were discovered by an army observation balloon. The government of Banacan is totalitarian in nature, and multiparty elections and freedom of expression are not tolerated. Thus, a number of their citizens are engaged in a rebellion against the dictatorship. Apparently mistaking us for guerillas, the army balloon's two-man crew fired on us and radioed back for reinforcements. Once these hostile armed forces arrived at our location, we inflicted three casualties on the enemy ground troops, while sustaining none ourselves. Technician Shaka and Quartermaster Boudica distinguished themselves in combat, the latter killing an enemy with her bayonet."

Some cheers and clapping for Boudica's bravery followed.

Romo paused for a few seconds and continued, "During our firefight with the local dictator's forces, we saved a young woman who had been abused. Her name is Nova. She's an eighteen-year-old orphan who was on her way to join the guerrillas. She has a background as a nurse's assistant, and she'll begin her training tomorrow with Doctor Akina. She has been issued a universal translator that's standard to the crew. That is all!"

Looking directly at Romo, Doctor Akina said, "Nova is a smart, sweet, and good-looking young lady." She pointed at Romo. "Nova was inquiring about the handsome young man who helped rescue her. I smell romance in the air." As Akina finished, Boudica whistled a sexy catcall. A few chuckles followed.

I then cut in. "Thanks for your report, Mr. Romo. Now Navigator Nax will report on our route from here to planet Sapiens, which was identified to us as a safe haven by the friendly time traveling alien Chaika."

Nax was a female humanoid Amigo aged thirty-five. The Amigos were close in appearance to humans on Earth. The main difference was that their navels were off center. The reader may want to have a tummy check amongst friends to check for any Amigos.

Nax began, "Our mission on Terruno went well, with no damage. Our mother ship *Zeta's Hope* orbited around the planet, monitoring nearby activity, while the landing module went to the surface to collect fuel minerals and food. We are currently cruising to planet Sapiens at about a hundred times light speed. Fuel consumption is at the specified nominal rate. Our fuel tanks and food storage compartment are full. Arrival at Sapiens estimated in about twenty days."

I thanked Nax and proceeded to brief the bridge officers on the planned initial contact with the Sapiens. "After a twenty-day trip, *Zeta's Hope* will arrive at Sapiens and begin orbiting around it. Communications Officer Faith established contact with ground control at Sapiens and got the coordinates of the landing site. I have selected three of you to come with me for the initial landing party: First Officer Romo, Doctor Akina, and Chief of Security Amie. Chief Engineer Jang will be in charge during our absence."

The two-months-pregnant Akina interrupted. "My husband in charge of the ship? Honey, don't run off and leave us stranded!"

Laughter was heard for a couple of seconds.

I then went on. "We'll bring down additional personnel after establishing housing arrangements for our crew with the Sapiens government. During preliminary arrangements, we will be employed as contractors for the Tri-Interplanetary Alliance (TIA), whose members are from the planets Sapiens, Verde, and Proxima per our friend Chaika. She warns us that there may be remote-controlled kidnapper spaceships operated by space pirates from the Malian star system. The pirates have seized cargo spaceships, later demanding a ransom for the return of the crew and cargo. The pirates are armed with relatively slow-moving heat-seeking missiles, and their crews possess conventional firearms similar to ours."

Quartermaster Boudica enthusiastically exclaimed, "If we run into them, we'll give them a whipping!"

Security Chief Amie, the android, noted, "Our vessel has no weapons. However, per intelligence from Chaika, we have a faster ship than the pirates and better long-range sensors. They also have no deflection shields. It's possible that the pirates may fire upon us, for we may not resemble the configuration of cargo ships they have attacked in the past, and they may mistake us for a new Sapiens warship."

After a pause I went on. "We have about twenty days before we arrive at Sapiens. Let's discuss next week contingency plans against the possibility of running into the pirates. Does anybody have any issues to bring up before adjourning?"

After a few seconds of silence, I declared, "Meeting adjourned!"

After twenty uneventful days, the Greys arrived in the vicinity of Sapiens. They decelerated and started orbiting Sapiens, which was a moon circling a giant gas planet named Grande that revolved around their Sunlike star in the Goldilocks zone.

Before they finished the first orbit, Navigator Nax exclaimed, "A bogie just came from behind Grande. It's approaching us. It has the configuration and engine signature of a Malian pirate. It's a thousand miles from us. A Sapiens spacecraft is pursuing it from about a thousand miles behind."

A few seconds later, she added, "The pirates just fired a heat-seeking missile at us."

Captain Noah shouted, "Maneuver One! We rehearsed this. Everybody knows what to do."

Helmsman Ben turned *Zeta's Hope* around and slowed as they passed by the missile, making sure it was tracking them. Then proceeded at reduced speed toward the pirates and cut the engines to allow the spaceship to glide behind the pirate vessel.

Then Noah ordered, "Navigator, shields up!"

Nax activated the deflection shields. Within a moment, the pirate ship was hit by its own missile, which perforated the vessel and exploded, scattering some debris. The pirate ship tumbled and was slowly pulled into Sapiens's atmosphere, igniting as it disintegrated.

The blast wave from the explosion was felt in *Zeta's Hope* for a couple of seconds, without causing any damage, thanks to the deflector shields. After a moment of silence and seeing that they were all well, cheers rose from the crew. After they settled down, Communications Officer Faith said, "Sapiens ground control is sending us landing instructions."

After months of wandering thru the galaxy, the Greys had arrived at a planet that they could call a safe haven.

CHAPTER EIGHTEEN

A DAY IN THE VIGASIA STRIP

After traveling for a few months, the Greys arrived at planet Sapiens, about halfway between their home world of Zeta and Earth. Sapiens is a habitable moon orbiting a giant gas planet, much like Saturn. Sapiens is about the size of Earth. The planet is in the Goldilocks zone, a region in which a planet is the right distance from its sun so that its surface is neither too hot nor too cold, so as to favor the existence of liquid water. The planet has an atmosphere nearly identical to Earth's, and its surface is 70 percent covered with water. Most of the landmass consists of five large continents and several island archipelagos, like the Caribbean islands. Like Earth, Sapiens's magnetosphere protects the planet from the charged particles of the solar wind and cosmic rays, which would otherwise strip away the ozone layer that protects the planet from harmful ultraviolet radiation coming from a Sun like star.

Sapiens had a population of seven billion humanlike inhabitants and over one hundred countries that agreed to exist under a central government based on the principles of universal rights and shared knowledge and resources, including space exploration that spanned several millennia. Their aerospace technology had developed slowly and was a notch behind that of the Greys. By the mid-1900s, Sapiens had enjoyed a few millennia of worldwide peace and space exploration.

The friendly time traveling alien Chaika had suggested Sapiens to the Greys and Amigos as a potential safe haven. For over a century, planet Sapiens had formed a partnership called the Tri-Interplanetary Alliance (TIA) with planets Verde and Proxima. Member planets collaborated with each other in matters of trade, technology, military assistance, and cultural exchange. Their weapons included aircraft and armor about as advanced as that of the Reptoids, including a nuclear weapons arsenal. But they also had advanced technology in computers, communications systems, and food replication.

The alliance assigned a liaison to the Greys. This individual from planet Sapiens was a man in his forties, one Colonel Rick Patel. Members of the Sapiens race resembled earthlings, with the exception of an elongated skull that on average was one to two inches longer than a human's. Rick was educated in psychology and a background in law enforcement. He later became an astronaut and commanded several missions, including a victorious encounter with pirates from planet Malia. In mid-1947, he would be part of a mission to Earth. Rick tells us of his initial impression of the Greys:

> Two days after the arrival of the Greys to our home planet in mid-September 1944, we went to the city of Vigasia, where Mayor Irma invited us to a gala reception dinner. The three highest-ranking members of the Greys' crew (Captain Noah, First Officer Romo, and Chief Engineer Jang) and their romantic partners were the guests of honor. I, Colonel Rick Patel, had been selected

as the Tri-Interplanetary Alliance's liaison with the Greys. At a reception dinner for us, I would be publicly introduced by the President as the Alliance's liaison with the Greys.

We arrived at Vigasia in a military passenger plane a day early to get acquainted with the fine cuisine and a couple of local museums of the arts. The Greys had spent their first couple of days on our planet with high government officials from the state and defense departments, so I hardly knew anything about the Greys' culture and history. With technical knowledge passed to us from the Greys, I'd been busy preplanning technical and operational details in preparation of a trip to Earth, scheduled for mid-1947.

I was told the Greys consumed little meat compared to a Sapiens. We made a reservation for lunch at a fancy restaurant, in an area known as the Strip, which had the finest fruits and salads! But they also had a good reputation for beefsteaks, my favorite main dish.

The main avenue of the Vigasia Strip looked like an ocean of flickering neon lights hanging from the frontage of many casinos, hotels, restaurants, nightclubs, and other businesses. The streets flowed with heavy traffic, and the sidewalks were crowded. A young couple had large two-foot glasses of colorful alcoholic drinks.

I wondered, *What will the state of their minds be like after they finished their drinks?*

Curious tourists freely took pictures—and many of them flashed their cameras at our tour group with the Greys. As we got off the van that had transported us, there were a couple of guys handing out cards with pictures of beautiful top-less women, with the contact information im-printed on them as to where these ladies could be reached by any fellow who felt lonely.

Atop the door of our destination, a restaurant called O'Veggies, there was a gigantic statue. It was that of a large winged woman (Lady Luck?) with a small smiling man riding on her back, whose outstretched hand was loaded with money.

I asked myself, *Does he represent a typical gambler? Is he obsessed about becoming wealthier? Will he be among the few blessed with good fortune by Lady Luck?*

As if reading my mind, Noah turned to me and asked: "Is he going to pay for dinner?"

We chuckled at his ingenious comment!

His wife Faith added: "We are amused by all this activity!"

At the lobby by the entrance of O'Veggies there was a piano. While waiting to be seated, I recall hearing a song by earthling Consuelo Velazquez titled "Bésame Mucho." A wooden plaque on the wall had a Virginia Woolf quote that read: "One cannot think well, love well, or sleep well if one has not dined well."

We sat down for lunch at our restaurant table. After a few minutes I commented to the waitress, "What a fine beefsteak! My compliments to the chef and the steer!"

Then, turning to the Greys, I jokingly told them, "Have no fear of us. We Sapiens eat lots of meat, but we have no plans to put you on the menu."

For a few seconds the Greys' faces went blank.

Captain Noah then explained to me, "Forgive us for not laughing at your joke Colonel Patel. But our home planet was invaded by an aggressive species, the Reptoids, that liked having us for dinner. During initial contact, we had a trade relationship with the Reptoids, who bought pharmaceuticals, medical equipment, tools, and computer and communications systems from us. The Reptoids had a closed society, and travelers there were not allowed outside their capital, so we knew very little about their home planet.

"But to our surprise, the Reptoids invaded our home world without any warning. We fell to this threat in a matter of days, their conquest culminating in their use of a nuclear weapon on our capital, which refused to surrender. Only twenty-five of us Greys, and twenty-five of our Amigo allies, escaped in the nick of time. We left behind many kin and other loved ones to be murdered by the merciless invaders!"

My face grew red with embarrassment. It was not good to start a liaison by offending our guests' sensitivity! After this misstep, I might as well look for new employment. May be the restaurant where we were had an opening for a dishwasher!

Trying to recover from such an awkward moment, I said, "My apologies. I was not aware of that fact. It will not happen again. And please, feel free to simply call me Rick. All my friends do."

After pausing for a moment, and looking to change the subject, I asked, "How did you folks like the arts museum we visited this morning?"

Noah's wife, Faith, then came to my rescue in my state of distress, answering, "That was a fine international collection of paintings and sculptures from your Renaissance period to modern times. I was impressed."

Then Doctor Akina innocently asked, "I saw a lot of nude paintings and sculptures. Are you folks nudists?"

A few chuckles were heard around the table. As the laughter died off, a waiter came with the food and saved me from answering the question about nudism. For a while all the hungry mouths concentrated on their food. Everyone pronounced it excellent!

I thought of asking some questions to get to know them better. Considering my earlier blunder, I figured that I'd better stay away from talking of recent atrocities that the Greys had suffered during the invasion of their planet. I believed that questions concerning the Greys' history and culture preceding the invasion would be safe subjects at the dinner table. Thus, I asked, "What can you tell me about the Greys' home world?"

Visibly saddened, Noah reflected and answered, "Our home world is Zeta. It's twenty light-years from Sapiens in the Zeta Reticuli star system. We had nine countries that agreed to exist under a central government based on the principles of universal rights and to share our knowledge and resources, including our experience of nearly two centuries of space exploration. We prospered in a free market system, but we also cared for the sick and elderly."

Curious about their history, I queried them, "Any wars in your history?"

Noah's wife Faith proudly replied, "By the mid-nineteen-hundreds, we had enjoyed four centuries of worldwide peace. Through space travel, we had trade and cultural relations with another friendly planet called Amigo. Our first officer Romo and a couple dozen others in our crew are from there. We recently became capable of space travel at about a hundred times the speed of light. We also possess advanced technology in computers, communications systems, power generation, food replication, and medical technology. We will share our technology with you in exchange for your generous hospitality and your weapons technology."

I inquired further, "Certainly—but what about sports and other forms of entertainment?"

Enthusiastically, Chief Engineer Jang raised his webbed hands and answered, "Our leisure activities included water sports, camping, hunting, and games resembling volleyball and water polo. Families would gather at home to play table games like Ping-Pong, pool, cards, dominoes, chess, and checkers. We also enjoyed music, theater, singing, and dancing. Each of the nine countries in the planet had annual festivities similar to arts and crafts fairs and carnivals."

Then I changed the subject, trying to gauge the Greys' willingness to collaborate with us in space exploration, "Chaika, our time traveling friend, mentioned that you have the fastest spaceship in this part of the galaxy. In the next few days the Interplanetary Alliance's President Ronnie may be interested in talking to you about hiring you to explore a star system called Sol, where the inhabitants of planet Earth recently developed nuclear weapons."

"About five thousand years ago, sixty leaders of a group of fanatic religious terrorists were banished to Earth. Our time traveling friend Chaika confirmed this information. They were a bunch of warmongers who loved enslaving others, digging for gold, and building pyramids. Our political leadership think it's about time we check on that planet's inhabitants, with your help if possible."

Captain Noah reflected for a few seconds and replied, "Sure. We are willing to explore space together with our new friends in the Interplanetary Alliance. Of course, we expect you to help us with logistics support for the journey and some currency for our personnel to help pay for food, rent, utilities, furniture, transportation, clothing, and a few minor luxuries." Noah ignited a cigar as he finished his last sentence.

At this point, a pudding dessert was served. After enjoying the last few bites of our lunch, we still had about thirty minutes to kill. I asked First Officer Romo to join me for a smoke. After we had lit up, I said, "I was told about the death of your wife a few months ago. My condolences for your loss."

He replied, "Thanks. It was a tragic way to die, but I'm slowly recovering."

I went on. "Glad to hear that. If you feel up to it, after the gala dinner tonight, I'll show you some nightspots. We have everything—from musical performances by world-famous artists to busy nightclubs, where you might meet some new lady friends."

Romo replied, "No, thank you for your kind offer. But I actually have my first date with nurse

Nova, who is part of the crew of our spaceship *Zeta's Hope*."

"Good for you," I said, took a draw of my smoke, and added, "Let's finish our smokes and rejoin the others. The tour bus could be here any minute!"

Following our rich lunch, we were scheduled to be taken by bus for a tour of history and science museums, where I took the opportunity to share some details of the trip to Earth planned for mid-1947. After nearly three hours of this, we were ready to rest before the gala dinner at a large and luxurious hotel.

At the hotel, a police cordon shielded us from protestors, some of them carrying signs that read "Out with the Freeloaders" and "ET Go Home." The police did a good job in keeping them at a distance.

As we sat at the head table with Noah and several high government officials, we heard three twenty-minute speeches—first by Mayor Irma, followed by Vice President Bonzo and President Ronnie of the Interplanetary Alliance.

The president's turn to speak came. He had dark-skinned features, like somebody with the mixed heritage of a black and a native American, a heavily lined face, and a distinguished-looking mustache. Ronnie shared some pleasantries before, pointing to me, he said, "Let me introduce you to Colonel Rick Patel, who will be our alliance's liaison with the Greys and Amigos. He will be our mouth, eyes and ears with them."

I stood and bowed to the applauding audience, savoring my few seconds of fame.

As Ronnie drew his speech to a close, his face turned serious. "To those protesting outside, let me tell you that the greatness of our people is reflected in the way that we treat both our fellow citizens and our neighbors. Our Grey and Amigo friends are *not* freeloaders! We'll benefit from them in four ways. First, their power generation technology will reduce our energy costs. Second, their medical technology will help heal our sick. Third, we'll use their recycling and disposal methods on land, sea, and space waste that has been piling up for many decades. Fourth, their space technology will expand our knowledge of this galaxy. And don't forget to thank them when all these things happen! Good night everybody, and may God bless you all!"

**Drawing of Colonel Rick Patel
(Artwork by Roberta Lerman)**

A round of applause followed. An orchestra began to play, and the dance floor quickly filled up. Nurse Nova and First Officer Romo distinguished themselves dancing to the sound of "La Cumparsita," an old tango song by Gerardo Matos Rodriguez. The harmonic sound of violins, piano, and accordion filled the air. The fluid movements and footwork of the dancers were synchronized to the rhythm of the music.

Soon it was well past nine o'clock in the evening, and the reception hall became less crowded, as many a tired guest headed home. After a few minutes, Captain Noah and I were ready for a smoke and looked for a place to enjoy our cigars. As we arrived at one of the ample balconies at the hotel, we found nurse Nova and First Officer Romo, both halfway drunk, sharing a warm embrace and a tender kiss. They had just embarked on a heated romance that would have its ups and downs. Here is their story per Romo's account.

CHAPTER NINETEEN

THE ALLURE OF THE NIGHTLIFE

With twenty years of recovery under my belt, I was in the Tenth Galactic Narcotics Anonymous Convention on planet Sapiens during an evening in late 1969 —an event attended by thirty thousand recovering addicts. The theme for the convention was "The Promise of Freedom," which was appropriate for an event addressing recovery from addiction. As the clock struck eight, the convention chair, Peter, introduced the main speaker, an addict with umpteen years clean. The speaker shared about how addiction had brought her down to rock bottom and how she had asked for help to embark on a journey toward a joyous, legitimate, and productive life in recovery.

After the speaker ended her speech, Peter led a countdown of clean time. It started with experienced recovering addicts with over fifty years clean. As the number of years was called out, addicts would stand up to form a circle around the large sports stadium. Meanwhile the crowd enthusiastically stumped their feet and shouted out: *"Keep coming back! Keep coming back!"*

All sorts were in attendance—men and women of every race; rich, middle-class, and poor; gay and straight—for addiction is an equal opportunity disease. After a few minutes, there were nearly thirty-thousand recovering addicts forming a circle.

Eventually Peter got to the point in the countdown where he called out for those with one day clean. A lonely, slim fellow in his thirties slowly got up from his chair, dragged his feet up to where Peter was standing, and picked up a copy of the Narcotics Anonymous Basic Text that was being handed out to newcomers. This young man was wearing a baseball cap, a raggedy pair of pants, worn-out sneakers, and a sweaty T-shirt. He looked dead tired as he embarked on the first day of his journey of recovery. I felt tears in my eyes. My mind wandered twenty years back to when the seed of recovery was planted in me, after I humbled myself to ask for help.

By the way, my name is Romo Agrox, first officer of the Greys' spaceship *Zeta's Hope*. I'm from planet Amigo, allies of the Greys. With me at the convention was Captain Noah, with whom I walked to an area in the upper bleachers where smoking was allowed. After taking a draw from his cigar, Noah asked me to share about my experience with addiction and recovery—just before we were to go later that evening to a comedy show at the convention.

I took a draw of my cigar and began telling my story: "Alcohol was my original poison of choice. As far as I remember—I've always wanted to drink. I recall my parents drinking and laughing when I was a child. It seemed fun! My functionally drinking dad told me alcohol would cheer my spirits. My enabling mother would remind me that the son of God turned water to wine as his first miracle. Heck, I thought it was cool to have a winemaker as a divinity!"

Noah chuckled. I went on. "My first drunk occurred at age thirteen with older teenage playmates. The obsession and compulsion of addiction was obvious. Once I took that first one, I had a problem stopping. Puking and passing out were occasional occurrences during my binges. Waking up with a hangover became routine. Yet I figured that sleeping after one binge was all I needed to get ready for the next one. My research for a greater buzz later led me to illicit drugs. It was typical for a trusted playmate, a school buddy, or co-worker to make the introduction.

"My personal christening into the world of illegal drugs was through high school classmates, who introduced me to some wacky weed in a graduation party. Later, during my college years, I would meet many beer drinkers and weed smokers. During the first few months aboard *Zeta's Hope*, we had no mind-altering chemicals; thus, I remained clean. But soon after my arrival on the friendly planet of Sapiens, I got reacquainted with drugs. Here is my story."

One evening in the fall of 1944, my bud Benny and I got together. He was a drug-using college mate of mine from planet Amigo, and a crewmate, the helmsman on *Zeta's Hope*. He was smart and well versed in many topics; from technology to drugs. After we settled down for a week on planet Sapiens, he invited me to join him and some of his friends for a weekend evening of drinking and dining. We were both about twenty-five at that time.

As the sun set on an early evening in mid-October, we arrived at Benny's friend's home for a dinner party. Benny knocked on the front door of his friend's house.

Within seconds a fellow in his mid-thirties opened it. Benny sad, "Hi, 420. This is Romo, my old pal I told you about."

420 smiled and replied, "Welcome, guys! Please come in, and get comfy in the living room. The television is on, and the ball game just started."

We sat down to watch the TV. The game looked like baseball on Earth, the main difference being that there were only three bases and seven players in the field.

The living room was spotless. Through a glass sliding door we saw two young girls splashing around in the pool. One looked twelve and the other two. Soon thereafter, an attractive lady in her mid-thirties brought us a twelve-pack of cold beer and a tray heaped with sandwiches.

420 introduced her. "This is my dear wife, Mary, the queen of my home and the mother of my two precious daughters."

She smiled and said, "Here's the wine. On the table, you'll find nuts and fruits. That tray has a few joints and some stimulant powder. I love Barry White. Let's listen to his music."

She went to the CD player and played some of Barry White's top hits: "You Are the First, My Last, My Everything"; "Never Gonna Give You Up"; and others.

Attentively listening to the music for a minute, Mary turned to her husband and says, "I believe we made our last baby to Barry White's music."

We chuckled at her comment. Mary smiled, snorted a line, grabbed a beer and a doobie, and went to join her children at the pool.

Sipping on his drink, Benny commented, "I understand that Chaika, the friendly alien we encountered on our way here, owns the copyright to all these earthling songs on this planet. She must be making a killing!"

"True," replied 420. "Chaika said that when crossing a wormhole a couple of years ago, she accidently traveled nearly seventy years into Earth's future. During her short time there, she and her crew downloaded many songs, films, and books. Coincidentally, I finished reading an interesting book, *War of the Worlds*, by the earthling author H. G. Wells. And I just ordered *1984* by George Orwell. War and dictatorships are not pretty, on whatever planet!"

420 took a sip of his beer and went on. "I doubt Chaika's paying them any royalties. Within a few years, she and her crewmates will retire with a few million bucks in their pockets!

420 then asked, "Romo, what kind of work do you do for a living?"

"I started my career as an electrical designer of control and instrumentation systems for our Spaceship *Zeta's Hope* with the Space Agency on planet Amigo. Upon completion of the spaceship, I was made the First Officer. So here I am! What about you?"

"I'm a Navy veteran. Currently the wife and I own a small gift shop."

420 sipped on his drink and asked, "So, Romo, are you married?"

After a moment of sad reflection and a big gulp of beer, I answered, "Five months ago, my wife was killed by a sharklike creature while swimming near a beach on planet Avalonia. Her violent death freaked me out! I have been depressed for the last few months. But I just started dating a young woman from planet Terruno called Nova. We'll see what happens!"

Following our meal, we kept drinking and talking and then watched an earthling movie on TV called *Saturday Night Fever*. We also lit a couple of joints and did a few lines of stimulants.

420 jokingly said, "These drugs are illegal in this state. We must be criminals!"

Benny added, "Back on our planet, drug-related arrests doubled our prison population—not to mention economic inequality. We had a successful experience with decriminalization. We enacted extensive drug law reforms that decriminalized low-level possession and use of all illegal drugs. No one is arrested or incarcerated for drug possession. Now many more people are receiving treatment, and addiction, related diseases, and drug overdoses have been drastically reduced. Our experience demonstrated that ending drug criminalization—along with investment in treatment and harm reduction services—can improve public safety and health."

We went on talking about various topics such as music, travel, sports, and space travel. Within two hours, I had buzz! And it was time to go see my new girlfriend Nova!"

On the hunt for that next buzz and the affections of a lovely lady, I found myself drawn to the allure of the nightlife in planet Sapiens that cool October evening in 1944. During that evening, I was to meet my future girlfriend Nova in a local watering hole called Earthlings—where they played anything from easy listening to rock, country, and disco. Chaika, the time traveler, had made millions selling earthling music to places like this.

It was a weekend night. A wooden plaque by the door contained a Shakespeare quote that read: "If music be the food of love, play on." I pushed open the door, and the hideous stench of stale beer hit my nostrils. The nightclub was crowded with customers dancing or playing pool or darts. From the DJ's booth came the sound of a tune called "Looking for Love" by Johnny Lee. The song told of looking for love in all the wrong places. I wondered if that was a hint from the Almighty questioning my lustful purpose in that singles bar.

Many of the patrons were under the effect of alcohol and perhaps other mind-altering substances. The drinkers huddled along the club's countertop, keeping the two bartenders busy. The faces of loyal customers were softened under the dim artificial light. These faces belonged to people whose callings ranged from business, professional pursuits, the military, blue- and white-collar work, and perhaps the drug trade—to satisfy a need for anything other than alcohol. Most of them were in their twenties and thirties, but a few who were older loved the bar's dim lights, which hid any wrinkles. Perhaps we were all in a race with time, yearning for a little loving to fill a void in our lives.

As my companion for the evening, I had brought our attractive android crewmate Amie.

After she sat down, a drunk came over and whispered to her, "Honey, you look so good. I'd love to make a baby with you!"

Instantly, Amie replied with her robotic voice, "Negative. I was manufactured with no reproductive systems. You'll have to ask a biological female for that function."

Puzzled by her answer, the drunk scratched his head and said, "I believe I've had too much to drink. I'm going home!" With that, he exited the bar.

Shortly thereafter, Nova entered the club with all the splendor of a model on a fashion show runway. She had previously joined our ship's company on Terruno. The band played a Beatles' song titled "Something." As she moved through the crowd, heads turned to catch a glimpse. Her teasing, disarming smile warmed the hearts of those around her. She exuded the glamour of a classy temptress, mixed with the look of the girl next door. Nova was a woman for whom a man would conquer new worlds!

She approached the bar and sat on the empty stool next to mine. "A drink for the lady," I told the bartender.

"A mimosa, please," she asked with a smile.

"A mimosa for the lady," the bartender repeated as he lit her cigarette.

Her intense look invited intimacy. The smooth movement of her hand as she raised the glass to her ruby lips was an act of seduction. I suspected that she seldom paid for her drinks.

She was a young woman, with the face of a Hollywood star, the body of a beauty pageant contestant, and the wit of a late-night comedian—a combination that acted on me like an enchantment. Nova's skin was as white as that of a Nordic fairytale princess and as soft as flower petals. She was wearing a simple but elegant black dress revealing bare shoulders with a few sexy freckles that begged to be counted. Her black hair fell in long curls down her back. She had long, shapely legs, and her slim built featured soft, feminine curves.

When she flashed one of her contagious, sexy smiles, her rich red lips opened to reveal her sparkling pearl-white teeth. Often her sensuous mouth would stay halfway open, as if asking to be kissed. Her captivating angelic blue eyes seemed to light up her surroundings. My eyes followed her every move like a magnet. Nova was a beautiful woman in her physical prime.

The band began playing a catchy Miami Sound Machine tune called "Conga." The loud sound of drums, horns, piano, and guitar filled the air with an infectious rhythm. Several couples, all seemingly happy in diverse states of intoxication, went to the floor and moved to the beat.

"Would you like to dance?" I inquired.

"Sure, I would love to," she replied with a sexy voice and smile that reminded me of the young earthling actress Lauren Bacall.

Her moves on the floor were energetic but sensuous. Back on Mount Olympus, Aphrodite, the goddess of love, would have envied Nova. I thought I'd died, gone to heaven, and met God's greatest and most beautiful creation!

We came back to our seats after dancing. I asked, "What do you like to watch on the tube?"

"I like old earthling sitcoms," Nova replied. "*I Love Lucy* is my favorite."

She took a draw of her cigarette, and then asked, "I haven't had the chance to ask you why you went into the aerospace industry."

By then the buzz from the alcohol was starting to kick in. So, with a smile, I humorously replied to her inquiry, "Since I was a kid I loved comedy and sci-fi. But I flunked comedian school and committed many grammar mistakes when writing. Thus, I went into aerospace."

She giggled. But something was bothering me like an itch that I could not scratch. After a few moments of reflection, I felt there was a question I had to ask. "Captain Noah told me you were fired as a nurse from *Zeta's Hope* because allegations of theft of painkillers."

Nova quickly replied, "A lady has to do what she has to do to get what she wants."

I bit my lips, disturbed by her answer.

After a pause, she cleverly changed the subject. "I moved into an apartment here in Sapiens."

I took a deep breath to calm down. Then I casually posed another question, "Have you found new work?"

"Had a gig modeling. But tomorrow I begin work as an exotic dancer at The Trap."

It was no surprise that Nova was modeling. She was a tall and slim woman with a pretty face. But for her to be working as an exotic dancer was a shocker, for she had moderate "assets." But what did I care? I was always more of a guy who went for pretty faces and tall slim bodies! Besides, the idea of dating a stripper gave me a thrill! I'd be the lucky guy taking her home!

There was a last call for booze as the DJ started playing Semisonic's "Closing Time."

I asked Nova, "My buddy Vet and I scored some stimulant powder, and we were saving it for an after-hours party at his condo on the beach. Would you like to join us?"

Nova replied, "Sure. But I don't have wheels. Can you give me a ride?"

I answered, "Sure. We'll go after we finish our drinks."

Those attending Vet's after-hours parties were typically working people ranging from their mid-twenties to their mid-thirties. They were well behaved and not noisy—not exactly the dangerous, gun-toting criminals that drug users were portrayed as in earthling movies like *Scarface* and *Colors*. My partying friends would sit around and talk, occasionally dance to the music, and sometimes play cards, while drinking alcohol and maybe passing a joint around or snorting stimulants. Music would be playing on the stereo—anything from the Rolling Stones' "Satisfaction" to Madonna's "Vogue."

Eventually, I took Nova home. I was tired and suggested we go to sleep. Nova disrobed, sexily smiled at me, and told me, "What makes you believe you'll get any rest?"

We made love—in the Jacuzzi and then in bed to the sound of Chris Isaak's "Wicked Game." Thus, began our love affair, which followed a pattern of sex, drugs, and loud music typical of young people at the time. During the initial months of our relationship, we would spend nearly an hour on the phone, like a couple of school sweethearts, before we went out on a date. We could be together and exchange small talk or just cuddle up and watch TV.

Every date was a slow act of seduction. Nova was a sexy woman who could get a rise out of a dead man! As time went by, memories of my deceased wife faded, and I developed a great fondness for Nova. Was she going to be the new special lady for me to fill that void? Was I on a delusional rebound? Or was I blinded by love?

Lovers Chatting (Artwork by Roberta Lerman)

CHAPTER TWENTY

DESCENDING INTO DRAMA AND CHAOS

First Officer Romo's account continued:

> During the next few weeks I got to know my girl-
> friend Nova better. She told me she'd had her
> first love affair at age fifteen with a senior in her
> high school back on planet Terruno. Things went
> well until her boyfriend was drafted and sent to a
> faraway war, where he died. She mourned his loss
> for a few months and began using alcohol, which
> was available at her parents' or friend's homes. I
> recall having the same attraction to alcohol by the
> time I was in college.
>
> Two months into our relationship Nova pro-
> posed shooting stimulants. I said no, having had
> fear of using needles, particularly when in a state
> of intoxication. Then she suggested smoking it—
> better known as freebasing. I'd never heard of this,

but with the thought that smoking drugs was more acceptable—and wanting to show I was cool—I agreed. At the time, freebasing seemed to be the newest fad in the drug scene. After a few weeks, I concluded that freebasing was to snorting stimulants as hard liquor was to beer. The writing was on the wall for our fall!

One day after work, I came to see Nova.

I opened her refrigerator, thirsting for water. "Shoot! This fridge is empty!" She lowered her head. She had that hungover look. I asked, "Are you spending all your money on drugs?"

She whispered, "I'm broke. And I'm short for rent."

"Golly! You need to control yourself!"

Later, in recovery, I would learn there's no control once an addict takes that first drug. I went on. "Okay, I'll help with rent and food."

Later I would learn that paying the bills of an addict enables their addiction. And the line between enabling and unconditional love is very thin!

My dealer Vet also went down with this new habit of freebasing. Being around the product that he sold did not help him. This was analogous to putting a drunk in charge of a bar or liquor store. He got to a point where he was using more than he was selling. By late 1944, he was broke. Vet sold his car, his motorcycle, and his furniture. His phone was disconnected, and he was about to get kicked out of his place. And his girlfriend left him because of his self-destructive, addictive behavior.

While shopping at a local mall, I ran into 420. He'd just finished shopping. He called out my name from about twenty yards away and made a beeline toward me. He seemed upset and started talking fast.

"Romo! Glad to see you! I'm in a bad situation and don't know what to do!"

"Hi, 420! What's going on?" I said, puzzled.

"Freaking Vet—he's having an affair with my wife! I've driven by his place the last couple of days, and I've seen her car there. I should kill him! The only reason I didn't was because my wife Mary had our two-year-old kid with her. But if I see that son of a gun again, I'll shoot him on sight! I know that you are good friends, but people who hang out with Vet may get a bullet meant for him!"

I understood my friend's pain, seeing his marriage ruined by Mary's addiction. His hopes and dreams of having a home, wife, and kids were broken up by her extramarital affair. Also, part of his disillusionment was with Vet, whom he'd considered a longtime friend.

"I understand your pain," I said, "but delay any shooting for now. Vet's broke and about to get kicked out of his apartment. He's going back home tomorrow to live with his parents up north, about a thousand miles away from here! I know that because he asked me to drive him to the bus station."

420 paused for a few seconds and reflected on what to do next. Deep in his heart, he did not

want to go through with his plan. And juries are known to convict jealous husbands!

"Okay. I'll hold off on the bullets. But if I see that son of a gun around next week, I'll shoot him!"

I sighed with relief. 420 probably did not know that Vet, despite being a small-time drug dealer, did not have a gun. But I felt that a tragedy had been prevented; now I would not have one friend dead and another one in jail.

I bade farewell to 420, went home, had dinner, and went to bed. Before going to bed, I prayed that things would turn out okay.

Next day, I drove to Vet's place to give him a ride to the bus station. Knowing that he would need money for the trip to his parents' house, I lent him forty bucks.

We got to the bus station about fifteen minutes before the bus left. It was an overcast afternoon, perhaps foreshadowing bad news to come. The bus station's public address system was playing a Naughty by Nature tune called "O.P.P." (meaning other people's partner). Figuring that we had a few minutes to spare, Vet and I took a walk to smoke cigarettes and chat.

Once we were about twenty yards away from the crowd at the bus terminal, Vet took a draw of his cigarette, turned to me, and said, "Thanks for the cash."

"No problem, Vet. What are friends for? I think a change of scenery is good for you. You've been drinking and using a bunch of drugs these last couple of months."

I didn't know it at the time, but within a few weeks I would be told in rehab that geographic changes don't work for an addict. Wherever you go, your addiction follows!

"Yeah. Breaking up with my girlfriend was a bummer. She left me for a lesbian who works with her at the strip joint! That really bummed me out and hurt my ego. But I guess I have to let go of my feelings for her. By the way, how are things going between you and Nova?"

"So-so. She seems to be spending most of her money on drugs. I had to lend her money for rent and food."

Vet paused for a few seconds. He then stepped back a bit from me and said, "Romo, I have a confession to make. I was a lonely man after my girlfriend left me. Nova came to my apartment a few weeks ago to buy some stimulants. We got high for about half an hour and started flirting around. One thing led to another, and we started having an affair."

For a few moments, we stared at each other in silence. Mixed feelings of shock and anger came over me. I'd just been told that my girlfriend was a drug whore and that she was cheating with one of my friends! But that's where her addiction had brought her. After some reflection, I thought that if it was not with Vet, Nova would have screwed any other likable man who offered her drugs. I raised my arms and put them over my head and looked up at the sky, hoping for some sort of divine guidance.

Somebody once told me that with friends like Vet, I needed no enemies. The guy seemed to jump from one trouble spot to the next. However, I admired his honesty. My conclusion was to stick with my original plan of getting Vet out of town before an angry lynch mob of jealous men would harm him.

Finally, I broke the silence. "It's odd for me to say this, but I'm relieved to find out the truth. Thanks for telling me. It's best to know the truth, no matter how much it hurts."

I paused, took a draw of my cigarette, and told him, "I suspected she was having an affair. The initial passion in our relationship was gone. It just didn't occur to me that you, a friend, could be the other man."

With a guilty look, Vet just stood there for a few seconds. At last he said, "I'm sorry. I wasn't thinking of the consequences of my actions."

We were quiet for a little while. We made some small talk until the bus driver called for passengers to board. We said our farewells to each other.

Had things been different, I might have been the guy on the bus, leaving town with a trail of burned bridges. That was the last day I saw Vet.

By the next afternoon, I'd settled down a bit from Vet's upsetting revelation and showed up at Nova's apartment. Christina Aguilera's "What a Girl Wants" was playing on the radio. I confronted Nova about the affair. After a few seconds of silence, she said, "Romo, I like you. But a lady has to do what she has to do to get what she wants."

I bit my lips in anger. I was disappointed, hurt, and upset by her lack of commitment to our relationship. But I respected her honesty and her quickness to admit her infidelity. And I wondered if my own addiction was leading me down the same path behind her and Vet.

Nova just happened to be a drug-using lady friend with whom I became excessively codependent in a relationship. Was I in a situation where my unrequited love was just too one-sided? Did she like me some, or was she in love with me?

Afterward, Nova and I stayed on friendly terms. But the affair left me emotionally scarred. Any emotions that I felt as a result of her betrayal—such as disillusionment, anger, self-pity, and low self-esteem—rationalized my drowning in a sea of alcohol and other drugs.

CHAPTER TWENTY-ONE

HITTING BOTTOM

First Officer Romo's account continued:

On a cold February evening of 1945 after dinner, I was sharing with my sponsor Anonymous about how I hit bottom:

"By December 1944, I was a messed-up twenty-six-year-old. I thought I had a drug problem. My obsessive drinking and compulsive use were dominating my life, and I felt I had to stop using to end my misery."

My sponsor Anonymous interrupted me with a question: "What happened to you when you first tried to stop?"

I replied: "My initial attempts to quit were focused on my poison of choice—stimulants. I didn't realize that once I picked up any drug, including alcohol, the compulsion to get high would return, and I would be off to the next binge."

Anonymous sympathetically nodded and added, "It's common for a newcomer to have a reservation about not having a problem with alcohol, a legal drug."

He reflected for a moment, and then asked, "Did you have any emotions before you started the binge that led you to rehab?"

I related, "The ups and downs of my codependent relationship with my addict girlfriend had an effect on me. I wasn't handling the rest of my life well either—whether work or grieving over the deaths earlier in the year of my parents and my first wife. I was dwelling on negative feelings and not looking at the positive things in my life. I was alive and free, physically healthy and employed; I had food on the table, owned a car, and had a roof over my head. Despite all these blessings, I was emotionally underdeveloped, with a spiritual void—much like an immature teenager with a dark cloud over his head who's too proud to ask for help. I thought that I found an escape in drugs, but this brought only temporary relief, with the same problems staring me in the face the next morning when I woke up hungover and out of cash."

Anonymous then asked me, "How about telling me about your last few weeks using and hitting bottom, before you asked for help?"

"Because of an infidelity, I broke with my now ex-girlfriend three weeks before I went to rehab. I used alcohol and other drugs daily. I used alone nearly all the time—an indication of my worsening addiction. I did not sleep well. I was frequently tardy or absent from work, resulting in verbal reprimands from my supervisor, who was aware of my alcohol use but not my illegal drug use. Fortunately, the design and development projects assigned to the teams I led were within budget and on schedule—thanks to outstanding contractor support."

As he finished his coffee, Anonymous remarked, "Some of us reach a moment of clarity that brings us to recovery after a traumatic event—be it a romantic breakup, overdose, jail, the death of a loved one, or a failed suicide attempt. But I believe that for staying on the path of recovery it is important to keep up the willingness to stay connected to the program on a daily basis, whether through meetings, reading literature, and working the steps, even using the phone or social media."

Then Anonymous asked a final question: "How about elaborating in detail about the last day you used?"

The last day I got high was New Year's Eve 1944. I had broken up with my addict girlfriend Nova and isolated myself. I had become excessively codependent on her. Was I in a situation where my unrequited love was just too one-sided? Did she like me some, or was she in love with me? I was extremely depressed as I listened on the radio to a Lee Ann Rimes country song called "How Do I Live?"

I had two grams of rock stimulants. So, I began freebasing while locked up in the bathroom, a pistol at hand to fend off intervention by either cops or robbers. At that point in my addiction I was willing to die—not for family, God, or country but for my next high. Such is the extreme of insanity to which addiction takes you, a disregard for your own life and the life of others.

After a few hits, I started hallucinating; I heard whispering voices in my home's hallway. I glanced at the light coming from under my bedroom door and saw a shadow move. Instantly, I grabbed my gun, pointed it at the door, and yelled, "Freeze! I got a gun on you!"

A soft female voice whispered back, "Officer Romo, this is your android Amie. It's well past midnight. I hear noises from your room. Are you okay?"

I called back, "I'm okay, Amie. I just have the runs!"

Holy cow, I thought to myself, *I almost shot my concerned android!*

I was overwhelmed by feelings of embarrassment and guilt. My mind ran through events that had had a negative effect on my life—whether work, a failed romantic relationship, or grieving over the deaths earlier in the year of my parents and my wife. I was not handling my emotions well. And now I felt guilty and worthless, on top of the sudden, crushing depression that normally follows a stimulant high.

I considered myself a failure in my romantic affair with my girlfriend. **And thoughts of my space agency's motto came to my mind that 'failure was not an option.'** Thinking that life was not worth living anymore, I arranged myself neatly on the bed, took my gun, put it to my mouth, and pulled the trigger.

Click.

Nothing happened. I then realized that the safety was on, so I unlocked it and repeated the process.

Click.

Nothing again—the darned gun had a double lock mechanism!

Frustrated, I threw the gun on my bed and went to the bathroom to get one last hit. Shortly after that, I passed out and fell into a deep sleep. That was a rare time in my life when my desire to get that next hit saved me from shooting myself!

I woke up noonish with my usual hangover and empty pockets. I washed my face, got dressed, and headed for the kitchen to eat my brunch before I went back for a nap. This was typical hangover behavior when my body and mind were worn out after a long binge.

At nightfall Benny, my dealer and aerospace coworker, dropped by to collect money I owed him for stimulants he'd fronted me. He often gave me coke on credit, and I was fortunate never to have fallen behind in my account and gotten on his bad side. Some addicts are less fortunate and end up facing fatal consequences for debts to a dealer!

At the lower levels of the illegal drug market, it is the addict with the better connection that becomes the dealer. I had known Benny since my college years; he was a family man with a good job. We knew each other's parents back in planet Amigo, and we had shared drinks and small amounts of drugs through the years. It's odd that most people who are unfamiliar with the drug scene picture a dealer as some crazy, gun-toting, shady-looking, tough ethnic minority hanging around street corners in the inner city. That stereotype may be true in some cases, but quite often a dealer is as white as a bedsheet and lives and works in the suburbs. He may be a close friend, a neighbor, a schoolmate, a coworker, or even a family member.

I served Benny a drink, as he sat down at the table across from me. There I stood, sweating and a bit shaky—the physical effects of my weekend of heavy drinking and freebasing, a combination some people called a "workingman's speedball." After paying him his money, courtesy of an automated teller machine, I spilled my guts to Benny,

"Hey, man! I've been getting really messed up the last few weeks—drinking and doing coke every day. During the last three weeks, I've been late to work, and I've called in sick a few times."

A concerned Benny replied, "You, look sweaty and a little shaky. You need to control yourself!" He paused. After some reflection, he added, "Maybe you should slow down a little bit."

Later in recovery, I would learn there's no control once an addict takes that first drug.

Then I exclaimed: "Oh man, I went crazy last night. I can't understand why I can't stop after I start a binge. I'm going crazy! I tried shooting myself twice last night, but I was too messed up to work the double safety mechanism in my gun. After the second attempt, I just got high and passed out!"

Ironically, Benny was the guy who recommended that I get a gun with a double safety feature. Perplexed at my revelation, he went silent for a few moments, looking at me with great concern. I wondered what he was thinking.

Depiction of Addict (Artwork by Roberta Lerman)

"You are messed up," Benny finally said. "You need to see a therapist!"

That was good advice. For several months, I never told another person about my suicide attempt. I guess that I did not want anybody else to know that at one point in my addiction I was a crazy, suicidal fellow.

I was strung out and sick and tired of being sick and tired. The next day I went to see a therapist. He referred me to a twenty-eight-day rehabilitation program. Going to rehab was perhaps the best decision I made in my life. Today, with over twenty years in recovery, I've heard many people talk about having a moment of clarity when they first asked for help and embarked on the road to recovery. In my case, I would like to credit a concerned android and my compassionate dealer for having that moment of clarity on my behalf. In a way, it was an unconventional sort of divine intervention.

CHAPTER TWENTY-TWO

CONVERSATIONS
WITH A THERAPIST

First Officer Romo's account continued:

> I remember the days of my youth, when I worked hard and partied harder. Eventually I hit bottom and asked for help with my problem. Asking for help with my drug problem was perhaps the best decision I made in my life.
>
> My name is Romo, a human ally of the Greys from planet Amigo, and First Officer on our spaceship *Zeta's Hope*. Knowing that I'm a recovering addict who is over twenty years clean, Captain Noah asked me to share about my early experiences with addiction and recovery on planet Sapiens. So, I continue with my story—following my hitting bottom, having a moment of clarity and humbling myself to ask for help at age twenty-seven.

In January 1945 I'd been using alcohol and other drugs for three weeks on a daily basis. I used drugs to escape the drama and chaos of my life, whether at home or work. By then my frequent absenteeism and tardiness were noticed by my boss, who seemed worried about me.

I humbled myself to ask for help about my drug problem and entered a twenty-eight-day inpatient rehab program. Somebody at rehab mentioned that I suffered from a chemical dependence problem. I thought that they were going to give me chemicals to counteract the chemicals I was using—and that after twenty-eight days I would be converted to a social user. Oh man! Was I wrong!

At rehab I met my drug counselor Conseil. He was about sixty, with well-trimmed gray hair and a mustache. He had a friendly demeanor and smiled all the time. I felt I could warm up to him.

But that feeling quickly came to an end after a revelation from another rehab client. She warned me to be discreet around Conseil, as he was a retired narcotics officer. Knowing this fact about him planted a seed of distrust in me. It took a while for me to begin trusting him. As a matter of fact, my first assignment from my therapist was to learn how to listen to others. That says something about the sorry state of my closed, distrustful and self-centered mind at the time.

During our introductory session, Conseil filled me in about the daily routine at rehab. Then he asked questions about my childhood, my parents, romantic relationships, my job, and more.

After a while, he asked, "What is your favorite television character?"

Being a fan of Earth's future TV programs provided by Chaika, the time traveler, I replied, "*Star Trek*'s Spock."

He chuckled. I was puzzled by his reaction. Was he making fun of me?

After a few seconds, he said, "You don't like the idea of having feelings, do you?"

These words surprised me and lingered in my mind for years.

But he was right. My inability to deal with negative feelings was an issue that I had to come to grips with. Whether it was resenting my ex-girlfriend's infidelity, grieving over my parents' death, or simply having a bad day, I was always carrying some emotional garbage that I didn't know how to deal with. He interpreted my liking Spock as a subconscious desire not to feel negative emotions. Was that some sort of self-imposed denial of my emotions?

Over the next twenty-eight days, Conseil worked on some of those issues with me. In the second week, he started the conversation rolling as follows: "Nearly one out of four people in this country suffer from mental health issues."

Trying to be humorous, I said, "In the last few months, I believe that I became acquainted with most of them on my way to rehab!"

Conseil kept a serious face. "In case nobody has told you," he said, "addiction is a disease, not a moral deficiency. Obsession and compulsion to use are characteristics of the disease."

"I'm relieved to hear that!" I exclaimed.

Then I began to ask rambling questions. "What medicine do I take to get well? Does therapy include training on how to become a social drinker? Will I ever get rid of my craving for alcohol, women, and other mind-altering substances?"

Not blinking an eye, he said, "No pill or prescription medicine will ever cure you of your addiction. In our twenty-eight-day program, you will learn the basics about how to change your behavior. Some of these include guidelines such as not using alcohol and drugs and not hanging out with your old drinking and drug-using friends."

"Heck," I interrupted, sounding hysterical, "I'm not going to leave my friends! And nearly everybody in my family and at work drinks. Some of the local bars where I hang out are like second homes to me!"

Conseil went on. "Once you complete your twenty-eight-day program, we'll ask you to come once a week to our six-month aftercare program. We may ask you to bring along any loved ones. During that time, we strongly recommend that you go to recovery meetings regularly, stay in touch with people who are clean, and get a sponsor—kind of a big brother or spiritual guide—who can provide you with direction on how to stay clean. Maybe you can talk your sponsor into coming to aftercare with you!"

"You mean that I will not be cured after twenty-eight days here?" I exclaimed with some indignation, as if I had been deceived when I agreed to come to rehab. The thought crossed my mind to get out of there!

Conseil said, "No, this program only provides you with basics on how to stay clean. Think of it as a seed of recovery that's been planted. You'll have to water and fertilize this seed by going to recovery meetings, staying in touch with people who are clean, and getting a sponsor to help you. You will do this, a day at a time, for the rest of your life until the day you die!"

"How about drinking?" I asked.

"No," he answered.

The boozer inside me started to panic!

I asked, "Not even a cold beer here and there? Or wine with a nice holiday meal? What am I supposed to do if I'm having a bad day? Anyhow, booze is legal, unlike the street drugs I used."

With a look of concern, Conseil said, "Romo, if you want to put your life back together, you'll have to abstain from using alcohol, in addition to any other mind-altering substances!"

Then he continued with his mild but still assertive manner, "I want you to think very seriously about this."

During the next few seconds, my crazy, partying personality went wild. I thought to myself: *Not one drink for the rest of my life? Heck, I'll throw one last party before making a commitment to this! I'll invite my friends. We could have fireworks, belly dancers, male and female strippers, clowns with balloons, a donkey, a dwarf on a trapeze, and the fire department on hand, just in case things get out of hand! We'll have a block party and invite the neighbors, form a conga line, and have one last big drunk!*

"What's on your mind?" Conseil inquired, bringing me down from the clouds.

"Oh nothing," I lied, thinking that he would recommend locking me up in some madhouse if he ever read my thoughts. "I'll think about it. At this point, I'll only commit to doing the twenty-eight days here in rehab."

"Willingness to stay clean a day at a time is all you need. Our session is over!" he said.

I sighed in relief.

"I want you to think about this," he continued. "I repeat, you only have to stay clean a day at a time. Recovery is about getting better in baby steps."

"Staying clean a day at a time sounds more doable than staying clean the rest of my life."

"Well," he said, flashing his calm, charming smile, "that is one thing we can agree on!"

By the third week of my stay in rehab Conseil started our session by handing me a pamphlet and saying, "Tonight, there will be some folks hosting a recovery meeting from an anonymous recovery organization. Before the meeting, I would like to go over the questions in this pamphlet with you. And I want you to answer them honestly."

The first piece of recovery literature that I picked up in rehab, Information Pamphlet Number 7, was titled "Am I an Addict?" I remember filling out the simple yes or no answers to those twenty-nine questions and how this helped me believe that I had a drug problem! For the sake of keeping it simple, let's just show a sampling of four of these questions. Question #1: Do you ever use alone? Question #9: Has your job or school performance ever suffered from the effects of your drug use? Question #13: Have you ever tried to stop or control your using? Question #20: Have you ever thought that you couldn't fit in or have a good time without drugs? I answered yes to all these questions.

After discussing my answers to the questions in the Informational Pamphlet, Conseil told me, "After a couple of weeks of observing you, I got together with the other therapists and came up with an analysis of your personality."

I was perplexed at this but silently listened as he continued, "On the good side, despite your addiction, we think that one aspect of your personality is that of a hero. You are a smart, conscious person, warm, caring, selfless, agreeable, dependable, dutiful, and helpful to others, and you also have a sense of discipline."

My ego got a little inflated at his revelation. *I'm starting to like this guy!*

Conseil continued with his analysis. "On the other hand, you grew up in a somewhat dysfunctional family and we think that you have the traits of a lost child. Your mother was delusional schizoaffective, and your dad was a functional drinker who worked long hours. You learned to escape tension and emotional stress by what you thought were fun but unhealthy activities, like going nightclubbing and getting high with your drug-using buddies and ex-girlfriend on nearly a daily basis. By next week, we'll come up with a list of healthy activities to replace these unhealthy activities."

I felt a little uncomfortable with this truth but kept my ears open as he went on. "And last, but not least, you have a clown personality. Occasionally you like to make jokes and humorous observations with bits of sarcasm in them. Your humor is a way to connect with others and could be considered a survival tool when you are faced with negative emotions or situations, whether at home, at work, or elsewhere. Through additional therapy and a twelve-step recovery program you should be able to deal better with these negative emotions and feelings."

I was still somewhat uncomfortable but impressed by all this analysis of my personality. Our conversation for the next few minutes focused on clarifying those three aspects of my personality: the hero, the lost child, and the clown.

After a brief pause, I curiously asked him, "Why are you a drug counselor?"

He replied with a sad face, "A few years ago, I found out that my son was an addict. That fact created lots of pain and hurt within me."

At that point the barrier of isolation around me broke down. From that moment on, our common pain was to be our bond. After that revelation, I opened up to him, and we began to make some progress.

At the beginning of my fourth week in rehab, Conseil told me, "Romo, you need to plan your spare time activities for when you get out of rehab. Instead of going to bars and parties with your old drug-using friends, you need to plan to get involved with healthy activities, be it recovery meetings, sports, moviegoing, or board games. That way you'll meet new people who don't center their activities around alcohol and other mind-altering substances. We can come up with a list of these activities before you leave this facility."

I answered, "Yes sir. I'll prepare a list of these activities before I leave."

Then he handed me a book called *When I Say No, I Feel Guilty*, a bestseller by Dr. Manuel J. Smith.

I looked at the book for a few seconds and asked, "Why should I read this?"

"You have an introverted personality, and you are not assertive. You aim to please others, including your now ex-girlfriend and your other drug-using buddies."

"What is this assertiveness stuff?"

Conseil answered, "Assertive people express themselves and their rights without violating the rights of others. They establish boundaries for their own behavior and the behavior of others. There are some stories in this book that will tell you how to say no without feeling guilty. This is a problem with you."

I mumbled, "Now I'm confused."

"You have trouble saying no when somebody passes you a drink or a joint. You have trouble saying no to your ex-girlfriend when she asks you to give her money to help pay her rent—thus enabling her addiction. You seek acceptance from these people; they know you are a pushover, and they use that fact to manipulate you. When you get fed up with them for helping themselves to your home, your paycheck, or your car, you get angry and frustrated and feel sorry for yourself, and you escape those negative feelings through your next binge. You also feel shy about asking your boss for a promotion. Then you get whiny about it when it goes to someone else! For the last three weeks, I watched you interact with other inpatient clients and noticed this unassertive behavior. Do you want me to go on?"

"No, that won't be necessary. I get it," I said, surprised by his detailed analysis of my behavior.

That concluded that session. Many years later, I'm still working on my lack of assertiveness!

I vividly recall my last one-on-one session with Conseil. He showed me some bags of fake drugs. Was he testing my resolve to get clean? Suddenly tears came to my eyes, and I broke down crying.

"Hey, don't worry," he said, trying to calm me down. "They're not real."

"I know," I said. "I know enough about drugs that I can spot a poor fake a mile away! Had it been the real thing, I probably would have made a quick offer to buy it, or perhaps I would have tried to pull your arm off trying to get at it! I would have thrown you out of your office until I used all the stuff or passed out or overdosed or died defending my last hit."

Conseil seemed surprised by my revelation. Nowadays, over twenty years clean, I would assertively say no and walk away in a situation where I was presented with drugs.

I added, "Hell, my drug dealer thought I was so crazy that he was the first person to tell me I needed to go get help from a therapist." Conseil chuckled at my new revelation.

He then asked me to stay two extra days so we could continue working together. On those extra days, I elaborated on the last few sad, lonesome nights using drugs—puking and shaking in front of the toilet bowl, pistol by my side, ready to risk my life to defend my next hit from cops or thieves who never materialized. Back when I hit bottom, my only fear was running out of alcohol and other drugs! Today, more than twenty years clean, my only fear is to relapse.

It was in rehab that I embarked on the road to recovery, a journey I continued with the support of a twelve-step program. My gratitude goes to Conseil and others on the rehab staff for putting up with my stubbornness and planting in me a seed of recovery that helped me stay clean those first few days.

CHAPTER TWENTY-THREE

GOING TO MEETINGS, GETTING A SPONSOR, AND THE FIRST STEP

For months after going to rehab, I had a hard time abstaining from drugs. My initial attempts to quit were focused on stimulants, my poison of choice. But I didn't realize then that once I picked up any drug, including alcohol and mind-altering herbs, the obsession and compulsion to get high would return, and I'd be off to the next binge. The ups and downs of my codependent relationship with my addict girlfriend and drug-using buddies also kept me in active addiction. I had a hard time letting go of them.

Other areas of my life were not going well either—whether work or grieving over the deaths of my parents and my wife. I was dwelling on negative feelings and not looking at the blessings in my life. I was emotionally and spiritually immature and had a hard time asking for help.

Drugs were like an escape from personal issues, whether at home or work. But the drugs only brought temporary relief, with the same problems staring me in the face the next day. Then I would wake up depressed, with empty pockets and with a big hangover. By that time, I was beginning to get sick and tired of being sick and tired. It was after a failed suicide attempt that I discussed my situation with a close friend. Then I realized that drugs controlled my life and that I needed professional help from mental health specialists.

After staying at rehab, I was instructed by therapists to seek further help in a recovery fellowship in order to stay clean. I was given a list of twelve-step group meetings in the area where I lived. A meeting occurs when two or more addicts meet regularly for the purpose of recovery. Going to meetings, addicts learn the therapeutic value of talking to other clean addicts, who share problems and share how they recover from their addiction.

The first meeting I attended in my early days was a small group that averaged an attendance of about ten. I arrived at my first meeting location early and parked my vehicle next to a car with a bumper sticker that read: "The longest journey begins with the first step."

A fellow was standing by the door, who turned out to be the meeting chair. I had previously met this guy when he brought a meeting to rehab. He welcomed me with a hug, and we chatted for a few minutes.

When I was in rehab, I had asked this fellow, who I'll call Anonymous, to be my sponsor. A sponsor is an addict with perhaps a year or more clean time, someone with whom a "sponsee" can share his hopes and life experiences. As a sponsor, Anonymous helped me understand things about the program, from language, meeting formats, and the service structure to the meaning of the fellowship's principles. Sponsorship is simply one addict helping another.

At the start of the meeting the chair, my sponsor, introduced himself and said, "Welcome to this Step meeting. The steps are a spiritual process where we surrender our ego to a Higher Power in order to transform our behavior from a suffering addict to a recovering addict. Our understanding of a Higher Power is up to us. We can call it the group, the program, or we can call it God. Please check the schedule for other types of meetings, such as open discussion or speaker. No cross talk is allowed."

He momentarily stopped and then introduced himself in more detail. "My name is Anonymous, and I'm addicted to alcohol, women, and other mind-altering substances! I would find in a recovery program that negative behavior—such as controlling, anger, self-pity, gossiping, and character assassination—were part of my addiction. I'll tell you about myself for no more than five minutes.

"I was born into a household where my parents were loving and caring and had traditional values and work ethic. They were not mean or cruel, and I believe that they tried their best as parents. But we were a somewhat dysfunctional family. My dad was a daily functional drinker, who'd had a small bar at home, where I helped myself to my first drink when I was six. My mother was a delusional schizophrenic who was institutionalized a couple of times when I was growing up. As a small child, I had feelings of shame about Mom's mental illness and guilt about those feelings of shame.

"During my teens I hung out with older boys, with whom I played ball and board games. They had access to alcohol. I sought their acceptance as a friend and had my first drunk with them at age thirteen. By age fourteen, I was working part-time at a liquor store. My original poison of choice was alcohol, but in college I often partied and occasionally used a psychoactive herb. I obtained a college degree and found a good job in the aerospace industry. But my addiction slowly led me to use more and different types of drugs. After a few years I became sick and tired of being sick and tired and asked for help. Hope for a better life brought me into recovery through a rehab program five years ago."

Anonymous paused, sipped on his coffee, and went on. "I was told that changes were needed in my choice of people, places, and things. Was I an addict? Here is Narcotics Anonymous'

Information Pamphlet Number 7, titled "Am I an Addict?" Like myself, after filling out the simple yes or no answers to twenty-nine questions there, most people in these rooms figured they had a drug problem. But that's a question every addict has to answer on their own. You cannot rescue addicts from their addiction. They have to rescue themselves by taking that first step of honestly 'accepting' the disease of addiction and developing the willingness and open-mindedness required to live in a recovery program.

"After a few days in the rooms, I realized that my worst enemy was between my ears and that the solution to my problem was an inside job. I had to open my ears and mind to others' experience, strength, and hope. Now I'm clean and serene for five years. In the same way that there are principles in science, there are guiding spiritual principles called the steps that teach addicts to live life on life's terms. To study and incorporate the Steps into our new way of life, this group uses literature from the anonymous fellowships from Earth made available to us by a time traveling addict who visited that planet about seventy years in the future."

Ending his brief introduction, Anonymous looked around and proceeded to read the First Step from the *Basic Text* of Narcotics Anonymous,

"**We admitted that we were powerless over our addiction, that our lives had become unmanageable.**"

He went on to read the material on Step One, and halfway through it, Anonymous asked me to finish the reading. After I was done, he said, "An addict is a man or woman whose life is controlled by drugs. We are not responsible for our disease, but we are responsible for our recovery."

He momentarily paused and then went on. "And since we are responsible for our recovery, it's a good idea to go to meetings, review our literature, and learn to live by those spiritual principles called the Steps. Are there any questions, or would anyone like to share about Step One?"

After a few seconds of silence, Anonymous turned to me and

asked me, "Would you like to describe to us the physical, mental, and spiritual aspects of addiction?"

I had studied the First Step during my last week in rehab. After some thought, I provided a reply: "The physical aspect of the disease of addiction is the compulsive nonstop use of drugs. An addict has a problem stopping once he has picked up that first drink or drug. Once we get started, we don't stop until we either pass out or get in trouble."

Being a bit of an insecure newcomer, I momentarily stopped and stared at Anonymous to gauge his reaction to my answer. He looked at me with an approving smile. I continued. "The mental aspect of the disease of addiction is the obsessive thinking about drugs. From my personal experience during my first few days of abstention, I could hardly go on for fifteen minutes without having a casual thought about using."

I drank a sip of coffee and went on. "The spiritual aspect of the disease of addiction is our total self-centeredness focused on our drug-using lifestyle, regardless of the consequences. Our selfish self-centeredness takes us away from our relationship with God, family, friends, work, or school."

Three for three! I was proud of myself!

Another newcomer then asked, "But what are the spiritual principles behind Step One?"

"Good question!" Anonymous said before going on, "Acceptance that we have an addiction problem is most important in Step One. On the subject of acceptance, the book *Alcoholics Anonymous* tells us: 'Unless I accept life completely on life's terms, I cannot be happy. I need to concentrate not so much on what needs to be changed in the world as on what needs to be changed in me and in my attitudes.' Thus, an addict must understand that recovery is an inside job that requires constantly practicing the principle of acceptance.

"Accepting that we are powerless over our addiction is key to moving forward in the recovery process. Most of us addicts spend years denying that we have a problem with our addiction, and this wall of denial has to be surmounted if we are to recover. The spiritual principle of open-mindedness is also key to success. We have to be open-minded to a new way of life where our concept of fun does not involve the use of mind-altering substances. And of course, if we are not willing to fully embrace recovery, we are doomed to fail."

A lady with about a year clean then asked, "What about the principle of surrender? I hear it's very important!"

Anonymous smiled and replied, "Thanks for the reminder. Yes, surrender is a very important principle. I had difficulty with the concept of surrender and admitting my powerlessness over my addiction, as it went against the macho culture in which I grew up. Surrender means not fighting anymore. We accept our addiction and life the way it is. The road to victory in our struggle with addiction is paved with white flags of surrender! Only after surrendering are we able to overcome the disease of addiction and start on our process of recovering from it."

A moment later, a newcomer woman raised her hand. "Today, I celebrate sixty days clean with the help of God and the fellowship."

Applause spread across the room. The newcomer went on. "When I was using, my life was unmanageable. I was in a state of spiritual, mental, financial, and physical bankruptcy. And this addict was like an Olympic athlete in dysfunctional relationships! My parents, boyfriend, neighbors, teachers, and employers disowned me. The death of my younger brother by drowning in his own puke shook me up. Today I live in a recovery house, learning the tools to live life on life's terms. I have a job and pay my rent and other expenses. I'm still working on issues with relationships and old debts. Things will get better every day I'm in recovery. I have God and you guys to thank for this!"

A few seconds passed, and the hand of another newcomer went up. Anonymous acknowledged him, and the newcomer said,

"I was discharged from detox after five days there. Now that I'm in recovery, is it okay to occasionally have a social drink or a joint to relax? Someone told me I have a reservation. What is that?"

Anonymous instantly said, "Heck no! When I first came to the rooms, I had a reservation that alcohol was not a drug! I thought I could drink socially with my distinguished aerospace coworkers after being clean for a few weeks. Thus, I relapsed. When I came back, after my mind cleared up a little bit, I realized that when I had that first drink, the old obsessive and compulsive patterns of addiction took over! It was a hard lesson in my early days in the rooms five years ago!"

After a pause, another newcomer asked, "What about isolation? I have been told that that is not good!"

Anonymous turned to his wife next to him, as if hinting for her to give the answer. She turned to the group. "If I had a middle name during my old using days, it would have been *Isolation.* During my active addiction, my isolation reduced my physical, mental, and spiritual contact with my Higher Power and my fellow human beings. Today, I reach out to other recovering addicts. I avoid old playmates, playgrounds, and playthings that endanger my program. Today I do not isolate, and I stay in touch with others in recovery, church, and social clubs on a regular basis. Only by reaching out to others can I get the support I need to recover from my addiction."

At that point, Anonymous interrupted by announcing, "We have reached the end of the meeting. To stay clean please keep coming back to meetings, network with other recovering addicts, get phone numbers and use them, get a sponsor, read the literature, and learn the spiritual principles of the program. Let's now close with a prayer."

After the closing prayer in that evening meeting, we all went home to rest. It was another day alive and clean in the life of this addict.

For many years I followed these recommendations in order to

stay clean. I had to keep coming back to meetings, network with other recovering addicts, get phone numbers and use them, get a sponsor, read the literature, and learn the spiritual principles of the program. Today, I have over twenty years clean. I owed it all to God, and other addicts, who helped me out with their suggestions. And it all began with that First Step, admitting that I was powerless over my addiction, and that my life had become unmanageable. My new way of a drug-free life started with that humbling, simple first step!

Attention, Earthlings!

If you believe that you are an addict, humble yourself, and decide quickly to ask for help in a treatment center and/or a recovery fellowship, such as Alcoholics Anonymous or Narcotics Anonymous. It could be the best decision you ever made!

CHAPTER TWENTY-FOUR

INTERSTELLAR CRUISE

Back to the galactic neighbors of Earth: planets Sapiens, Verde, and Proxima. By 1941 these three planets had formed a partnership called the Tri-Interplanetary Alliance (TIA). Members collaborated in matters of trade, technology, and military assistance. The planetary governments agreed to exist autonomously under a central government based on the principles of universal human rights.

After the Greys arrived at planet Sapiens in 1944, the alliance assigned them a liaison, Colonel Rick Patel. When he met the Greys, he was aged forty. He'd been nine years with the interplanetary police, and nine in the space program, achieving fame in the latter during a victory over Malian pirates. Though suffering PTSD (post-traumatic stress disorder) and undergoing counseling, he was a confident, lighthearted man who rose through his government's bureaucracy. But President Ronnie, a former astronaut himself, recognized in Rick a mixture of the diplomatic and military skills of a potential leader. Rick would later be part of the crew that would undertake a mission to Earth in mid-1947.

The overall situation in our galaxy was good, but with some sensitive issues with a couple of races recently encountered. The alliance's initial encounter with the Greys and Amigos in 1944 flourished into a good friendship. However, other races, such as the Reptoids and Malians, were bent on either expansionist conquests or piracy. But even between the friendlier species, minor flares would occur when races would move from one planet to another, causing an adverse reaction at the destination planet from those concerned about the loss of jobs, a possible rise in crime, or possible security threats from these newcomers.

Specifically, on planet Verde a fanatical religious minority wanted to keep the planet isolated from outside influence. This fanatical group had committed acts of terrorism, causing increased security measures in government buildings and places of public gatherings.

Rick told us of a cruise to planet Verde with his Amigo and Grey friends in late 1946:

> I embarked with my friends on the space cruise ship *Sunflower Galaxy* on a journey from planet Sapiens to planet Verde. The 900-foot-long nuclear-powered interplanetary vehicle resembled the *Discovery One* spaceship in the earthling film *2001: A Space Odyssey*, a preliminary design concept that NASA developed in 1968 for interplanetary space travel. It was comprised of a cylinder, with the propulsion system on one end and a large two-hundred-passenger two-deck rotating sphere crew compartment on the other end. Attitude thrusters controlled the 400-foot diameter sphere's rotational movement, which provided artificial Moon-like gravity. The large vehicle required on-orbit assembly for a period over a year.

In our tour group on Sapiens, nearly all the *Zeta Hope*'s bridge officers were rewarded with a two-month vacation after working nearly continuously for two years on the design and development of a new generation of spaceships for the Tri-Interplanetary Alliance. With me were the Greys' Captain Noah; his wife, Faith; Chief Engineer Jang; and his wife, Doctor Akina. Also, with us was First Officer Romo, from planet Amigo. We were looking forward to a vacation at Verde, going on horseback rides, visiting ancient ruins, sunbathing and snorkeling at the beach, and enjoying full-blown feasts, munching on roasted rodents while sipping on milk. Oh, yeah. I forgot to mention that Verdes look like five-foot bipedal cats. Meow!

As we neared the end of our dinner on the *Sunflower Galaxy,* Doctor Akina commenced, "I'm impressed with the work you guys have done designing and developing new spaceships for the alliance. The *Sunflower Galaxy* is a futuristic one-of-a-kind interstellar cruise ship, with crew and passengers that number about two hundred. I understand that you also worked on a cargo version of this starship and an armed military/explorer version similar to our spaceship *Zeta's Hope!*"

A smiling Captain Noah added, "I see that your husband, Chief Engineer Jang, has kept you informed of our projects."

Jang chuckled and told us, "Yep. I even told her that I put in my name in the hat for leader of the landing party on the mission to Earth scheduled for mid-1947. In the future, I see my name on schools and streets honoring first contact with the earthlings. I'm so humble! Hopefully, they won't nuke us with their dangerous new toys!" Akina turned to Jang with a look of concern and lovingly squeezed her husband's hand.

Noah then said, "But how about you, Akina? I heard lots of good things about you in the field of medicine, particularly in the field of microbiology!"

"Thanks, Noah!" replied Akina, "But we sure were ready for a two-month vacation!" She sighed with relief as she finished this last sentence.

Faith, Noah's wife and *Zeta Hope*'s Communications Officer, turned to me and asked, "How about you, Colonel Patel? A famous, single guts-and-glory astronaut like you should have no trouble with the ladies, particularly after posing as the centerfold for your planet's leading women's fashion magazine! Inquiring minds want to know!"

Faith and Akina giggled as they waited for an answer.

Recalling being drunk nine years ago when posing for the centerfold, I was startled by the unexpected question. A bit flustered, I replied, "I was a drunk when I posed for that centerfold in a women's fashion magazine nine years ago. A few weeks after that, I went into rehab and got into a recovery program. I recently broke up with my girlfriend, Carol, who relapsed and abused alcohol and other mind-altering substances. I'm over eight years clean now and need to protect my recovery by not rebounding immediately into another dysfunctional relationship. For now, I need time to heal before I get into a committed relationship!"

As I spoke, I sadly reviewed memories of my ex-girlfriend's relapse and our eventual breakup. By that time, we were done eating.

Then Romo came to the rescue. "Hey, Rick! Let's go to the cigar lounge for a smoke!" With that, we turned to the ladies and excused ourselves.

Romo and I went to the smoke lounge to enjoy a couple of cigars. As we sat down, I pulled a piece of paper out of my pocket and told Romo,

"I just wrote an Inner-City Kids' Code of Conduct. Let me read them to you, and let me know what you think …."

> "Inner-City Kids' Code of Conduct:
> 1) God is a loving and caring dude. He did not go on vacation and leave you in charge.
> 2) No need to kiss up to him. He knows what you are doing.
> 3) If you have to curse really bad, avoid do-ing it in front of a lady.
> 4) Be grateful for everyday above the ground.
> 5) If you don't think that mom would ap-prove it, don't do it!"

Romo chuckled and said, "I used to think that way when I was a kid!"

I went on,

> "6) If somebody throws you under the bus, don't go back asking for more.
> 7) If somebody ticks you off, love them at a

distance.

8) Don't steal or freeload. Work for it!

9) Don't lie, gossip, or assassinate the character of others.

10) Don't be envious of other man's woman. He may have a gun!"

Romo laughs, telling me, "I think that's pretty good. I'll need a copy of that."

At that moment, the TV began to broadcast an Earthlings' 1950s nostalgia show from the main salon. The host was a fellow impersonating Ed Sullivan. He announced to the audience the line of performers impersonating Bill Haley and the Comets, Chuck Berry, Paul Anka, and some Elvis guy.

The show started with Haley and the Comets performing a song called "Rock Around the Clock." The sound of guitars, horns, and drums filled the air. A crowd of Sapiens, Verdes, Proximans, Amigos, and Greys moved to the beat of dances known as the bop and the jitterbug.

In between songs, Romo told me, "Rick, that time traveler, Chaika, made a fortune selling music from Earth's future!"

He paused and added, "On Earth, this music will be illegal in several countries and banned by some radio stations. Also, a famous performer like Chuck Berry had to sit in the back of the bus in many cities and go to segregated bathrooms because of his race!"

I took a puff of my cigar. "Good point! I see that you've been reading up on planet Earth. The president of the Tri-Interplanetary Alliance will be proud of your preparations for our mission to Earth in mid-1947."

After another puff on my cigar, I said, "But before we go to Earth, let's talk about an important matter."

I looked around as if I was about to share a big secret and said out loud, "Let's talk about women!"

After a brief pause, I continued, "My new lady has a roommate with enough curves to strike out a baseball lineup of sluggers! Let me hook you up with her. There is nothing like a new romance to bury memories of past romantic failures. She seems fun, knows how to dance, plays water polo, and excels at a few other things." I smiled coyly, winking at Romo.

He raised his eyebrows, shrugged, and said, "Thanks for the offer, Rick, but no way! I'm on the rebound from a dysfunctional relationship with my ex, Nova, so I'm taking a vacation from dating. If I get in another dysfunctional relationship and marry again, I get the feeling that I'll go through a nasty divorce!"

He paused, gave me a reproving look, and added, "But look at you! You just broke up with Carol, a nice, well-educated lady, and in no time casually bounced off to a new fling! What are we going to do with you? You are like a crazy young buck with excess testosterone! Don't you ever think of a committed relationship, perhaps with marriage and kids?"

Romo was right! His last question stayed with me for years! But in my early time of recovery, women were like an addiction to me, and it took me a long time to change my womanizing behavior.

As Romo finished his sentence, the actor impersonating Chuck Berry started a song called "Carol," which began with a verse that said, "Oh, Carol, don't let him steal your heart away!" Upon hearing the words of the song, Romo chuckled heartily.

I smiled and raised my arms as if the song had been God-sent to remind me of an adventure cheating on my former girlfriend, Carol. Maybe the Almighty was suggesting through this song that I should make amends to Carol.

I took another draw on my cigar, exhaled, and leaned forward with a smile. "Romo, you are such a square! You remind me of some of the traditional values of my older kin and family friends! Don't you worry about a thing! Be a free spirit like me! Come on! Let's have some fun! Let's go double-date with my new lady and her roommate!"

As I said this, I gestured with my hands to suggest the body of a curvaceous woman and added, "Let's ask them if they want to go out with us to dine, dance, and who knows what else!"

As I finished this last sentence, the bang of a large explosion nearby shook the walls of the cigar lounge. It shook us deeply, and our faces turned to reflect worry and confusion.

CHAPTER TWENTY-FIVE

RUN FOR YOUR LIVES!

What began as an interstellar cruise vacation for the Greys and their friends from planet Sapiens to planet Verde took a downturn shortly after dinner. As the spaceship *Sunflower Galaxy* began orbiting planet Verde, First Officer Romo Agrox and Colonel Rick Patel, the Alliance's liaison with the Greys, were shook up by an explosion as they enjoyed an after-dinner smoke in the spaceship's cigar lounge. Of this event, Rick relates:

> Following the confusion caused by an explosion near the interstellar cruise ship's *Sunflower Galaxy*'s cigar lounge, customers headed out the door, with Romo and I tagging along close behind. My heart was thumping like a drum!
>
> In the midst of the panic, someone screamed, "Run for your lives!"
>
> But shortly thereafter, the ship's captain made an announcement over the public address system:

"Ladies and gentlemen, an explosion occurred by the engine room near the rear of the ship. That area is suffering decompression, but we have isolated those compartments. No need to panic! We have orders to abandon ship. Please proceed rapidly toward the closest shuttle lifeboat!"

I turned to Romo and said, "You heard him! Let's go to the shuttle lifeboats!"

At the moment, we were in a hallway full of people moving at a brisk pace. As we approached our destination, a second explosion nearby shook the hallway, causing many to lose their balance. The explosion apparently came from the ship's kitchen, blowing the door into pieces of shrapnel, wounding some. A fire ensued, and dense smoke filled the air.

I thought for a moment and then said, "That looks like an incendiary bomb! Let's keep moving on and try to reach one of the shuttle lifeboats."

Romo pointed out, "We have wounded here! Let's help a couple of them reach the lifeboats!"

Near us was a young Verde couple, identifiable from their feline appearance. They'd been hurt by small shrapnel fragments and had flesh wounds in their faces and arms. They also looked a bit shook up. With the help of a first aid kit in the hallway, Romo and I quickly bandaged their wounds and helped them toward the lifeboats. A couple of crew members with fire extinguishers passed us in the direction of the burning kitchen. The young Verde woman said to us, "Thank you for assisting us. So much for the honeymoon with the husband!"

Romo, the Verde couple, and I worked our way to one of the shuttle lifeboats. It was two thirds full. These lifeboats were built like a free-fall lifeboat of Earth's twenty-first century but had wings that would allow them to glide for a landing, much like the US space shuttle. It had a homing beacon to help rescuers find it. In the event it could not land on a landing strip or grass field, the lifeboat could land on any large body of water, and it had seaworthy engines that could carry it as much as fifty miles after landing on water. The *Sunflower Galaxy* cruise ship had two of these shuttle lifeboats, and each could carry a hundred passengers, enough for the two hundred people on board the *Sunflower Galaxy*. Its control panel near the front window resembled an airplane's.

In the pilot's seat there was a young black Sapiens that I recognized as the Chuck Berry impersonator in the earlier after-dinner show. Being a pilot himself, I walked up to him and asked, "Do you know how to fly this thing?"

The young man replied, "Yes sir. Call me Ensign George. The cruise line trains several members of the crew to fly these babies, and I'm one of them." Reassured by the fellow's words, I returned to the entrance door to aid others coming in, a number of them requiring help because of their injuries.

Moments later three figures entered the lifeboat, a couple of crew members helping a tall Verde seriously hurt and bleeding profusely from shrapnel wounds. He was wearing a cook's apparel. By that time, the Greys' doctor Akina and her husband, Jang, had come in. She checked the tall Verde's large chest wound and said, "This man is not going to make it unless we get him to a hospital at once!"

I approached the injured one. To my surprise, I recognized a tattoo with a black flag on him and exclaimed, "This fellow has the tattoo of a terrorist organization on his chest! I'm with the interplanetary police and would like to talk to him after we tend to his wounds!" But the injuries were too much for the fellow. Within a few seconds, his body began twitching as he exhaled his last breath and died.

The ship's captain came into the lifeboat and said, "We are on the last lifeboat left on this ship. The flames are only ten yards away from it."

He paused, glanced at the hundred people present, and started issuing directions. "Everybody, please sit down and secure your seat belts." He headed for the last empty seat near the pilot and strapped himself in. Everybody else followed suit, strapping in within the next few seconds.

The captain then gave his final order on the deck of the *Sunflower Galaxy*: "Pilot, release the shuttle lifeboat, and set course for the landing strip at Verde's space center."

The pilot simultaneously ignited the pyro-technic controlled hold-down bolts and a second later fired two small hyperbolic liquid propellant rockets, releasing the shuttle lifeboat away from the *Sunflower Galaxy*. Within a minute they reached the Karman line, the boundary between the Verde's atmosphere and outer space approx-imately sixty miles above sea level. The pilot maneuvered the craft into position to enter the atmosphere, where it would be protected from the heat of reentry by a ceramic thermal protection blanket on its bottom. Reentry was quite shaky but successful. As we descended, we could spot through the pilot's window the wreckage of the *Sunflower Galaxy* falling and breaking up, fragments igniting as they entered the atmosphere. Within a minute they saw the three-mile runway at Verde's space center.

After hearing instructions from traffic control, the pilot turned to the captain and said, "Traffic control at Verde warns that another lifeboat is attempting an emergency landing. They advise us to glide in at any body of water, such as a river or the ocean near the launch complex."

After a moment the captain replied, "Take the ocean glide-in option."

Ensign George steered the shuttle lifeboat for a landing in the ocean. Fortunately, it was a sunny day with good visibility and calm seas, with waves of two feet or less. As the shuttle lifeboat landed on the water, there was an initial splash, but within seconds the craft was calmly floating along the ocean within a mile of the launch complex. The pilot activated the lifeboat's engines and turned it toward the shore.

Just then I got a call from Admiral Powell. The Admiral informed me, "I have been named the chair of an accident investigation team. At an early headcount it's estimated that all but three of the two hundred passengers and crew members made it alive to the lifeboats. A few others are injured but expected to recover soon."

I interrupted him, "We have the dead body of a Verde who was bearing a terrorist tattoo on his chest. He suffered many shrapnel injuries, as if he'd been close to the source of an explosion."

After a moment of silence, Powell said, "Yesterday, the Verde chancellor informed us that a confidential informant had alerted them to the possibility of extremists performing unspecified acts of terror against the Alliance in an attempt to spoil good relations between the interplanetary partners. The Verde government just sent in photos, fingerprints, and DNA samples of a number of the most dangerous extremists. Bring in the suspected terrorist's body for identification, and report as soon as possible to the accident investigation board we've formed at Verde's space center. Powell out."

The shuttle lifeboat arrived near shore about ten minutes after splashdown and settled on a shallow four-foot sandbank. The pilot deployed the emergency water slide and instructed us to use any of the four large uninflated life rafts stored in the ship. Romo and I deployed one of the rafts and helped load some of the injured onto it, along with the dead terrorist suspect. Upon landing, we spotted a patrol car and a few ambulances. A security guard approached and greeted us by saying, "Glad to see that you all are alive and well. Welcome to Verde Space Center!"

Ensign George, still in his Chuck Berry outfit from the show earlier, grabbed his guitar and joyously began playing "Roll Over Beethoven"!

CHAPTER TWENTY-SIX

CONSPIRACY BY THE BEACH

A young college student from planet Verde arrived about ten minutes early to his lunch appointment with some friends. On that late fall day of 1946, they had agreed to meet at noon by the entrance of the beach pier. The cruise spaceship *Sunflower Galaxy* had made its flaming entrance into planet Verde's atmosphere near there on the previous day, pundits in the press alleging that the terrorists had done that with the intention of making sure that the planet's inhabitants had personally witnessed their act of terror. Various boats and helicopters could still be seen near the position where the ship had crashed into the ocean, working to recover bodies and pieces of the wreckage. Other than that, things appeared normal, with an average number of beachgoers, surfers, and volleyball players; others were either fishing or coming in and out of restaurants.

The young student was about twenty and dressed in a T-shirt and swimming trunks, through which one could see the muscular profile of someone who exercised regularly. His hair hung to his shoulders, and he was listening to earthling rock and roll tunes on his smartphone. His name was Neo. He had bought several CDs from Chaika, who accidentally had travelled through time into the future through a wormhole, a shortcut connecting two separate points in space-time. The song that played on his smartphone was a 1970's American soft rock tune titled "Free Bird" by a band known as Lynyrd Skynyrd. It was a song about lovers who had just broken up. When the lead singer announced that he was "free as a bird now," Neo was reminded of Eyeshi, with whom he'd just ended a four-year relationship to which he felt unready to commit for the long term. He felt free as a bird too. He would join a great number of youths in their experimentation with sexual freedom, mild-altering substances, and the wild nightlife of the club scene—a lifestyle that he thought would bring him great joy.

The young Verde man thought nothing of the crash-and-burn lifestyle that he had adopted. He believed that today his primary purpose in life was to study hard and party harder. But his ideas of fun would lead him to rock bottom, jail time, and rehab within days. During those exuberant days, full of socially libertine dreams and ideas, Neo still perceived himself as a fun-loving college guy. But within him were planted the seeds of addiction—along with its associated obsession and compulsion—to both sex and drugs.

He had been taking computer science courses since early summer at a local university. By now he was quite familiar with Verde's space coast and the easygoing and relaxed life at the beach. He liked the beach, admired the beautiful ladies, and enjoyed seeing the smooth waves from the ocean caress the sandy shores.

But unknown to others on that beach, Neo was part of a group of extremists assigned to perform covert activities among his fellow citizens and their interplanetary allies. He belonged to a group that rebelled against modern ideas of tolerance in politics and freedom of religion. His real name was Mark, but he had created the false identity of Neo Green, a young man who had come from out of state to attend a local college, enjoying life while spying on his countrymen and their interplanetary allies. Neo specialized in identity theft and had also created false identities for the other Verde terrorists for whom he was waiting.

Within five minutes of his arrival, two of his friends arrived, their leader, Zarqa, and his sidekick, Dorf. An odd pair they were. Zarqa was the six-foot-tall muscular personification of a warrior. He was proud and ruthless in combat, but with an added touch of hatred and sadism equivalent to the fanatic supporters of Nazi Germany and Middle Eastern extremists on Earth. Zarqa deeply resented the authorities, as a few years ago they had killed his fundamentalist rebel dad in the Battle for Rackqa when Zarqa was a preteen. Since his passing, Zarqa seemed obsessed in a quest for obsessive vengeance like that felt by the character of Ahab in Herman Melville's *Moby Dick*.

On the other hand, though equally proud and with military training, Dorf was about a foot shorter in height and less intimidating. His personality showed an occasional sense of humor, mixed with an old-fashioned sense of honor.

Neo hugged them warmly, as one would old friends, and immediately asked, "Where is T'agono?"

Zarqa responded, "T'agono didn't make it. He hired onto the *Sunflower Galaxy* as a cook, where he could easily set a small secondary incendiary explosion in the kitchen. But he apparently had a problem setting his bomb, which apparently blew up prematurely. Our explosives were disguised as sticks of butter and required great expertise in setup. As a clergyman, he had little training in such things."

Dorf interrupted by saying, "May he live a happy afterlife, where he can eternally battle and feast!"

Then Dorf turned to Neo and lightheartedly said, "Your many ex-girlfriends and the association of bartenders in Verde send their greetings to you," alluding to Neo's reputation as a drinker and womanizer.

Zarqa smiled in one of the rare moments he ever showed joy.

Then he looked around, seeing there was nobody near them, and said, "Neo, you should have seen the result of our deed on the *Sunflower Galaxy*! A few dead and many wounded all over the place! I most enjoyed hearing an injured Sapiens squealing like a pig! Too bad most of the crew and passengers escaped thru the shuttle lifeboats on that interstellar cruise ship! We needed more explosives!"

Dorf added, "We are a small group now, but many are joining us through social media, particularly after the abuse of our comrades at the Bubu Gra prison! The mistreatment of our comrades in the prison is good advertisement for our cause!"

Zarqa went on. "Our deed will shake that tenuous alliance between our Verde home world and the Alliance! We will continue to terrorize them here on Verde with more acts against soft targets, including a matter of honor that we'll discuss later this evening. Eventually public opinion about the interplanetary Alliance will change, and perhaps we'll go to war with the foreign infidels on those other planets! Then glorious victory awaits us, and we'll conquer and enslave these inferior people!"

Zarqa paused and then asked, "Neo, did you get those additional explosives in the black market for our next mission?"

After looking around to see if any unwelcome ears were nearby, Neo responded, "Yes, I got them from one of my drug connections. I killed the man, so we don't have to worry about any witnesses from that transaction."

Dorf said, "Glad to hear that! You are a valuable asset in our quest to purify our world! My only regret is that we had to kill all those innocent civilians! I would rather gloriously battle armed Alliance soldiers!"

Zarqa spat on the sandy beach and said, "Don't you warriors feel ashamed about blowing up the *Sunflower Galaxy*! It was full of those from inferior species—Sapiens, Proximans, Amigos, and those disgusting amphibians that call themselves Greys! They all deserve to either die or be enslaved! Let's go to the pier and eat! I hear they have some fine restaurants and that one of them has a good spicy roasted rodent special!"

As they walked toward the pier, a Verde biker with dark glasses that was checking them out walked away from his observation point fifty yards away at an outdoor bar. He looked cool with his leather jacket, blue jeans, and boots. The fellow blended well with the crowd, which included a few bikers, surfers, tourists, fishermen, and sunbathers. He went by the name of Harley. He was an undercover agent for the Space Coast County Drug Task Force.

Harley picked up his cell phone and reported: "Harley here. I've been tailing that small-timer Neo that one of our confidential informants told us was dealing. I'm not sure if he's got anything to do with the dead gun dealer he knew, but we can keep eyeing him up to see if there's any connection. Neo just got together with a couple of his friends and they are all heading for the pier, perhaps for food or liquor. I don't have any audio, but I took pictures. I'll email them to you; see if anybody there recognizes them. I'll stay here observing them until my replacement arrives at one o'clock. Harley out."

CHAPTER TWENTY-SEVEN

HONOR OR FALSE PRIDE

On a fall day in 1946, at the Verde home world in the country of Rabia, a few extremists gathered in the large rural home of a skilled surgeon called Gabby after attending an opera. The opera's story was set in medieval times, about a thousand years ago. Its hero, Michael, fought and killed several tribal leaders, unified the nation of Rabia, and became their first king. Michael had allegedly said that battling God's enemies enriched the spirit and paved the way to paradise. His story was a cornerstone of Rabian mythology.

At Doctor Gabby's home, the Rabian guests were dressed in feudal attire with swords and were consuming lattes and snacking on beef jerky. This assemblage of characters somewhat resembled the fanatic supporters of old Nazi Germany and Middle Eastern extremists on Earth.

The leader of this group was named Rhino. He stood up in the middle of the large living room and started a conversation with a short report: "Zarqa tells us that our clergyman T'agono died in the process of setting explosives on that cruise spaceship known as the *Sunflower Galaxy*. May T'agono live a happy afterlife, where he may eternally battle and feast!"

All those present stood up and loudly said, "May a loving, caring, and merciful God welcome to paradise those who died in the name of our noble cause!"

After a minute of silence, Rhino went on. "Zarqa reports that there were many dead and wounded. He mentioned enjoying hearing an injured Sapiens squeal! Too bad most of the crew and passengers escaped on the lifeboats on that interstellar cruise ship! We did not smuggle enough explosives to cause greater damage!"

Rhino took a sip of his latte and continued. "We are a small group now, but we'll grow! The more people join us, the more we'll terrorize the Alliance planets of Sapiens and Proxima! We are getting many new recruits through social media, particularly after the abuse of our comrades at the Bubu Gra prison! Our deeds will shake that tenuous truce between us and other Interplanetary Alliance members! We'll continue to terrorize the Alliance infidels with attacks on soft targets, including an honor killing of a woman that may be occurring as we speak. Other attacks will include one on a major city's railroad station and power grid. Eventually public opinion about the Alliance will favor a full-blown war with planets Sapiens and Proxima! Then glorious victory awaits us, and we'll conquer and enslave those inferior peoples in the Alliance!"

The small party went on for two hours. After everybody left, Gabby cleaned up and sat down to finish his latte. In his hands he held a secret recording of the evening's feast. He'd earned their trust when they came to him to treat wounded extremists. But unknown to his guests, he was a deep undercover informant in service of the current Rabian government, which wanted to maintain the peace and improve relations with neighboring countries and the Alliance.

Gabby and his wife had their own motives to betray the trust of his colleagues. A few years ago, they had lost their only son during one of the terrorists' skirmishes with the Rabian government. These extremist elements on the planet of Verde tried to undermine the Alliance with acts of terrorism.

In a moment of despair, Gabby's wife said, "I'm glad that they are gone! There was a moment I felt like saying that it's time to stop feeding into the insane cycles of terrorist violence and warfare. People are dying by the thousands! But saying that would have been our death sentence at the hands of these crazy terrorists!"

Of all nations on planet Verde, Rabians had the highest death rate due to acts of terror. Gabby and his wife felt it was time to end the cycle of violence and start looking for spiritual and peaceful solutions that required greater tolerance of diverse religious and political views. He felt this was the only way to stop the growing number of widows and orphans!

The next day Gabby and his wife would meet another couple for a card game, something that they had done routinely for several years. The other couple were secret government intelligence agents. At that time, he would provide fingerprints, photos, and DNA samples of extremists plus the secret recording he made that evening. To avoid arousing suspicion, Gabby was instructed to meet with this couple only once a week, unless they discovered details of a major terror plot. He had to be careful: one of the rebel sympathizers and his family were neighbors across the street! Before he went to bed, Gabby prayed for the victims of terrorism.

Back in the space coast area, a young Rabian lady named Fatima was coming back home from her gym workout. She was a second-year student majoring in computer science. Fatima had fallen in love with a local college fellow who was of a different religious faith than her family. By dating him, she was breaking a promise her father, Umax, had made to an old Rabian business-man to give Fatima as a bride in a prearranged marriage. But being in love with someone of her choice felt wonderful to her.

Her boyfriend was at a local chess club, so Fatima was plan-ning a quiet evening catching up with her studies. But at that point, she was fed up with old values that she felt made women second-class citizens in Rabian society, where she could not drive a car and needed her father's consent to wed. She hoped and prayed that sometime down the road her dad would be more accepting of her decision to date and marry her college boyfriend.

She headed into her apartment building. In the hallway she saw a man on his cell phone (Dorf). As she passed by him, Fatima courteously said hello and kept on her way to her apartment.

Fatima walked through the threshold of the door of her apart-ment. To her surprise, she found Umax in the kitchen, wearing oven mitts and struggling with pots and pans while preparing a seafood chowder.

She exclaimed, "Daddy! What a surprise! I did not know you were here!" She leaned forward and kissed him on the cheek.

Umax replied, "I had some business dealings here on the space coast. I wanted to surprise you. How are your studies coming along?"

Fatima responded, "So-so. Got a B in calculus and an A in assembly language programming over the summer courses."

Apparently happy with her grades, Umax changed the subject and inquired, "Where is your new boyfriend?"

She answered, "He'll be playing chess with a friend for at least another hour."

"Do you insist in dating that infidel? He's does not practice our religion! This is a dishonor to our family!"

"Yes, Dad. It's not a matter of honor. Don't let your false pride blind you! I was hoping that you would accept us. He's such a nice guy! Wait until you meet him!"

Her father raised his voice as he asked her again, "For the last time, is that the way you want it?"

Sensing something wrong, she nervously replied, "Yes. That is the way I want it."

As if on cue, her dad's friend Zarqa emerged from hiding in a bedroom behind Fatima and shot her in the back of the head with a silenced pistol. She fell to the floor dead, blood gushing out of her head and splattering on the kitchen floor. After they walked out the door, her father Umax and Zarqa removed their gloves and put them in a gym bag with the gun and silencer. Before they left the apartment, they handed the bag to young Neo, who was hiding in a bedroom.

Zarqa told him, "Weigh the bag down with about ten pounds of rocks, and throw it into a deep body of water."

Neo bade them goodbye, went downstairs to the parking lot, and put the bag in his car. He drove off, while Zarqa and Umax left in a different vehicle.

Watching them from a distance in front of the apartment's laundry room, in an adjacent building, was Officer Harley Wesson, an undercover agent for the Space Coast Drug Task Force. He had changed from his biker outfit to a flannel shirt and blue jeans.

He picked up his cell phone and reported, "This is Harley. I've been following Neo, who one of our confidential informants told us was dealing. Something is going on in apartment 119 at Skylab Apartments. A fellow was outside with a cell phone, perhaps acting like a lookout. A young lady went into the apartment with a gym bag. A few minutes later, an older guy and two young men came out. One of them was Neo, carrying a gym bag. I speculate the bag may have illegal drugs, guns, or money. I don't have any audio, but I took pictures. A couple of the guys look like those I saw earlier today by the pier. I'll email the images to you and see if anybody recognizes the young lady and the older gentleman. Also sending you images of the suspects and plate numbers of the two vehicles they are driving. I'm going to keep tailing Neo. I'll report within an hour. Harley out."

CHAPTER TWENTY-EIGHT

NEO'S SLIP

Stoned from the joint he'd smoked earlier before an honor killing, young Neo felt his compulsion to get high take hold of him that late autumn evening of 1946 on planet Verde. Instead of following his terrorist cell leader Zarqa's instructions to weight with rocks the bag containing the honor killing's murder weapon, silencer, and gloves and ditch it in a deep body of water, Neo decided to go to a strip joint called The Trap. Heck, he figured, it was still early in the evening, and he had no college classes the next morning. He might as well go party!

As he walked into the nightclub, the disk jockey introduced four lady dancers to the sound of earthling music provided by Chaika, the time traveler. As Ernesto Lecuona's *Malagueña* played, the dancers' performance resembled a mix of Spanish flamenco and a Turkish belly dance. Their fluid movements and footwork were synchronized to the rhythm of the music. In their hands, they held hardwood castanets that produced a rapid series of clicks whenever required by the act. Their dancing style seemed to be a combination of prima ballerinas and burlesque performers like Josephine Baker.

Their audience crowded into the bar were men under the influence. Their faces belonged to people who made their living in diverse ways. They were businessmen, professionals, sailors, airmen, bikers, surfers, and perhaps even a drug dealer, to satisfy their need to get a buzz from anything other than alcohol. A number of them were in their fifties and sixties, and they all loved the bar's dim lights, which hid any wrinkles in their faces.

Neo sat on a barstool and ordered a drink. A man in his seventies next to him was having trouble lighting a cigarette. Neo turned to him, offered him a light, and cheerfully said, "What's up, Grandpa? What brings you here?"

Verde Dancing (Artwork by Roberta Lerman)

The old fellow replies, "I'm in a race with time, a few steps ahead of the reaper, numbing the pain of the death of an old flame who committed suicide more than three decades ago, dreaming that I could go back in time and relive our romance." The old man swallows a shot of liquor and continues, "I'll do so until I kill myself drinking! After all, I hear that they don't serve alcohol in alcoholics' heaven!"

Neo chuckled at the old gent's last sentence. He then reflected for a brief moment and then asked the old man, "She must have been quite a lady!"

The senior gentleman replied, "She may not have been special for anybody else, but she was to me!"

Neo smiled at the drunk preacher of the Church of Intoxication and turned to watch the ladies dancing. The Trap was his regular waterhole, where his girlfriend worked as a waitress. Her name was Barbara, and he'd dated her for a few months. Neo figured he would have fun there and make some cash selling small amounts of drugs to both strippers and customers. After the bar closed, he would take Barbara home and have a roll in the hay with her.

He thought that their lovemaking was the ultimate experience, culminating in a glorious mutual bliss. Had there been more sparks and fireworks, they would have set their bed on fire! Driven wild with lustful desire, they did it everywhere except on top of the refrigerator. Neo was surprised that they did not break any bones or furniture! Sex was like an addiction to him!

But after a few months on the nightclub scene, this aspiring terrorist got deep into drugs, compelled by his addiction. Thus, Neo went about his business, got a bit drunk, and sold a few packages of drugs to some of the strippers that evening, a few of them giving him free personal dances in the nude. He did not know that one of the strippers was a confidential informant to local law enforcement.

During one of the personal dances, he asked the stripper, "Do you have any children?"

Startled by the question, the young lady replied, "No."

Flirtatiously drunk and admiring her assets, Neo went on. "I have a steady income and I'm potty-trained. Will you adopt me?"

His girlfriend Barbara overheard this and became upset at him. Thus, Neo went home alone with some drugs he had left. He consumed every bit of them by his sad and lonely self. It was an unmemorable one-man party!

Thus, Neo began his self-destructive drug using ritual. Within a few seconds he had an intense buzz, known to addicts as "a bell ringer." He kept going at it for nearly three hours. He had side effects; such as the shakes, diarrhea, and vomiting. Neo also hallucinated—he'd hear sounds or voices and see moving shadows outside his window. But despite all the side effects, he insanely went on, compulsively chasing that next high, until he passed out.

Late the next morning Neo woke up with a big hangover. As he tried to get up, he realized that his hands were handcuffed and his feet shackled. On one side of his bed the Greys' Doctor Akina was scanning him with her medical tricorder, analyzing his vital signs. At the foot of his bed was undercover officer Harley, dressed in a golfer's outfit, drinking a cup of coffee. By the door stood a uniformed and armed Space Coast County deputy sheriff. Neo's initial instinct was to flee, but he realized that he was powerless in his constraints. Resistance was pointless!

Doctor Akina exclaimed, "This fellow has good vital signs! A miracle he's alive and healthy despite all his drinking and drugging. God must love this guy despite his desire to self-destruct!"

Harley interrupted, "Neo, here is a warrant for your arrest for selling illegal drugs to a confidential informant. You have the right to remain silent and the right to an attorney."

He briefly paused while Neo remained silent. Harley went on. "We've had you under surveillance the last twenty-four hours after an anonymous tip that you were selling drugs. Last night we recorded your sale of drugs to an undercover operative at the strip club. You have possession of drugs and paraphernalia in your apartment. And in your vehicle, there is a bag with the murder weapon used to kill a young college woman named Fatima at apartment 119 in the Skylab Apartments. You have a lot of jail time facing you, buddy—unless you cooperate with us in the murder investigation."

Then Harley asked, "Who were your two buddies at the Skylab Apartments last night? They are suspects in the destruction of the interplanetary cruise ship the *Sunflower Galaxy!*"

As Harley finished the last sentence, the Interplanetary Alliance's Colonel Patel walked in with a smartphone in one hand and a cup of coffee in the other. He said, "Good morning, Neo. Golly, you and your friends have ticked off lots of law enforcement officials and prosecutors all over the galaxy! I've made a lot of phone calls trying to get the best deal we can for you from both local and Interplanetary Alliance prosecutors."

Neo listened attentively.

Patel got close to Neo, smiled, and looked him straight in the eye, adding, "The victim's father, Umax, a Rabian businessman who solicited the honor killing, will be detained as soon as his plane arrives back in his country. And we've got a surveillance team and bugging devices on the large mansion he has here in the space coast, where your other two terrorist buddies are—Zarqa and Dorf, right?"

Patel paused and continued, "We got their pictures, fingerprints, and DNA samples for them from the country of Rabia while you were sleeping last night. Authorities in their homeland seemed to have an interest in them for alleged violent crimes! On the other hand, you currently have no criminal record. But you will have one now as Officer Harley courteously informed you about two minutes ago. We know that you are just a small-time addict dealer working for very dangerous violent extremists!"

Patel smiled. "Here is a proposal you can't refuse! Should we have your cooperation testifying against your high-ranking terrorist buddies, we'll drop all charges related to your assisting the bad guys, except for the drug-related charges. You could enter a witness protection program and do your time in jail here for selling illicit substances. We'll provide you protection under a new identity, and you come out of the slammer in three years or less, plus a year probation—where you may be submitted to random drug tests. At that time, you may enjoy all the sun, surf, food, and female companionship as you can for many decades to come until the natural end of your life!"

Neo smiled back. He was not crazy about either going to jail or going back to live an austere life in hiding should he be able to escape. But Neo liked the idea of enjoying the sun, surf, food, and ladies for many decades to come until the natural end of his life. He concluded that life as a jihadist terrorist was not for him!

Colonel Patel was right. It was a deal he could not refuse!

CHAPTER TWENTY-NINE

A QUEST FOR VENGEANCE

It was a late autumn afternoon in 1946 on planet Verde. The view of the Ais River was gorgeous from the mansion of Umax, a businessman who allowed two members of a terrorist cell to live there with him. These guys were responsible for the honor killing of his daughter, plus the destruction of the spaceship *Sunflower Galaxy*, all in the last forty-eight hours. The two extremists, Zarqa and Dorf, enjoyed drinks, traded stories, and made plans for further acts of mayhem and terrorism with the purpose of sabotaging the alliance between their home world of Verde and their allies on planets Sapiens and Proxima.

They'd spent several hours on a computer. Using fake accounts, they engaged in activities of misinformation, identity theft, and fraud—while they drank themselves silly. In one of their schemes, they emailed out fake notices saying that recipients had won a multimillion-dollar lottery—and that they should provide them with their name, birthdate, and Social Security number to receive the prize money! In another scheme, they created a dating site called "ET Babes," where they got people to register and thus obtained personal information from them. Occasionally they would hack a computer by sending a message to update software applications, which once downloaded would extract personal and financial data from the victim. A couple of their victims were high-ranking engineers in the Verde Space Agency!

That afternoon, Dorf researched a data base provided to the Verde government by Chaika, the time traveler. He'd come across the name of a few notorious earthlings. After a couple of drinks, he said, "In social media, I'm going to blame this guy George W and the military industrial complex for the attack on the *Sunflower Galaxy* spaceship!"

Baffled by such a suggestion, Zarqa asked, "Won't that look a bit incredible?"

"Heck no!" replied Dorf as he typed and added, "He's an infidel! They'll believe it!"

If somebody posted anything they disliked, they used a technique called forum sliding, where they used several prepositioned 1- or 2-line comments, such as "That's nonsense!" or "You must be part of a government conspiracy!", causing the unwanted post to slide down out of view.

Having being on planet Verde's space coast for only two days, they were curious as they observed the view from their balcony facing the Ais River, where they saw a lush line of pines, palm trees, and cabbage palms receiving the last flickers of late afternoon sunlight. There was some activity visible on the river, which hosted a myriad of leisure seekers boating, fishing, and waterskiing among the friendly dolphins and water hogs. In the background a song began playing on their recorder, titled *"Push It to the Limit,"* by an earthling called Paul Engemann.

Gazing on the slow-moving water hogs, Zarqa started a conversation, "Dorf, look at those two slow-moving creatures, lazily overgrazing on river grasses. No wonder that one fisherman on the shore was complaining about the poor fishing, as those animals eat the river grasses that serve as hideouts for small fish. I wonder when hunting season is for those useless animals! Centuries ago these water hogs were relied upon among the indigenous population as a source of food, and their hides were made into leather shoes. What do you think? Should we go hunt for one of those creatures and dine on it for the next few days?"

Dorf replied, "Not any time soon! There are laws protecting these destructive animals! When we win our holy war, conquer this country, and enslave these weak and irrational people, we and other jihadist warriors can stake out large holdings of land for us. We'll start water hog farms and sell their meat for profit at restaurants, as done for chicken and mutton. Heck, the best way to save any species in danger of extinction is to make it edible!"

Zarqa chuckled and then replied, "Dorf, under our false identities we got ourselves jobs in our next target about a week from now at Yorkia's central train station. Strange rituals these infidels have of going on shopping sprees for a religious holiday!"

Zarqa paused for a moment of reflection. His hatred of nonbelievers was deep in his heart. His father had died at infidel hands in the Battle of Lepian in 1936 when Zarqa was in high school. He worshipped his dad's memory. The man was his hero, idol, and role model. But since his passing at the hands of nonbelievers in a battle a decade ago, Zarqa was obsessed in a quest for vengeance similar to that felt by Captain Ahab in Melville's *Moby Dick*.

With an expression of concern, Dorf interrupted his friend's train of thought. "I don't know, man. I'm concerned about these attacks on soft civilian targets. From where I see it, it's braver to engage in battle with armed men, as we did back when we attacked that military post in our homeland. I prefer guerrilla warfare on an armed opposition over these acts of terrorism on unarmed civilians that we've committed lately."

Zarqa replied, "Don't worry, Dorf. Our acts of terrorism will cause a collapse of the peace between our home world of Verde with planets Sapiens and Proxima, and we'll have plenty of opportunities to fight glorious battles at that time. Anyhow, Neo should join us by eight thirty this evening. We still have time before we sit down and discuss our next project. We'll assume new identities and move to Yorkia and get jobs at its central train station as we prepare for another attack there. We'll simultaneously do a cyberattack on that city's power grid, plus we'll blow up Yorkia's central train station. When we do so, we'll send messages in our native Rabian language claiming responsibilities for these attacks. It will be a glorious day! For now, let's go inside and watch the early evening television news."

The two extremists went back inside the house, sat in the comfortable living room, and turned on the television set to watch one of the news channels. The news program was about to start, and a young lady anchor began: "Breaking news this evening! Prominent businessman Umax Norg has been detained in Rabia. We show a picture of this individual on the screen. Authorities report that he's a person of interest in the terrorist attack on the interstellar cruise ship *Sunflower Galaxy* and the honor killing of his daughter. Please report any recent sighting of him to local law enforcement. Two other individuals have also been identified as persons of interest. They go by the names of Zarqa and Dorf, and authorities report that they are responsible for several murders back in Rabia. They are also persons of interest in the terrorist attack on the interstellar cruise ship *Sunflower Galaxy* and the honor killing previously mentioned. Should you see any of these individuals, please report this to law enforcement authorities. They are armed and dangerous!"

As the anchor woman finished saying this, Zarqa and Dorf looked at each other with an expression of great concern. After a moment of reflection, Zarqa screamed, "We've got to get out of here as soon as possible! This house is in the name of Umax's corporation. It should not take long for the authorities to figure out that we are here. We should leave this area as soon as possible! Let's head north to our next target in Yorkia. It should be easier for us to hide in that large city! We'll call Neo from one of our cell phones once we are a couple blocks away from here!"

Dorf added, "Let's get our guns, smartphones, and the laptop and forget about anything else. Our vehicle is parked two blocks back in the apartment building complex. In the trunk are explosive devices, clothes, and cash we can use."

Within half a minute, Zarqa and Dorf collected their smartphones, guns, and the laptop. They climbed out of the house through a first-floor window where some shrubbery provided cover from any curious eyes.

After they moved through the bushes a few feet under the cover of darkness, two blinding lights shone on them, and they heard Colonel Rick Patel's commanding voice: "Hands up! The house is surrounded by Alliance and law enforcement officers!"

Tipsy from hours of heavy drinking, Dorf was slow as he pulled his gun out. He was simultaneously hit by shots from Patel and Harley. Unseen by Patel and Harley a few feet further ahead, Zarqa acted faster against a deputy sheriff that got on his way. He wounded him in the shoulder as he ran into the waters of the Ais River. There he spotted a small island about fifty yards away and swam toward it, planning to rest there momentarily while trying to figure out his next move.

As Zarqa swam toward the island, a large quadcopter drone with a bright searchlight began circling around the house. Barely three yards from the small island, Zarqa looked back as he heard the quadcopter drone approaching. He sensed a slight movement on the water on his left and turned in that direction. The last thing Zarqa saw before dying was the large jaw of a fifteen-foot gator that

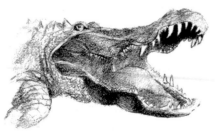

dwelled in the river, feeding mainly on dolphins, water hogs, and other marine life there. Because of his large size, locals had named the gator *Moby Dick*.

Drawing of gator (Roberta Lerman)

CHAPTER THIRTY

WHAT TO DO NEXT

It was an early autumn Monday morning in 1946 on planet Verde. The Interplanetary Alliance's Colonel Rick Patel woke up and rubbed his eyes. His new girlfriend, Shessi, slept on her side next to him. He pulled the bedsheet off her and admired her smooth skin, the long soft curly hair cascading down from her head, and the curvaceous contours of her body. In his mind he recollected the details of their amorous encounter from the previous evening, recalling that she was screaming the name of the Lord for some odd reason. The companionship of pretty ladies was like an addiction to him! In a way, he looked at this as his reward for having his vacation interrupted the last four days with the investigation of the terrorist attack on the *Sunflower Galaxy* spaceship, which concluded with the arrest of three terrorists and the death of a fourth one.

The question in Rick's mind was what to do next. For now, he intended to rest for a few days of a well-deserved vacation, before taking on his new assignment: mission to Earth. Life was good to

Rick. He looked forward to his next adventure, whether exploring the galaxy or his next romantic encounter. No commitments, except for his career as a space explorer!

He had started his vacation on the wrong foot by breaking up with his now ex-girlfriend, Carol, who complained about his flirting with other women. But he felt that Carol fell in love with the man that Rick could be, not the man he was. All his friends knew that he was a free-spirited playboy who was not ready for a committed relationship. When not saving the Galaxy, he habitually moved into the arms of the first pretty woman who caught his fancy. But as he would find out today, some personal issues would have to be addressed.

As his girlfriend Shessi cooked breakfast, his cell phone rang. It was Rick's mother, Winona, who'd become close friends with his ex-girlfriend's family.

Winona said, "Hi Rick. It's your mother. Are you going to come spend the holidays with us?"

"Yes, Mom. As previously planned, I'll be home to see you for a few days when I arrive back at Sapiens. After that I'll be reporting to my new assignment in the mission to Earth to be launched from planet Proxima in the summer of 1947."

"Nice to hear that son. But I've learned from Carol's mother that you left her for some home-wrecking temptress. Carol is such a nice, beautiful, and intelligent young lady with a career in molecular biology! And she would make a great daughter-in-law and young mommy to my future grandchildren!" Winona sighed. "Are you planning to settle down with that new girlfriend? When are you going to give me some grandchildren?"

"Oh Mom, I agree with you about Carol! But I'm not ready for a commitment. I want to enjoy my life as a single man and focus on my career as an astronaut! In a way, at this moment of time, I'm married to my career." Then Rick sarcastically added: "And don't you worry about grandbabies with the new girlfriend. We are having safe sex!"

"Rick, you are terrible! Anyhow, I gave Carol your new cell phone number, and she will be calling you soon after I hang up! Bye, son," Wynona said as she hung up.

He shook his head as he hung up. He realized it might take his mother some time before she accepted the fact that his relationship with Carol was over. Rick went up to the kitchen and kissed Shessi as she fixed breakfast. He poured a cup of coffee and turned on the radio to a music station, which was playing The Bangles' "Manic Monday"—courtesy of Chaika, the time traveler. He grabbed the newspaper and sat down to read it at the dining table.

A few minutes later, the phone rang again. It was Carol, who cheerfully said, "Hi, Rick! I'm calling from my mom's. How are you doing?"

"I'm doing fine, Carol. I had to interrupt my leave the last four days with the investigation on the *Sunflower Galaxy* incident. But the culprits have been caught, and I'm on leave for a few days. Then I have to report for duty for the mission to Earth to be launched from planet Proxima next summer. It's so nice of you to call me to bid me farewell!"

"I truly wish you well, Rick. I recognize that things between us are over, and I accept that we both must go on our separate ways. I know that you like being single and that you aren't ready for a commitment. But I still care for you and wish you well."

"Glad to hear that you accept the situation, Carol. I know that my flirting with other women around was upsetting you, as was the fact that I was soon leaving for a long journey to Earth. I have a new girlfriend now, and I hope that you too can move on with your life. Perhaps it's best for us to part on good terms. How are you doing?"

"I'm doing well ... My drinking and partying days are over. In a few minutes, I'm going into a treatment center to help me recover from my substance abuse, so I'm having breakfast with Mom before we go."

"Good for you, dear. Glad to hear that you are taking care of that problem. My regards to your mother!" said Rick, expecting the call to end.

"Mom is fine. Thanks. But there are a couple of things that I need to tell you."

"Glad to hear your mom is well. What things do you have to tell me?"

"When we broke up, I got really drunk. A girlfriend turned me on to use drugs intravenously at that time, something I'd never done before. Yesterday, I found out from the doctor that I have hepatitis C. He said that though rare, it's possible to contract hep C sexually—so you may want to check with a doctor."

"Oh, I contracted hepatitis when I was a kid. I'm sure that through treatment you'll be cured within a few months at the most." Rick didn't know what Hepatitis C was.

"I believe that you are talking about hepatitis A, Rick. I read about addiction and its consequences in a book called *Out of Numbness*, where I'm told that hepatitis C is transmitted through contact with blood—often through intravenous drug use and sometimes through blood transfusions from an infected source. It also can be transmitted from a pregnant mother to her unborn child. Fatigue is the most common symptom, but depression and cognitive problems also occur. Because the body's immune system tries to destroy the virus, patients may experience muscle and joint pains, headaches, and dry mouth. The disease can cause severe scarring of the liver, a condition known as cirrhosis. But on the good side, there is better treatment today than decades ago."

Startled at his ex-girlfriend's revelation about hepatitis C, Rick reflected on this for a few seconds. Then in a low voice, he said, "I'm so sorry to hear that, Carol. This is really sad news! I feel for you, dear."

"Thanks, Rick! But there's a second thing that I have to tell you about."

A bit confused, Rick said, "Go ahead."

"We are pregnant. And our child may get hepatitis C from me."

For a few seconds, Rick went through a flurry of emotions. Despite his breakup with Carol, of all the women that he'd dated, he was glad that she was the one to get pregnant with his child. At that time, she would have been his top choice to get married and raise a family. On the other hand, the fact that their child had this disease he knew nothing about had him both baffled and saddened.

After his brief reflection he said, "I'd like to keep in touch with you and the child. I'll send you four hundred a month as a form of child support."

"That will not be necessary, Rick. I felt that I had to tell you this before I go to the treatment center. And they don't allow outside calls for the first week. Hopefully, I'll stay in recovery, have a healthy child, and live in comfort with a decent salary from a career as a molecular biologist. I may even find a cure for hepatitis C!" Carol paused for a couple of seconds and said, "Mom is calling me to give me a ride to the treatment center. I have to go, Rick. Have a nice day!" Carol was sobbing as she hung up.

Rick went into a deep state of reflection. Carol left no phone number. The only way to contact her would be through her mother, and she did not like him at all! Good luck with that!

He pondered what to do next. But despite Carol's civil demeanor, she apparently wanted him out of his life. There was nothing that he could do about it! He just hoped that someday she'd forgive him, let him back in her life, and let him meet the child.

The radio started playing a 1934 Billie Holiday jazz song titled "The Very Thought of You," which satellites from the Interplanetary Alliance had recorded from Earth's radio signals. The tune brought back sweet memories of Carol. But he concluded that he couldn't change his past—and that he must accept it, live life on life's terms, hope for the best, and move on.

CHAPTER THIRTY-ONE

A LATE-NIGHT TALK SHOW

First Officer Romo Agrox reported on the crew's arrival at Proxima:

> We arrived at planet Proxima on a cool January late afternoon in 1947 to prepare for our mission to Earth in midsummer. On the horizon we saw the dim light coming from the two red dwarf suns in this star system of Proxima. Beyond the airstrip, we saw a prairie with a herd of bisonlike creatures munching on the grasses a couple of miles away. As our spacecraft approached the passenger terminal, we saw a couple of Proximan ground crew on the runway. They were intimidatingly huge in size, about four hundred pounds each and seven feet tall!
>
> My name is Romo, first officer of the Greys' spaceship *Zeta's Hope*—a vehicle able to travel at a hundred times the speed of light, the fastest

around at that time. I'm from planet Amigo, which collaborated with the Greys in the development of our ship, half of whose crew of fifty was from my planet, the other half Grey crew members.

During our travels through the Milky Way, we visited three planets in the vicinity of Earth—Sapiens, Verde, and Proxima. They had formed an alliance of member planets collaborating with each other in matters of trade, technology, military assistance, and cultural exchange. This alliance asked the Greys and Amigos to partner with them in a mission to Earth scheduled for summer 1947.

In January 1947 Captain Noah's wife was expecting their first child, and he did not want to leave her side. So, he asked me to fill in for him in a public relations appearance for a television show and to bring with me the Grey ensigns Boudica and Shaka, who would take part in the mission to Earth. Little did we know that on that evening we would get a lesson in the eccentric and light-hearted culture of the people of Proxima. What follows is my account of our appearance on that late-night talk show:

After arriving at the theater, we were led to the stage and told to sit on a large couch. Above it was a wooden plaque with an e. e. cummings quote that read: "The most wasted of all days is one without laughter." Our smiling show hostess, Thally Nightly, came to greet us before the curtains opened. She was a retired galactic wrestling champion who was about seven feet tall and weighed about four hundred pounds, all muscle and bones—typical of Proximan females, who typically were a foot taller, had facial hair, and were twice as heavy as their relatively frail male counterparts. But I was to find out that, despite her intimidating size, Thally was a warmhearted lady with a rather eccentric sense of humor. And because the construction of their vocal cords resembled a duck's, Proximans produced funny sounds when speaking.

The time came when the curtains rolled open. The house band started playing a happy tune, as the announcer shouted out with his squeaky voice, "And now, here is our show hostess—Thally Nightly!"

After a warm applause, Thally started her monologue about the daily news as follows, "A drunk wakes up and has not had a drink yet. He goes to an ice cream shop and eats a half a gallon of rum raisin. He's now suing the ice cream shop because he did not get a buzz."

Some laughter came from the audience. Thally went on. "Thanks to the latest health pro-grams and advances in medical science people are living longer. This was done so that people have extra time to pay their bills."

Chuckles were heard from the studio. She then turned to Boudica and Shaka, saying, "Today we have with us a romantic couple of our Grey friends that are part of the crew of the spaceship *Zeta's Hope*. They are called Boudica and Shaka. As a matter of fact, they are married—to each other, I mean. Let's welcome them with a big hand!"

A round of applause was heard. Thally contin-ued, "You're married! Any children?"

"Yes, we have a four-month-old girl!" the Grey couple responded in unison, as Boudica proudly showed a picture of the toddler.

"That's a cute kid! So nice and peaceful she looks!" Thally paused briefly and added, "Wait and see what happens when she becomes a teenager! You come back and tell us how you feel then!"

The audience laughed. Then Thally made a request, "I hear that you guys are great dancers and that you have practiced dancing to earthling music. Can you dance for us? Maestro! Earthling music for our dancing couple!"

The band started playing a nice melody written by composer Jerome Kern titled Smoke Gets in Your Eyes. Boudica and Shaka get up and rhythmically move to the music, similar to Earth's Fred Astaire and Ginger Rogers. Applause is heard when the Grey couple finished dancing. Then they went back to sit on the couch.

Thally followed with a question, "What can you tell us about your home world?"

The Greys reflected for a few seconds, the question bringing up feelings of nostalgia. Shaka answered, "Our planet of origin is Zeta. It's about thirty-five light-years from Proxima in the Zeta Reticuli star system. That's over two hundred trillion miles from here! We are amphibians who give birth to live young. On land, we are not as athletic as humanoids, but in water we swim well with the aid of our webbed hands and feet. We have a well-developed sonar system, much like a dolphin's, which helps us locate either predator or prey. We also have high empath abilities, enabling us to sense the emotions of a person or animal. About the way we govern ourselves, the nine constitutional republics on our home planet agreed to exist under a central government based on the principles of universal rights; all shared our technology and resources, including our experience of nearly two centuries of space exploration."

Thally inquired further, "Tell me about the arrival of the Reptoids to Zeta."

Both Greys' faces saddened for a moment. Then Boudica replied, "Near the peak of our civilization by mid-1944, a crew of twenty-five humanlike aliens came from a friendly neighboring planet called Amigo to join us on a venture to the uninhabited planet Avalonia. They were intelligent and as advanced as the Greys. The Amigos told us of a catastrophic event in their home world a couple of days before they arrived on our planet. They were invaded by an alien race of Reptoids. The aggressors brought with them modern weapons, like armored vehicles and fighter-bombers. Like the Greys, the Amigos had not fought a war in several centuries, and their weaponry consisted mainly of antiquated six-shooters and hunting rifles, which few people possessed. In a matter of days, the invaders overran their home world and either murdered or enslaved their inhabitants. Our Amigo refugees feared that this army of invaders would embark across the universe to conquer other species and obtain their technologies! We lost many loved ones on Zeta to the Reptoid invasion nearly three years ago. We miss them and mourn their loss!"

Boudica paused briefly. After collecting herself, she continued, "Within two days of the arrival of the Amigos, our orbiting long-range sensors showed a large fleet of ships approaching Zeta. We had no idea that what was to follow was the beginning of the end of our civilization as we knew it! This was in mid-1944, when we were ordered to escape and embark on our long journey to other worlds! To those of us who escaped the invasion and survived, it was the beginning of a long and arduous odyssey that would eventually bring us in contact with a number of other intelligent species!"

The audience applauded.

Then Thally turned to me with a sexy wink and asked, "Mr. Romo, are you married?"

I sighed, responding, "I was widowed two years ago, in 1944, when my wife Luciet was attacked by a sea predator while bathing in the ocean on planet Avalonia. God bless her soul!"

After a moment of silence, Thally said, "We are sorry to hear about your loss—but it's been two years of mourning by now. Are you ready for a new relationship?"

Not waiting for an answer, she got up from her chair and shouted to the audience with her funny, squeaky voice, "You may want to try dating some of us big mamas in Proxima! Maestro, some sexy earthling music! All single ladies in the audience: Stand up and shake your booty for our lonely bachelor from planet Amigo!"

The house band began playing a 1991 song by Right Said Fred titled "I'm Too Sexy." About twenty four-hundred-pound bearded Proximan women stood up in the theater audience, shaking their bodies, throwing kisses at me, and flexing their muscles. At that moment I became highly concerned for my safety, being in the proximity of so many muscular Proximan females, all apparently in a state of sexual excitement!

Perhaps sensing my high anxiety, Thally signaled the ladies in the audience to sit down, which they did. She sat back down and changed the subject. "We were just busting your chops! So, Mr. Romo: How do you like our home world of Proxima?"

**Depiction of Proximan female
(Artwork by Roberta Lerman)**

Relieved at the change of subject, I quickly responded, "We find it a rather interesting world. Your home planet closely orbits your host stars, a red dwarf pair, every eleven days. Your days look like twilight because of the low intensity of your suns. It does not rain much here because of light evaporation because of the dim light from your sun. Outside of your mountain ranges, your land masses are mostly prairies or dry desert. But life in your vast oceans is abundant with algae, kelp, and fish. It's interesting that vegetation here is black. Your plants appear black to our eyes, absorbing light across the entire visible wavelength range in order to carry on photosynthesis using as much of the available light as possible from your dim suns. But your species has adapted to this environment, having the night vision of an owl and the hearing of a dog."

Impressed by the informed description of her home world, Thally said, "You are right! And the fishes, land creatures, and vegetables on our planet are tasty!" After chuckles from the studio, Thally went on. "Mr. Romo, what motivated you to go work in the aerospace industry?"

I immediately replied, "Since I was a kid I was a stargazer. In the evenings I would look into the starry skies and wonder what was in those lights in the sky. As I grew up, I watched a number of sci-fi movies and television shows. The sciences and electronic workshops were my favorite subjects in high school, so I decided to go to engineering school. When I finished college, I received an invitation to work for my home world's aerospace agency. It was an area that always interested me, and they paid well. After all, I was a believer in labor capitalism, which allows workers to be paid according to their education, experience, skills, and productivity."

"Interesting answer, Mr. Romo!" said Thally with a smile, as she continued, "But I hear that you're a high wheel in the spaceship *Zeta's Hope*. Tells us *who* the key crew members are in this mission to Earth next summer."

The audience broke into a round of applause. Thally interrupted, "Two pregnant Grey females in the crew! These Greys must be really loving and caring people!"

Loud laughter was heard from the audience.

Then Thally asked what any good journalist would ask, "Okay, *why* go to Earth? Would not it be better to spend our tax money on our home worlds—in programs such as education, health-care, or public transportation?"

Actually, I was expecting this type of inquiry. I reflected momentarily and answered, "Space exploration is a driver of technology. Satellite communications, weather forecasting and GPS would not exist without space exploration. Robotics, computers, digital photography and video, fuel cells, and other technologies benefited from space-related research. Space exploration is also a driver of science education. Ask how many scientists and engineers were inspired by the space program and by the science-fiction books, movies, and television shows that fed off of it. I believe space exploration is important for fostering a constructive sense of wonder, collective purpose and hope for the future."

I stopped momentarily to catch my breath. Then I went on. "As for specifically going to Earth, they are our closest galactic neighbors, within five light-years of planet Proxima. They recently went through a global war, and the prodemocracy side won. They still have serious issues, such as race segregation. But the fact that they have developed nuclear weapons and that they are at the early stages of rocketry creates a sense of urgency for us to establish formal relations with them. We at the **Interplanetary Alliance** only devote about one-half percent of our budget to all things space-related. This may not sound like much, but it's up to the people, and their elected representatives, to decide if this is money well spent or whether it should be diverted elsewhere."

Thally opened her eyes wide and responded, "Nice answer! Now, please give us a quick rundown on *how* you guys will accomplish this mission to Earth in the summer."

I replied, "A launch vehicle will take the flight crew to a space station orbiting around planet Proxima. There they'll board our spaceship, *Zeta's Hope*, which is currently docked to the station. Flying at one hundred times the speed of light, the ship will take them to Earth's orbit in sixteen and a half days. From orbit the crew will communicate to earthlings of their arrival with a CD containing greetings in five languages. A landing craft with a crew of four will land and establish formal relations with Earth's largest democracy, America. This crew of four is made up of Ambassador Rick Patel, Chief Engineer Jang, and crew members Boudica and Shaka—the last two being with us here tonight."

After a round of applause from the studio audience, Thally asked another question: "What happens once you get to Earth?"

I answered, "We'll establish formal relations with them and present the people of Earth with gifts, which include medical, electronic, computer, and communications technology and a box of cigars for their living God, who's called George Burns, a very lighthearted fellow. We know this from Chaika, our time traveling friend, who made available to us a movie from their future called *Oh God!*"

Applause rolled through the audience. Then Thally stood and pointed to Boudica and Shaka, saying, "Perhaps our Grey friends are willing to do one more dance for us before the show ends. Earthling music, Maestro!"

The show's home band started playing a song titled "Swing, Swing, Swing" made famous on Earth by Benny Goodman's orchestra. Boudica and Shaka moved to the dance floor and began responding to the rhythm of the music. As the curtain closed at the end of their performance, it was time to bid farewell for the evening to our new Proximan friends. Our first contact with them was a lesson for us in that appearances deceive and that their large intimidating appearance hid a warm and lighthearted character!

CHAPTER THIRTY-TWO

THE NIGHT BEFORE THE LAUNCH TO EARTH

On planet Proxima, it was dinnertime at the astronaut quarters before the launch to Earth during early June 1947. The top officers of the crew along with the launch director Romo, and Chaika—the friendly time traveler—were dining and chatting. These officers included the Grey's Captain Noah, their new first officer Patel from planet Sapiens, and Chief Engineer Jang. Chaika was the Ambassador at Large from planet Leza to the Interplanetary Alliance—planets Sapiens, Verde and Proxima—with whom the Grey and Amigo crew of the spaceship *Zeta's Hope* also had friendly relations. In the background was heard a recording of Spyro Gyra's "Morning Dance" and "Shaker Song"—courtesy of Chaika, who had been specifically invited to that dinner to share her knowledge of planet Earth and its inhabitants.

The main course of their modest dinner consisted of crab cakes and vegetables. Some chitchat followed about how everybody's health and spirits were and what they'd been up to.

After coffee and dessert were served, Noah inquired, "Chaika, you are known as a time traveler. How did you travel through time?"

She calmly sipped on her coffee and then answered, "It was by accident. About four years ago my spaceship got pulled into a wormhole that appeared out of nowhere! After some tumultuous minutes, my crew of three and I found ourselves on Earth's orbit on December 21, 2012. We intercepted communications from a country right below us called America. They had a constitutional republic and had recently reelected as president a black fellow called Obama. We intercepted their internet communications and recorded general information on the planet's history, politics, economics, military, and some of their arts—anything from music to books and films. After about thirty minutes, we were drawn back into the wormhole and reappeared where we had been before. To this day we have no idea how that happened!"

After a few seconds of silence, Captain Noah addressed her. "Chaika, please fill us in on your knowledge of humans in Earth, the planet we'll be visiting within three weeks."

Chaika replied, "Sure. I believe that humans evolved away from the other great apes in the continent of Africa about five million years ago, developing such unique characteristics as erect posture, bipedal locomotion, and manual dexterity. They eventually started using basic hand tools and language. From Africa early humans moved to the Middle East and on to Europe and Asia and later reached the Americas some twenty thousand years ago. Early humans hunted and fished for meat and gathered fruits and vegetables. About ten thousand years ago humans domesticated plants and animals, which supported population growth and the beginning of large settlements. Over three thousand years ago four main civilizations developed in Mesopotamia, the Indus Valley, around the Nile River, and China. These civilizations developed complex architectures, economic, political, and military systems. A notorious feature of their history seems to be occasional wars between various political entities, from the time of sticks and stones to a modern military equipped with ships, armor, flying machines, and—as of 1945—nuclear weapons. Any questions?"

After a moment of awed silence, Romo asked, "Humans recently underwent a global conflict. What can you tell us about it?"

Chaika answered, "Earth just went through a global war that lasted from 1939 to 1945. Two opposing military alliances were formed: the Allies (led by America, the Soviet Union, and Great Britain) and the Axis (led by Nazi Germany, Japan, and Italy). The major participants threw their entire economic, industrial, and scientific capabilities behind the war effort. It has been the deadliest conflict in Earth's history, with over fifty million fatalities. It included acts of genocide, strategic bombing, use of early missile technology, and the only use of nuclear weapons in war—so far."

Chief Engineer Jang interrupted with a question: "Was not Earth invaded in 1938 by a hostile alien species we know nothing about?"

Chaika quickly replied, "On the thirtieth of October 1938, we listened to a radio station broadcast monitored from our just-deployed first spy satellite, telling of an invasion by aliens from another world! The broadcast came in a series of news bulletins. First there was a report of an unusual object falling on a New Jersey farm. Then a report from that farm, where aliens emerged from a spacecraft and attacked onlookers with a heat ray, cutting off radio reports from the scene. A series of bulletins followed, detailing an alien invasion taking place across the world! After a commercial break, the last report told that the aliens, whom they called Martians, were defeated not by humans, but by bacteria. What a quick dramatic conclusion! You guys have to ask the earthlings for the full details of this Martian invasion when you get to Earth!"

Obviously, none of those present at that dinner were familiar with H. G. Wells's *War of the Worlds*, which that 1938 radio broadcast presented for thirty minutes after an introduction explaining that the radio program was a dramatization of that book on Halloween! Apparently, the Alliance's spy satellites missed that part of the radio transmission.

After a few moments of silence, First Officer Patel, who doubled as a liaison with the Greys for the Interplanetary Alliance, interrupted, "Back to the discussion of nuclear weapons. The Alliance spy satellites around Earth have been monitoring the use of these nuclear weapons by America. The first test detonation of a nuclear weapon was conducted by America on July 16, 1945. The test was conducted in the Jornada del Muerto Basin about thirty-five miles southeast of Socorro, New Mexico, on what is called the Alamogordo Bombing and Gunnery Range."

Captain Noah then inquired, "When our home world of Zeta was invaded by the Reptoids, they used a devastating nuclear bomb on our capital city. What is your outlook for Earth after the invention of this weapon of mass destruction?"

Chaika sadly reflected for a moment, sipping on her coffee, and then answered, "The various countries on Earth are currently engaged in some sort of Cold War. This Cold War is a state of geopolitical tension between the Eastern bloc (the Soviet Union and its satellite states) and powers in the Western prodemocracy bloc (the United States and its NATO allies). But high technology and military secrets are the most fleeting of all! I would not be surprised that the Soviet Union would soon test its first nuclear device, thanks in part to its intelligence gathering from both the Nazi and American nuclear projects. I believe that within two decades America and the Soviet Union will run the risk of a military confrontation that may result in the massive use of these nuclear weapons. Earthlings must learn how-to live-in peace with each other! The survival of their species and their planet depends on this."

Chaika sighed and continued, looking downcast, "Should this full-blown nuclear conflict occur, in a matter of minutes most of Earth's population would die, and modern infrastructure would be destroyed. This would be followed by a nuclear winter lasting for decades, ozone layer losses up to 50 percent, and famine and disease affecting any inhabitants that survived. I know this because that's what happened in my home world of Leza about a hundred thousand years ago! A few days before Leza's nuclear holocaust, a mission with fifty colonists was launched to colonize another planet. Communication with them was lost, and we thought we would never hear from them. But about three years ago, we found that their descendants, our Grey kin, survived and prospered, only to suffer from an invasion from the aggressive Reptoid Union, which also possesses nuclear weapons."

A minute of utter silence followed. It was late, and it was time to get some rest before the launch early in the morning for the mission to Earth. Thus, one by one the dinner guests left. After a few minutes, Romo and Jang were the only ones left chatting in the astronaut quarters. Romo headed for the door. He gave Jang a warm hug, telling him, "Goodbye, good luck, and Godspeed, Mr. Anonymous. Thanks for helping me in my recovery!"

Then Romo, the launch director, headed out the door to his quarters to get some sleep. After all, the mission to Earth was scheduled for launch early in the morning!

In the wee of the morning hours, while the ground launch team was loading propellants, a crowd of spectators was gathering on viewing sites six or seven miles from the launch pad. Among them was Doctor Akina, who was very pregnant with her second child. She was concerned about her husband Jang, who would be piloting the landing craft in the mission to Earth. She had been joyfully married to Jang for several years. But she felt that this mission to Earth would put her husband in the path of great danger. Her heart was full of worry.

Her opinion of earthlings was not too high; from her study of their history, she sensed they were barbaric, racist, paranoid warmongers. Human history during the last few millennia had shown many occurrences of enslavement and murder of those who belonged to different ethnic groups. And now these savages had nuclear weapons, which was a great concern for the Interplanetary Alliance's leadership and their reason for contacting them.

She prayed for her husband's welfare and that of his crewmates, during the launch countdown. As the sun rose above the horizon, the roar of rocket engines disturbed her silent prayer and caused a flock of nearby birds to take flight. It was a successful launch with clear skies at the launch center in planet Proxima on a beautiful summer morning in 1947.

Destination: Earth!

Akina viewing launch of Mission to Earth (Artwork by Roberta Lerman)

CHAPTER THIRTY-THREE

EN ROUTE TO EARTH

It was evening on a late June day in 1947. The Greys' spaceship *Zeta's Hope* was in geostationary orbit at a distance of some twenty thousand miles above their destination: Earth. From their vantage point they had an awesome view of the North American continent from coast to coast, the eastern half of the country shining with many lights from their urban centers, the distribution of city lights more scattered on the western half. Enjoying the panoramic view were Captain Noah and the crew that was to land in New Mexico the following day on the landing craft from the mother ship. Members of this landing crew were the alliance's ambassador Rick Patel from planet Sapiens, Chief Engineer and Lander Pilot Jang, and ensigns Boudica and Shaka.

The android Amie sat in the pilot's seat, keeping an eye on the control panels. In the background some earthling music played through the public address system.

After the group enjoyed listening to the music for a few minutes, Captain Noah asked Amie, "Any responses to our attempts to communicate with the earthlings, either the White House or the military installations in New Mexico?"

"No, Captain. No response from the White House or from either Army airfield."

Noah nodded, looking worried. "Not good news. Chaika gave us the comm links for all of these three places—the White House, and the two airfields with strategic bombers carrying nukes in New Mexico. The Interplanetary Alliance's leadership thought that our best chances for successful communications was with the prodemocracy Americans. But I guess these guys are not used to getting interstellar visitors. Their radio operators must think that our messages are some sort of prank! But our mission plan still calls for a landing tomorrow in order to establish contact."

They all remained quiet for a few seconds. Then Ambassador Patel broke the silence, "Nice-looking planet. Most of them must be sleeping like little angels. I wonder what earthlings dream about. A vacation? Sexual fantasies? Money? Attacks by monsters from outer space?"

Jang quipped, "They are dreaming of the reception party that they are going to throw for us upon our arrival. A great parade during the day with floats with people singing and dancing. Later in the evening, a gala reception where we'll all dance to music in great ballrooms and dine the finest foods, topped off at the end with gourmet coffee, sweet pastries, and the finest cigars."

Rick Patel said, "Maybe Boudica and Shaka can show off their dancing skills. They have been watching movies by Fred Astaire and Ginger Rogers."

Boudica and Shaka smiled. Shaka said, "We're going to bed. Please excuse us."

Captain Noah said, "That's fine. You are dismissed."

As they left, Jang called after them, "Save your energy to conceive your second child on Earth!"

They chuckle. Then Noah turned to Jang and asked, "Who going to pay for this party?"

Jang pulled down his hat and passed it around, saying, "I'll start a collection right now!"

As the hat came to him, Rick headed in the direction of his room and told Noah and Jang, "Excuse me, gentlemen, but it's time for this fellow to get some sleep."

Noah smiled. Then his face turned serious as he remarked to Jang, "Things may not turn out well. Many earthlings have issues with peoples from different races, not to mention that we are from another planet! Heck, they just went through a global war, where over fifty million people were killed. Humanity may not be ready to know that they are not alone. They're about as genocidal as the Reptoids that invaded our home world of Zeta!

Jang commented, "I don't think of Zeta as our home world anymore. Today my home is where my house, wife, and children are!"

Noah continued, "I sense earthlings are barbaric, racist, paranoid warmongers. You guys could get killed or taken captive. Your landing craft has no protection against their weapons! You are one of the brightest scientists in the galaxy. It'd be a pity to lose you to those guys."

Jang reflected and then began a brief speech: "Death or captivity is a risk that comes with our mission for contacting the earthlings! I'm aware that many of them are either racists or paranoid warmongers, or both. As for racism, I speculate that things will get better in baby steps. Earlier this year, a black baseball player named Jackie Robinson made his major league debut with the Brooklyn Dodgers. According to our time traveling friend Chaika, a year from now President Truman will issue Executive Order 9981, abolishing discrimination in America's military on the basis of race, color, religion, or national origin. Later in 1954 there will be a Supreme Court decision declaring unconstitutional state laws that establish separate public schools for students of different races. Bus segregation will also be declared unconstitutional by 1956, and so on. Eventually, institutionalized racial segregation in public facilities will disappear. And by 2008 they will have elected their first black president!"

Jang paused briefly for a sip of coffee. "As for being taken prisoner, I have been authorized by the president of the Interplanetary Alliance to encourage the invention of integrated circuit microchips by some guy called Jack Kilby, from Texas Instruments, and Bob Noyce, from Fairchild Semiconductor. This innovation will lead to the design of microprocessors and computer memory. Microchips will lead to the development of minicomputers, personal computers, television, cell phones, a global positioning system, tracking devices, and better communications and medical equipment. This may include the design of some really cool computer video games and helping some guy called Al Gore invent the internet. I have been instructed by the leadership of the Interplanetary Alliance to bring humanity closer to a computer revolution and to landing a man on the moon! But in the event of my death, I ask that my ashes be sprayed on that beach in Avalonia where my wife Akina and I went skinny-dipping that one night that we sneaked out. It's my hope that upon my wife's death, she will join me so that our ashes skinny-dip together until the end of time."

Noah couldn't help but chuckle at Jang's little speech. He then commented, "Yeah. About the internet, it's is a double-edged sword. On the positive side, it has enhanced communications around the galaxy, improved research, and facilitated online transactions. But on the negative side, I had my identity stolen by someone who committed fraud in my name. It has also been used for cyberbullying, espionage, and cyberterrorism. The computer networks in our critical space systems are isolated from the internet because of such negative aspects."

Then Noah gave Jang a probing look. "It sounds to me that you are really upbeat about this mission to Earth. Are you planning to move and settle there with your family?"

"As a matter of fact, I am," replied Jang, as he paused to sip on his coffee. "Akina and I have talked about doing that. Earth greatly resembles our home world of Zeta, with wonderful green forests and oceans where the bathing and the fishing are great! Akina could work as a doctor, while I could work in the high technology field, helping with the development of integrated circuit microchips, personal computers, and better communications equipment. And on the side, I could start a cigar exporting business back to planets Sapiens, Verde, and Proxima."

"You and your big dreams, my friend," Noah said with a smile. Then he looked at his watch and stood. "We have a landing on Earth early tomorrow. Time to go to bed! Captain's orders!"

CHAPTER THIRTY-FOUR

FIRST CONTACT?

On that early April evening in 2066, I was to meet Admiral Noah to work on the last chapter of our book about their 1947 journey to Earth. Previously, I did a web search to refresh my memory about 1940s Earth. After the end of World War II, there was tension between the Western democracies and Stalin's Soviet Union and his allies. The period between 1947, when the United States pledged to aid nations threatened by Soviet expansionism, and 1991, the year the Soviet Union collapsed, was known as the Cold War. And of course, I researched that specific event in 1947 widely understood as an Unidentified Flying Object (UFO) crash in Roswell, New Mexico.

About thirty minutes before the arrival of his wife, Faith, and their friend Doctor Akina, I met Admiral Noah for a predinner smoke at a park bench across from the Palace of Governors in Santa Fe. There we would hold our interview about that rough first contact between the Greys and humans; it had happened nearly 120 years ago, in mid-1947! But the old geezer, despite being 150 years old (the equivalent of seventy-five years as a human), had an excellent memory and would back up the facts with documentation of the Greys' mission to Earth he commanded back then.

After we exchanged greetings, he placed a compact disc player in front of me. I asked, "Is it a recording of the 1947 event near the Roswell army airfield?"

Noah's face saddened for a moment. Taking a long draw of his cigar, he replied, "Yes Mr. Wyatt, we recorded this from our starship. I wanted you to hear it before the ladies arrived. The recounting of that tragedy may bring them to tears."

I pressed the play button and listened to the radio transmission of the pilot of a P-51 Mustang fighter flying a routine dawn patrol on July 3, 1947, about ten minutes before sun up. The pilot reported: "Mustang 5 to Roswell ground control. I'm sighting what appears to be a meteorite burning through the atmosphere toward you from the northwest."

"Roger, Mustang 5. We just picked it up on our radar. We'll sound the alarm for personnel to seek cover. Beware that we have in a hanger a B-29 Superfortress bomber with a nuke. Keep us apprised of the situation."

"Mustang 5 to Roswell ground control. What I thought was a meteorite is slowing down! It looks like some sort of aircraft. It's still coming in your direction."

"Roswell ground control to Mustang 5. Protocol calls for first warning and then downing any unauthorized aircraft into restricted airspace. Heck, it could be commies!"

"Roger, ground control. Unauthorized aircraft, you are entering US military restricted airspace. Leave or we'll fire!"

After ten seconds, we could hear a hail of gunfire in the background. Then we heard a voice screaming, "Don't shoot! Don't shoot! We come in peace!"

Then came the sound of thunder. The pilot reported: "Mustang 5 to Roswell ground control. Aircraft was hit by my gunfire. I heard pleas from them not to shoot, saying that they come in peace. Then the aircraft was hit by lightning. Definitely not their day! It has deployed a parachute and is slowly losing altitude as it descends southeast past the village of Corona."

"Roger, Mustang 5. We still have it in our radar. Keep us apprised of its descent. I'll inform the base commander of the situation. We'll possibly send an army unit to the crash site."

Then the compact disc switched to a narration of the crash event by Sapiens Ambassador Patel, "The situation was chaotic among the volunteer crew of four in the Greys' landing module. The shots from the earthling aircraft caused a compressed air line to fracture, killing crew members Boudica and Shaka and wounding Chief Engineer Jang, the landing party pilot, in the right forearm. At that point, Jang screamed, in pain from his injury, 'Don't shoot! Don't shoot! We come in peace!'

"At that moment, a lightning bolt hit the landing module, causing a blackout. With primary power out, emergency battery power was turned on. Jang intuitively reached for the manual lever with his left arm to deploy the emergency chute. He felt the landing module slow down, looked back at me with a smile, and said, 'Good luck, friend! Tell my wife Akina that I love her and our babies.'

"I looked at him with tears in my eyes as we braced for impact. I sat in the back, with the android, Security Chief Amie, on my right. Then came the loud sound of a crash.

"After a few seconds of the chaos and confusion of the impact, I tried to get up, only to realize that the android Amie was lying motionless on top of me, her head cracked by a beam. Apparently, she'd been programmed to protect me at all costs! As I manage to move out from under Amie, I saw that there was only one other survivor: Jang. Within seconds, I located the first aid kit to bandage Jang's bleeding right arm.

"I took a minute to check on our two fallen crewmates, Boudica and Shaka. Jang and I said a short prayer for them and emerged from the landing module. It was truly tragic. Our fallen crewmates had just gotten married!

"It was in the wee hours of July third, 1947, just as the early morning sunrays came out. Outside we saw a blend of yellow and rose-colored semi-desert soil, dotted with small bushes and cottonwood trees and a couple of aspen trees against a background of gently rolling hills.

Hills near crash site in Corona (photo by Lester Overstreet)

"After taking in the scenery, an angry Jang broke the silence: 'Quite a reception from the barbaric earthlings. A hail of gunfire! And we got hit by lightning to add to our misfortune. Not our day, I say!'

"Jang reflected for a few seconds and turned to me. 'From that negative reception, I believe that we should follow our backup plan. You get your motorbike out, ride away to some big city, and blend in.'

"I replied, 'I can carry you on the back of my bike.'

"'Thanks. But forget about that! We Greys stick out like sore thumbs! I'll wait here for the Earthlings' military to come and get me.'

"He paused and then said, 'You look human. Sapiens intelligence provided you with the false identity of an electrician from New Jersey. Ride away on your bike to some big city and blend in. Remember to report to the mother ship at nightfall! You have a cell phone, a bag of clothes, and about a thousand dollars in counterfeit small bills. Keep in touch with our people in orbit. Rent a small apartment and get a job. May be a year down the road things will cool off and our guys will come and pick you up in some agreed desert spot around here or elsewhere.'

"After a moment he went on. 'Don't worry about me. If I die, I'll probably be reborn as an anticommunist cigar-puffing Cuban!'

"I chuckled at his comment. But I knew that I had to follow his advice to blend in. It was the backup plan. With tears in my eyes, I hugged Jang and went back to the landing module to roll out with my bike. I pulled out a map and laid out my journey in about a minute. I then turned to Jang and said, 'May God watch over you, my friend.'

"I rode north into the desert, reaching a small road within five minutes. In the westward direction, I saw the lights of an approaching military truck. I turned east toward the small town of Vaughn just before a P-51 Mustang fighter flew overhead.

"As I rode on, I watched in the rearview mirror as a military truck turned off the road toward the landing module. They didn't seem to have noticed me. But humans would soon find out that they aren't alone in the universe when they reached the crash site!

"After riding about thirty minutes, I arrived at the town of Vaughn, where I found a gas station. It was thirty minutes past six in the morning, and a few people were out in the street tending to their daily business. A bronze-skinned gas attendant came out and greeted me with a Mexican accent. 'Good morning, señor. How much gas do you need?'

"'Good morning,' I said. 'Give me 75 cents worth.'

As he pumped, with an expression of curiosity he asked, 'Señor, are you the famous actor Victor Mature?'

"I smiled, gave him his dollar, and said, 'No, I'm just an electrician from New Jersey called Pat Rossi. Keep the change, buddy!'

"I turned north on the lonely road to Santa Fe. With me, I had the address, phone number, and pictures of a notorious aerospace engineer and a couple of ingenious electronics engineers. The leadership of the Interplanetary Alliance thought that humanity should be brought closer to a computer revolution and to landing a man on the moon! I then prayed for the friends I had left behind as I moved forward toward an uncertain destiny."